THE WIND

BY
**DOROTHY
SCARBOROUGH**

INTRODUCTION:

In 1925, an anonymous novel entitled The Wind highlighted the town of Sweetwater in West Texas. The Wind told the tragic story of Letty Mason, a Virginian woman who settled in Sweetwater during the drought-stricken 1880s. At the end of the book, Letty committed murder and suicide, partly as a result of the relentless wind in West Texas.

Critics praised the book for portraying the West with a "cold truth. However, many Texas readers attacked The Wind and argued that only a Yankee could have written it.

The author of The Wind turned out to be Dorothy Scarborough from Texas. She spent several years of her childhood in Sweetwater, but lived most of her career in New York City, yet all seven of her novels were set in Texas.

By the time Lillian Gish starred in the 1928 film version of The Wind, the story had a happy ending - and the Sweetwater Chamber of Commerce invited Scarborough back for a visit.

Dorothy Scarborough was also a respected folklorist. She called herself a "song catcher". She believed that radio threatened the survival of folk songs and travelled to the Appalachians to record centuries-old ballads with a handheld dictaphone. Scarborough believed that these folk songs told stories about a community's values and its collective history.

A novelist, folklorist, and song lover, Dorothy Scarborough drew inspiration from regional American cultures and in doing so, preserved the creative expressions of ordinary people of the past.

SUMMARY:

In the 1920s, a young orphan had to leave her native Virginia with a rather mild climate to join a cousin who raised cattle in Texas. During the trip, she meets a wealthy merchant who describes to her a difficult region: merciless climate, sandstorms, rough cowboys and the wind, everywhere, forcing the men to hide in holes serving as houses ... girl will have to face this implacable enemy who pursues her like a specter emerging from the depths of herself; this wind which deposits the sand, harasses, locks in loneliness and boredom and makes each visit welcome, if only to forget about the cattle, the kitchen or the constraints of the desert ...

The young orphan in question is Lettie. Freshly disembarked from her native Virginia, following the death of her mother, here she is forced to impose her presence on Bev, her beloved cousin, who became a farmer in Texas and flanked by a wife and children.

Everything started badly for poor Lettie. As soon as the train journey, an attractive stranger warns her against the rigors of this state, and against the wind in particular. Lettie, small nature, is quickly and strongly impressed by Wirt Roddy's speech and by what she sees passing by the landscape. Stunted trees, dry expanses and lean cows.

As she gets off the train, greeted by a stranger and assailed by the wind, she sets off on a short journey to reach her cousin's farm.

To better enable us to sympathize with the misfortunes of the pretty Lettie, the writer alternates the descriptions of the places and the situations lived by the young girl, and the memories of this one, linked to Virginia. The contrast between these two states is cruelly obvious. The drought which rages in Texas makes nature hostile, the wind constantly carries sand, the dwellings are rustic, even rudimentary, and the manners of the men are very abrupt ... Virginia is the symbol of opulence, of the good manners. The valleys are green and sprinkled with pretty rivers, the flowers bloom there, we have tea with our friends and neighbors ... the sweetness of life in the south, when we are lucky enough not to come from a background poor.

Lettie has to do her part of the job, she ignores all household chores, you have to travel more than 30 km to see neighbors, and no question of going to town, it's quite a trip. The isolation, the promiscuity would be bearable without the volcanic wife of Bev, a strong and beautiful woman who despises weakness.

Lettie, a fragile young girl raised in cotton, who still believes in Prince Charming, gradually lets herself be devoured by this country so singular and wild. The wind blows its madness on this poor girl, unable to make the right decision and who, from disappointment to hardship, gradually loses her sanity. I came out of my reading as shaken as Lettie Mason, I must say.

Most of the passages on drought and nature are striking. We suffer for these isolated cowboys and more, for all these poor animals - cows and horses - condemned to die slowly of hunger and thirst, under the helpless eyes of their owners. The men and women of this ruthless Texas must show both resignation and strength to adapt to these harsh conditions. Lettie will have neither and his downfall is poignant.

an excellent preface, evokes the phenomenon of the dust bowl, this ecological disaster that affected the Midwest during the Great Depression. Droughts and dust storms that lasted a decade (!!) and forever changed the ecological balance of these regions. Something to think about, even today ...

Main Themes:

The climate and the time period are chosen by the author for a reason, as she explains that at the beginning of the book. According to the author, the weather during the 1880s was harsher than it is now (Scarborough 2). Human progress affected the nature as houses, farms, and fences created many obstacles for the wind to roam freely. Thus, the time period of the novel could cause the incidents that are described in the text, while the current weather is not as cruel. The description of nature in this book is essential to the plot. Scarborough gives many details while exploring the landscape of Texas and Virginia. Virginia is described with the use of various epithets and adjectives.

The protagonist's old home is portrayed as a place of exquisite beauty. Texas, on the other hand, is shown as a wasteland. Here, there are no rustling trees, blooming flowers, or singing birds. The author uses repetition to enhance the feeling of monotony, writing "sand, sand, sand" (Scarborough 52). Thus, such a portrayal is used to highlight the differences between the two states and explain the anxiety of the main character.

One of the central themes that are discussed in the text is madness that can overcome one's thoughts. Letty is a young woman that is not prepared to live in the harsh environment of her new home. Here, the wind is only a part of the problem, as the living conditions further pressure her into existing according to the new rules and norms. The audience can see the differences that surround the life of Letty and the lives of ranchers from Sweetwater. The wind gains traits of a man as it embodies Letty's issues because she does not know where to direct her concerns.

Furthermore, the way people speak to Letty is also interesting. It is clear that nobody takes her words seriously and she is often left without a choice. For instance, in a scene where both Lige and Sourdough propose to Letty, she initially believes that the men are joking.

After discovering that they are serious, she declines their offers and says that she does not want to marry anyone at the moment. The men do not treat that as a real statement as disregard her desire not to marry as Sourdough says to her "excuse me, but you do — only you just don't know it yet" (Scarborough 149). Furthermore, they continue to discuss a possible person that she would like, making this important decision for her. Other characters repeat this process as well by disregarding Letty's words and actions.

Here, Scarborough explores the place of women in a male-dominated society and their freedom of choice. Most characters that Letty encounters through the novel try to enforce their wants and needs on her. Wirt Roddy does not believe Letty when she threatens him with a gun, which only exacerbates her frustration and leads to her killing him. Lige and Sourdough disregard Letty's desire not to marry and believe that she does not know what she truly wants.

The author explores the idea that other people do not see the main character as an equal, treating her as a beautiful but mindless attraction instead. These actions contribute to Letty feeling isolated and misunderstood, and it leads to her being further consumed by her dialogue with the wind. She does not have anyone to speak to, so she turns to her own thoughts which are plagued by the wind.

Main Character

Letty Mason is a person that is not prepared to deal with the life that she encounters at the ranch. She is soft and naïve. Moreover, her previous life was devoid of hard labor and restrictions, as Letty lived at home, helped her mother, and spend her free time teaching, sewing, and reading. One could argue that she lived a somewhat privileged life in comparison to people of Sweetwater. However, her character may be soft by nature, while most people at the ranch have had a different experience in life.

Thus, the clash between her personality and their demands contributes to her becoming increasingly distraught. In the end, she recalls the words of Wirt Roddy who told her about the wind. She believes that these words planted the idea in her head and made her insane. However, it is possible that even without this thought Letty would not be able to get used to her new life. The wind becomes the subject of her thoughts and directs her frustration in one direction. Therefore, it becomes the center of her attention.

Conclusion

The book The Wind by Scarborough explores the themes of being trapped by circumstances, gender, and occupation. The use of the wind as both an issue and a metaphor for other problems is intriguing. Moreover, the gradually changing thoughts of the protagonist and her focus on the wind show an unusual side of one's mind.

THE WIND

Prelude

THE WIND WAS THE CAUSE of it all. The sand, too, had a share in it, and human beings were involved, but the wind was the primal force, and but for it the whole series of events would not have happened. It took place in West Texas, years and years ago, before the great ranges had begun to be cut up into farms and plowed and planted to crops, when there was nothing to break the sweep of the wind across the treeless prairies, when the sand blew in blinding fury across the plains, or lay in mocking waves that never broke on any howsoever-distant beach, or piled in mounds that fickle gusts removed almost as soon as they were erected—when for endless miles there seemed nothing but wind and sand and empty, far off sky.

But perhaps you do not understand the winds of West Texas. And even if you knew them as they are now, that would mean little, for today they are not as they used to be. Civilization has changed them, has tamed them, as the *vacqueros* and the cowboys changed and gentled the wild horses that roamed the prairies long ago. Civilization has taken from them something of their fiery, elemental force, has humbled their spirit. Man, by building houses here and there upon the plains, by stretching fences, by planting trees, has broken the sweep of the wind—by plowing the land into farms where green things grow has lessened its power to hurl the sand in fury across the wide and empty plains. Man has encroached on the domain of the winds, and gradually, very gradually, is conquering them.

But long ago it was different. The winds were wild and free, and they were more powerful than human beings.

Among the wild horses of the plains there would be now and then one fleet and strong and cunning, that could never be trapped by man, that had never felt the control of bridle, the sting of spur—a stallion that raced over the prairies at will, uncaptured and uncapturable; one with supernatural force and speed, so that no pursuer could ever come up with him; so cunning that no device could ever snare him—a being of diabolic wisdom. One could hear his wild neighing in the night, as he sped over the plains. One could fancy he saw his mane flying back, his hoofs striking fire even from the yielding sand, a Satanic horse, for whom no man would ever be the match. Some thought him a ghost horse, imperishable. But now his shrill neighing is heard no more on the prairies by night, for man has driven him out. He has fled to other prairies, vast and fenceless, where man has not intruded, and now one knows him only in legend.

So the norther was a wild stallion that raced over the plains, mighty in power, cruel in spirit, more to be feared than man. One could hear his terrible neighings in the night, and fancy one saw him sweeping over the plains with his imperious mane flying backward and his fiery hoofs ready to trample one down.

In the old days, the winds were the enemies of women. Did they hate them because they saw in them the symbols of that civilization which might gradually lessen their own power? Because it was for women that men would build houses as once they made dugouts?—would increase their herds, would turn the unfenced pastures into farms, furrowing the land that had never known touch of plow since time began?—stealing the sand from the winds?

The winds were cruel to women that came under their tyranny. They were at them ceaselessly, buffeting them with icy blasts in winter, burning them with hot breath in summer, parching their skins and roughening their hair, and trying to wear down their nerves by attrition, and drive them away.

And the sand was the weapon of the winds. It stung the face like bits of glass, it blinded the eyes; it seeped into the houses through closed windows and doors and through every crack and crevice, so that it might make the beds harsh to lie on, might make the food gritty to taste, the air stifling to breathe. It piled in drifts against any fence or obstruction, as deep as snow after a northern blizzard.

How could a frail, sensitive woman fight the wind? How oppose a wild, shouting voice that never let her know the peace of silence—a resistless force that was at her all the day, a naked, unbodied wind—like a ghost more terrible because invisible—that wailed to her across waste places in the night, calling to her like a demon lover?

1

A YOUNG GIRL was traveling alone on a westbound train one day in late December, between Christmas and the new year. Family loyalty had named her Letitia after a great-aunt, but affection had softened that to Letty, so that she had not suffered unduly. Until recently love had smoothed all things in her life. She was a pretty girl, who looked younger than her eighteen years—a slight and almost childish figure in her black dress, with her blonde and wavy hair, her eyes blue as periwinkles in old-fashioned gardens, and her cheeks delicately pink as the petals of peach blooms. She looked tired now, however, for she had come all the distance from Virginia to Texas. She had spent the night at Fort Worth to break her journey, and now she was on the last day of her trip. She would reach Sweetwater that night.

She had never seen Sweetwater, nor heard it described, and she knew of it only as a postmark on a letter. But the name was pleasant-sounding, and so she whispered it to herself from time to time, while her fancy conjured up pictures of what the little town would look like. There would be home-like houses with their dream-inviting open fires in big fireplaces, and their porches overgrown with vines, as in the Virginia villages she knew. There would be lawns and orchards, and gardens with all the flowers one loved, each in its season, a cycle of beauty from early spring to late fall. And trees, of course, whose great, benignant branches sheltered nesting birds in spring, whose leaves in summer laced the sky and rustled softly when the wind blew, and sometimes hung as motionless as pictured leaves when there was no breeze.

Would there be a little river, perhaps, slipping like a silver shadow through the town, where a girl and a boy might row a boat on summer afternoons?—or a creek that showed rainbow minnows in its shallows and ferns along the banks? Or a lake, if only a tiny one, or a pond where water lilies bloomed with creamy petals and hearts of gold, and water hyacinths purple-blue? One thing she was sure of—there would be water, sweet and cool and pure, for wasn't the place named Sweetwater?

As one visions heaven according to his dreams of loved earthly beauty, so Letty Mason pieced together a Sweetwater that was to contain all the things she cared for most. She had to do something to keep from being too bitterly unhappy. When there was nothing to look to but a past that grief and separation had broken up, and a future that held she knew not what, and only so much of a present as a ride on a train, what could a girl do?

She gave a look at her present in an impulse of panic to escape the sorrow of yesterdays and the terror of unknown tomorrows. The day coach with its rows of red plush seats, all turned the same way like people that dared not look behind them, would be all right for anyone who was not alone and unhappy and afraid. Until a few months ago Letty could have laughed and had fun in it, while now it seemed ugly and hostile. At one end of the coach there was a big blackened coal bin and an iron stove as huge and red as a Santa Claus, when the brakeman had stuffed it with coal. There were not many passengers in the car—a few men with broad-brimmed Stetson hats, several mothers with their babies, a few older children, and one grandmotherly gray-haired woman crocheting white-thread lace. A little girl in a red-plaid dress and hair braided in tight, serious pig-tails, kept pacing up and down the aisle, touching the tops of the seats as if in some mysterious game. An urchin of about five, with eyes as round and expressionless as glass marbles, spilled his plump body half over the seat in front of Letty and stared at her without winking. She tried to smile at him, but she could not manage the necessary energy, and in fact the youngster seemed to expect no response to his scrutiny.

A man across the aisle looked at her now and then over the top of his *Dallas News*, and smiled tentatively, but she turned away each time. He was a rather handsome man, with wavy black hair and dark eyes and a mustache that quirked up at the ends. He was proud of that mustache, she decided, for he played with it affectionately. He looked old, over thirty, she felt sure.

There was something faintly familiar about him, suggestive of someone else she had known, perhaps long ago. As she looked at him surreptitiously, she was sure that she had never seen this man before—because he was a person that she would have remembered if she had ever known him—but he was teasingly reminiscent of another. Who was it? She tried to analyze the impressions he called up,—half pleasurable recollections, half fear and repulsion, vaguely commingled as in the waking remembrance of a dream.

When she had been traveling for several hours, the conductor came along and stopped to speak to her, as if he thought she might be lonesome.

"Gettin' on all hunky dory?"

"Yes."

She contrived a smile for him, because he was so kind, and his eyebrows were so funny! They were black and they spurted suddenly out from above his eyes like mustaches stuck on in the wrong place. They fascinated her, because she had never seen any like them before. But she mustn't let the good man know that she was smiling at his mustaches instead of at him.

"What is Sweetwater like?" she asked. "Do you suppose I'll love it?"

His eyebrows arched themselves jerkily. "Well, h-mm, that depends on the folks you've got there, daughter."

"I don't see why," she contended. "There are lots of places you could like without folks. There are places—you know—where you never could get lonesome, even if you stayed there by yourself for hours and hours. They're so pretty and peaceful they rest you, and happify you, as the darkies say, so you feel right at home there. And you enjoy being yourself so much that you don't miss other people."

"Yes, that's right." The eye-mustaches twinkled at her cheerily and then the conductor moved off down the aisle without trying to prove his point, as if indeed he preferred not to.

Letty huddled again in the corner of her red plush prison and gazed out of the window. The train was scudding along what seemed to be abandoned peach orchards, where unkempt trees were growing, their leafless branches sprawled and scrawny, instead of being trimmed and tended as in the orchards that she knew at home. And there were no fences round them, no protection at all to keep thieves from stealing the fruit in summer when there was any. Queer!

They were the largest orchards she had ever seen, she reflected, for they stretched along both sides of the track for miles and miles. She hadn't noticed just where they began, and it seemed as if they never would end. The ground was covered with a dead grass that waved in the wind, bent low, as if water were rippling over it. The trees weren't planted in rows, but scattered irregularly in a wild and lawless abandon. She puzzled over the strangeness of it all. She thought illogically of a remark she had heard once from an old man, "All signs fail in Texas."

When the little red-plaid girl came by again, Letty put out a hand to detain her. "Why don't they have fences to their peach orchards?" she asked.

"Where?" the child wished to know.

Letty pointed to the trees on each side of the track.

The little girl stared at her in puzzled fashion for a moment, and then she giggled, with laughter as light and spontaneous as soap-bubbles of mirth.

The *Dallas News* was lowered and Letty saw that the man across the aisle was smiling in amusement somewhat carefully restrained. He had been listening, then, to what she said!

"Those are mesquite trees. Wild," he volunteered.

Letty blushed and drew back. When Letty blushed, the process was one to distract and delight the beholder—as if the pink of peach blooms had suddenly turned into rosy flame. It always scared and upset her when it happened, so that in consequence she blushed more vividly than ever.

As if to reassure her, because sympathetic of her emotions, the man erected the barricade of *Dallas News* again, though with manifest reluctance.

After a moment, when he no doubt thought that she had somewhat recovered, he ventured forth again.

"They do look like old peach trees. I've heard folks often say the same thing."

Letty made no answer.

With a lingering glance, which made her color flare up again, he retired behind his paper and made no effort to prolong the conversation.

As the miles slipped by, Letty noticed that the mesquites tended to grow smaller. At first they had been large, not like forest trees, of course, but good-sized, while now they were dwindling. Why was that? She looked for other trees, but saw none of her old familiar friends—only these stranger mesquites. She felt depressed and forlorn. Would life snatch from her even the trees she loved? But of course it was a long way yet to Sweetwater, and the landscape could change a lot before she got there. She needn't worry. Still, she leaned her cheek against her hand and gave herself up to unhappy premonitions. To go into a country you didn't know about was hard, and to leave a home you had loved all your life was cruel. Life didn't leave you much choice, but just shoved you around as if you hadn't any right to feelings.

Suddenly, when she was wiping away a surreptitious tear, she was roused by a touch On her shoulder. Starting up, she saw that the man from across the aisle had moved over and sat beside her.

He spoke casually. "Like to see some prairie dogs? Maybe you never saw any."

"No," she said, fluttering rosily. "I never have."

He pointed one forefinger toward the ground beside the track and her following gaze saw a stretch of land with small hummocks scattered over it like earthen breastworks thrown up for Lilliputian warfare. Queer little animals were disporting themselves about them, red-brown, dumpy creatures like young puppies that had not yet begun to lengthen into dogs—some sitting on their haunches on top of the mounds, some scampering about on the ground that was bare of vegetation and hard-packed as a floor. Some looked with suspicion at the train, and then dived down into holes in the ground. Some ran clumsily away, while a few held their place with impudent disdain of engines and human beings.

"This is a dog town," the man went on to elaborate. "They have a colony, you see, and they dig underground homes for themselves, and live down there. I reckon that's where the old settlers got their notion of dugouts. Sometimes rattlers live in the holes with them, or maybe only in holes they've left. And ground squirrels, and hoot owls. They have tunnels running between the mounds all over the place."

"Why, how cunning!" she cried, forgetting her woes and her faint fear of this stranger. To think there were such darling little animals she had never even heard of!

She leaned in excitement against the window and flattened her nose against the glass like a youngster, to watch them in their antics.

"Does a prairie-dog town have a mayor and a city council?" She laughed dimplingly. "I don't see the church, or the school house or the jail."

He grinned. "I reckon they're not much of a religious or educated bunch, any more than the rest of us out here. But they're sociable little cusses and mighty human in some of their ways. The children make pets of 'em-"

Her fancy flashed off to the government of a prairie-dog settlement.

"That fat, lazy one there must be the bigwig, the rich man," she hazarded. "His mound is higher than the others, and he didn't duck when he saw the train coming. Some of 'em are silly cowards."

"Like folks," he concurred, as he twisted his mustache with long, browned fingers, and smiled.

He settled back at ease beside her, as if there could be no possibility of his being unwelcome. His air was that of a man who had a lazy energy well controlled, beneath whose apparent indolence a superb strength lay concealed, whose interested indifference was not greatly accustomed to rebuffs. He smilingly looked down at her.

Letty, who had been but momentarily startled out of her shyness in the excitement of seeing prairie dogs for the first time, now gave a quick frown and drew back within her shell of reserve. But the stranger appeared not to notice.

Or was it that he noticed and disregarded?

"Live in Texas?" he asked.

"No," she said coldly. She wouldn't talk with him, and then he would go away and leave her alone. Who was he that he should speak to her like this?

And then, almost without her volition, her sense of truthfulness answered his question. "I —haven't—but I guess I'm going to," she faltered, facing the fact

[*...missing text pg 14 and 15...*]

trumpet vine with its wonderful red bugles, climbing up the trees and covering the fence posts and stumps.... And a vine we call the cigar plant, with its little, long red bloom like a tiny lighted cigar."

"That's a sensible-sounding plant," he threw in.

"Vines are all beautiful, I think. They're like charity, for they go covering up the ugly things and places, the dead trees, the stumps and rough fence posts, and make everything graceful."

Her tone was dreamily reminiscent now.

"That's right," he agreed, with smiling attention.

"And the flowers... There are all sorts of wild flowers there, too, so many I couldn't name them all, but I love everyone. There's the butterfly weed, that the darkeys call 'chigger plant.' How funny to call it that,—when it has gay orange blossoms like gorgeous butterflies lighted there for a second. You can almost see them fold and unfold their wings!"

"Yes?"

"Then there are the daisies that bloom everywhere in early summer, acres on acres of them, white, with golden hearts, nodding at you in the sun like children telling you to come and play with them. And wild tiger lilies in the shadowy places, like Indian girls in gay blankets... And the blue-eyed grass, and Jack-in-the-pulpit, and Bouncing Bet... And the

9

wild roses are the sweetest things in the world, so pink and delicate and perfect! And the jewel-weed in shady spots... and wild violets, and Queen Anne's Lace, with the flowers as fine as cobwebs, and the little birds' nests of green curled up. And wild morning-glory running everywhere, and black-eyed Susans. And, oh, I couldn't possibly tell you about all of them!"

She paused breathlessly, after her rush of words. Then she blushed to think how much she had been talking to this stranger.

"Guess I'll have to go and see them myself sometime," he rendered opinion.

So maybe he was interested, after all, and not pretending.

"And the trees—" she went on, not wishing to slight such dear friends. "I mustn't forget them. Such wonderful trees as we do have there! Pines that stand on tiptoe to peek into heaven, so I always feel like asking them what they see there. And tulip poplars that have such gorgeous blooms, and dogwood that makes the hills all white in springtime... And holly with its berries for Christmas.... There's a big mimosa on our lawn. Did you ever see a mimosa?"

He shook his head regretfully. His look seemed to hint that he recognized that not having seen a mimosa tree he had led a wasted life.

She tried to make it up to him.

"Its leaves are lacy, like ferns, and its blooms are tiny pompons like flowers of the sensitive plant, pinkish-yellow, soft as soft. There's a big magnolia there, too. You know a magnolia is such a joy, for you can write on the leaves while they are glossy and dark, and even after they've turned brown, you can still read what you've written.... And the flowers! When I see a magnolia blossom, it seems to me it must have fallen down from heaven in the night."

She caught her breath sharply. "I do hope there'll be magnolias in Sweetwater."

He cherished his mustache without enlightening her on that point. "What else is there?" he asked.

"There's a hedge of crepe myrtle by the garden. In late summer it has rose-colored blooms like silky, crinkled crepe, the prettiest thing you ever saw. You want to love it, and make little dance frocks out of it!... In the fall the trees in the town and in the woods are all colors, yellow and brown and bronze and red, so that I often wonder which I love best, springtime or autumn."

"What did you do all day?" he questioned.

"Oh, I wasn't idle! I took care of Mother, and made my own clothes, and taught a class in Sunday school, and helped with church suppers. And I read a lot, everything I could get, and I took music lessons, and had a good time with the boys and girls."

She turned to him suddenly, shutting the door on her past. "Now tell me about Sweetwater. And please tell me I'll love it there!"

The blue eyes, the scarlet fluted mouth, the tremulous dimple all entreated him to speak well of Sweetwater.

He uttered but one curt word, "No."

Her eyes widened in dismay and reproach. "Why not?"

He folded his arms and looked at her keenly. "Go back to your Virginia, little girl. This country's not like what you've been used to. Take my advice and vamoose—while the going's good."

Her chin trembled. "But I can't!" she jerked. "I haven't any money—and I haven't got anything to go back to!"

"Why did you ever leave?" he flung at her.

She looked at him with piteous eyes, defending herself against what she felt to be an accusation. "Mother died, and she was all I had left."

She caught her under lip with her teeth to stop its quivering. "And she'd been sick so long that after she was dead, the debts licked up the homestead and everything, just like an earthquake swallowing them."

"What are you doing so far down here?"

"Cousin Beverley owns a ranch in West Texas. I haven't seen him since I was a child, but the pastor wrote to him after Mother died, and asked him if I couldn't come out and live with them. Cousin Beverley said to come on, if I thought it best, that I could teach the children. He was afraid I wouldn't like it much, but the neighbors thought I'd better come. It would be a change for me, they said."

"It'll be a change, all right." His tone was grim. "A hell of a change!"

She felt chill with an indefinable fear of the future, as if some cold, dark wing had farmed her. She tried to ask him a question, but for the moment she could not find her voice to speak. Her blue eyes gazed enthralled at him, as if he could read for her the future, could reveal what lay for her behind the curtains of the coming days.

He turned to face her unsmilingly. "What's your cousin's name?"

"Beverley Mason."

Even the syllables of that dear name sounded unfamiliar to her, as if this strange environment had cast a spell over everything.

"I've seen him. He's a good hombre," he answered briefly. "But he don't live in Sweetwater. What made you think he did?"

"His letter was mailed from there."

He gave an unhumorous smile. "Out in this country a man may live a hundred miles from his postmark. He don't go for mail twice a day, y'understand. Bev Mason's ranch is over twenty-five miles from Sweetwater. I've got an outfit farther west myself, but I live in Fort Worth. Couldn't hog-tie me to stay all year round out here. *Savez?*"

The hands that lay loosely in her lap were trembling. "But what is the trouble with the country—that you tell me to go back?"

"It's all right for them that like it. Some do—mostly men, though. It's hard on the women. Folks say the West is good enough for a man or a dog, but no place for a woman or a cat."

"But why, why?"

"The wind is the worst thing."

She drew a relieved sigh. "Oh, wind? That's nothing to be afraid of."

He went on as though she had not spoken. "It's ruination to a woman's looks and nerves pretty often. It dries up her skin till it gets brown and tough as leather. It near 'bout puts her eyes out with the sand it blows in 'em all day. It gets on her nerves with its constant blowing —makes her irritable and jumpy."

She gave a light, casual gesture with one hand. "It blows everywhere, I reckon, even in Virginia. Sometimes in winter we have regular storms of wind and rain. But we don't think anything of them."

He gave her an amused sidelong glance, and twisted his mustache in silence. His air was that of an adult who disdains to attempt to make anything clear to a persistent but silly

11

child.

"What else is there so terrible out here?" she prodded. The man was just teasing her, of course, and she Would let him see that she wasn't so easily gulled.

"The work out here is hard on women. Can't get any help, and can't have the conveniences they have in other sections. Plenty o' cowboys to run the ranch, but no women to help in the house. And the chuck department on a regular ranch is no job to sneeze at, let me tell you."

"I won't mind that, either," she affirmed courageously. "I always worked at home, as I told you. I did the dusting."

"You'll have a chore on your hands if you keep up that end of it out here," he said sardonically. His white teeth gleamed in a smile.

She was rather breathless, but would not surrender. "What else?" she demanded.

"Women get lonesome. No neighbors if you live on a ranch. Just a few cowboys and too damned many cattle and coyotes. It's enough to run a woman loco."

"But the men stand it, don't they?"

"It's a man-sized job. And the cow-punchers can go to town every so often and get on a high lonesome and lose money at poker. That relieves 'em. But the women can't do that, poor calicoes. They got to stay bottled up, and it's liable to bust 'em, sooner or later."

She began to feel that he might be serious. She took a few moments to study the question, while she looked out of the window in silence.

Then she turned to him. "It's not what I'd choose, but I didn't know what else to do. Oh, why aren't girls taught to make their living and take care of themselves, the same as men?"

Her little black-bordered handkerchief dabbed at her eyes.

The man turned his searching gaze on her and spoke meditatively, with a sort of crisp drawl. "It'd be a pity for that pretty face of yours to be ruined by the wind—like I've seen some women's faces. If you stay out here, 'twon't be long before your skin won't be as pink and white as it is now. In a little while your hair won't be as yellow and soft, after the hot sun has bleached it and the wind has roughed it. Pretty soon your eyes won't be as clear and blue as they are now, after the sand has near 'bout blinded 'em—you stay out here."

She turned from him in bitter silence and gazed at the telegraph poles.

The man beside her whistled softly, a weird, haunting tune. Then he began to sing words to it.

"Oh, bury me not on the lone prai-*rie*,
Where the wild coyotes will howl over me!
In a narrow grave, just six by three.
Oh, bury me not on the lone prai-*rie!*"

Tears began to trickle down her cheeks.

He leaned closer and spoke softly, yet with a hint of savage constraint, as if he disliked his words. "If you don't want to go—you don't have to, little girl. Come back to Fort Worth with me, and I'll—fix up something for you."

The eyes lifted to his held no look of suspicion, but only reserve and a vague fear. His own lowered before their innocence.

"Thank you," she said with dignity, wiping away her tears. "But I couldn't do that, of course. I couldn't impose on a stranger. And Cousin Beverley is expecting me."

"You're right—better go to Cousin Bev," he muttered.

His eyes looked disappointed, yet relieved. His face of a sudden seemed younger, more boyish, as if a mask of years and worldly experience had dropped from it- Then, as he pondered, the mask slipped back in place, and the years laid their shadows over his eyes once more.

"I'll give you my name and address, so you can write me any time you feel you want to leave," he said hurriedly. "If you find you can't stand it, let me know, and I'll come running. I may come, anyhow."

He took from his pocket an envelope, extracted from it a letter which he threw out of the window, and then gave her the envelope. It was addressed to Mr. Wirt Roddy, Fort Worth, Texas. The writing was that of a woman.

Letty took it somewhat dubiously. "Thank you—but I guess I'll not need to use it. I'm going to try to like my—new home."

"Here's hoping you will," he responded, suave and unperturbed. "But keep the address, so you'll have it handy in case you want to make a getaway. I can always help you out. I've got spondulix to do what I like with. And even if Fort Worth's not so pretty as your Virginia, it's not as bad as the cow and sand country at that, where the wind comes larrupin' over the prairie like wild mustangs on a stampede."

"You talk about wind like it was human," she said with an attempt at bravado.

He chuckled. "No, 'tain't human. It's a devil. Seven devils sometimes, when it goes rampagin' round."

"Well—what of it—so long as you know it's nothing but wind, and can't hurt you?"

Her eyes had an upward appeal, and her voice a lilt like a little brook speaking softly to itself—the innocent candor of a child that has been protected and gently dealt with, so that it is not used to being hurt or afraid, and scarcely knows enough to feel apprehension of any danger.

His gaze expressed playful superiority. "Ho! Can't hurt you?" he scoffed. "Don't you know this is a cyclone country you're coming to? Hasn't anybody told you that the settlers dig themselves storm cellars to run to, almost before they build their houses?"

Her cheek paled a little, but the dimple near the corner of her mouth still twinkled intrepidly, and her voice was brave, though small. "What are cyclones like?"

"Well, a cyclone is a tornado of a special deadly brand we have out here," he bragged. "It's a bull buffalo of a wind that whirls in a circle like a dancing dervish, while it races ahead at the same time. It's shaped like a funnel, small at the ground, and spreading out wide at the top."

He gestured to illustrate, and paused in enjoyment of her dismay. "It's a regular wind, a snuff-dipper of a wind. It catches up sand so's you can see it plain as a tree. It goes upward toward the sky like a cloud. It whizzes faster'n an express train can go, and where it's passed, there ain't enough remains of anything to hold an inquest over. If it was a house or a town, it's in splinters, and if it was a person—well, there's nothing left but a grease spot."

He smiled in pride over this virile wind he had called up.

"Did you ever see one?" Her voice quavered in spite of her effort to keep it firm.

"Once. And once was a-plenty. I was considerable distance off, too, when I viewed it. You can see the thing for a mile, if it comes in the daytime, but if it comes at night, you don't know anything, till it swoops down on you, roarin' like a prairie fire,"

His tone was serious now. She tried to sift out the truth from the jest, and her thumping heart told her that he had not invented this Texas storm.

She sat with paling cheeks and hands tightly clasped in her lap. So she was coming to a cyclone country! And wind was not merely a thing to be hated because it would ruin your skin and your eyes and hair, and wreck your nerves. It was a terror that might pass by day or night, to leave death and devastation in its path! In the day, when you could see its frightfulness,—or in the night when you could only hear it roaring, and imagine!...

She shuddered as she pictured a vast, swaying cloud of sand that spiraled to the sky, a mighty engine of destruction sweeping over the land, before which human beings were as helpless as rag dolls, that tore houses and towns to splinters. A cyclone! As in a nightmare she saw herself, palsied with terror, watching the mad, immense whirlwind sweep toward her, engulf her!...

Her body quivered, and the little rounded chin was unsteady. "I think you're cruel to tell me such things to scare me!" she cried, with a catch in her voice.

He looked gratified at the effect of his eloquence, and magnanimously willing to temper the horrors a trifle in compassion for her tremors.

"We-ell, now. I'm only just telling you what you got to look out for in this section. But of course cyclones don't come so often. You might live here for a long time and never see one, and then again you might run spang into one the first rattle out of the box."

She turned from him and gazed out of the window. Even if all this was true, it wasn't kind of him to tell her, to scare her when she was coming out there to live.

The man folded his arms and sat in silence beside her, humorously tolerant of her resentment, with the air of a man who is sure of himself and of others, and hence need feel small impulse toward haste or awkwardness.

The girl felt a quiver of fear of him, she could not have told why. She had never been afraid of anybody before, since in her quiet world even tramps were just men out of work, who wanted food and a kindly word before they passed on their way. But this stranger made her giddily apprehensive in some inexplicable way. Why should he tease her, and scare her like this? She wouldn't notice him any more, she would forget what he had said, and then maybe it wouldn't be true. If she looked out of the window and let him see she didn't care to talk to him any more, he would go away.

Perhaps he was just teasing her, and presently would apologize, and tell her there was nothing to be afraid of in this West where she had to live.

She glanced at him to see if he had it in mind to apologize, but he only smiled at her and said no word....

She wouldn't speak, she wouldn't, at all. She would ignore him, she would forget him. But she couldn't, somehow. She was aware of his presence, even though she wouldn't look at him. Her spirit tremblingly closed up under his influence, like the leaves of a sensitive plant at an alien touch. Her very body knew that he was there!...

But she kept her face resolutely turned from him, her eyes fixed on the landscape that glided by. She saw a wide, flat expanse of prairie, with diminishing mesquites, dead bunch-grass, on which long-horned cattle were grazing in the unfenced pastures along the track— gaunt creatures that stopped their feeding to look in panic at the train as it approached them. The very cows seemed afraid of something, in this strange country!...

Presently she saw on the ground beside the track the carcass of a cow with long horns, and ribs prominently outlined beneath the hide, a starved-looking cow. She felt a thrill of pity for its fate, and thought of the sleek, well-fed cows in the pastures back home. Would the new owners of old Bossy, the brown-eyed Jersey that had had to be sold, be good to her? She had loved Bossy like a friend, and had wept at seeing her led away. But Bossy was fat and gentle, not like these wild creatures. Well, at least there would be plenty of cattle on a ranch, and maybe she could make friends with some of them. There would be little young calves to pet, with wobbly legs and cold, poking noses that nuzzled into your hand....

The mesquites were much smaller now, scarcely more than bushes, and the wind was blowing harder, for the gray grasses over the plains were bent lower in the sweep of it....

As the train rattled noisily along, some of the cattle galloped off to a distance and gazed back in timorous belligerency as at an enemy to be feared and distrusted....

There beside the track was another body, one that had evidently been there a long time, for the bones were showing through the hide. Who looked after all those cattle, anyhow? She couldn't see any houses near, any signs of human habitation. What a lonesome land it was!...

Presently the engine gave a shrill hoot, as if signaling, but there was no one in sight. Was it just practicing, to keep in running order? The distances between towns was so long out here that maybe the engine would forget how to hoot if it didn't clear its throat now and then. Engines were funny things, almost like folks....

In another instant they passed a cow that was staggering along the track from the direction of the engine, one hind leg hanging broken and useless, its back bleeding.

Letty cried out, "Oh, the poor thing!"

The man turned a careless glance at the animal. "Yep, train hit 'er."

She shuddered. "Why don't they stop and do something for the poor creature?"

He shrugged his shoulders and answered comfortably. "It'll die after awhile, likely, same as these others you see along the track. Train gets one pretty often."

"Why, how perfectly terrible!" she gasped. A lump moved up and down painfully in her throat.

He shook his head reassuringly. "These critters aren't worth much a head. No loss."

She flashed him a look of burning indignation. "And is that what has happened to the others I saw?"

"Sure. You see, there's no fence to the right of way along here. The durn fools try to cross in front of the train, an' they get what's coming to 'em. Too bad, but it can't be helped," he added, in concession to her evident disturbance over the matter.

She leaned her head upon her hand, of a sudden feeling sick and faint. Her mind followed the poor thing as it staggered along, hurt and terrified, to fall by the way in that lonely land, to die maybe of starvation, by slow degrees. And the train hooted on its way, not caring for its sufferings, a train full of people who ought to be kind!

Her hands clenched tightly. "Life is cruel!" she choked.

"Looks hard, but that's the way life is," he said, more sympathetically. "The engineer toots the whistle when he sees a cow on the track, to give her warning she'd better get off. If she don't tumble to it, the cow-ketcher catches her and throws her to one side, so she don't get ground under the wheels and maybe wreck the train."

She made no answer. She was facing for the first time life's possibilities of cruelty. How could this man talk so indifferently, when—

He went on in elaboration. "Most times they get off in time. And train schedules would be shot to pieces if they stopped to tend to all the old cows in this cattle country."

She couldn't argue the question with him, but she still felt vehemently that men should be more humane.... If she tried to speak she might begin to cry, and she mustn't do that.

She gazed steadily out of the window.... There was another prairie-dog town, its citizens coming out to watch the train come just as the boys and girls did when the afternoon train came in at home. *Home!*—

Her throat ached with suppressed sobs, but she held her head erect. She wouldn't give way, she wouldn't cry!...

Presently the man went on with the discussion as if there had been no pause. "And you never can tell. Sometimes they die quick and are out of their misery. But then again an old cow that looks ready for the boneyard will get over her broken leg and hop around spry as you please on three pins."

At last she spoke with repressed intensity of tone, "And is this the trail to your West—the bodies of the poor creatures you've killed?"

"Yes, if you was to fall off the train, and didn't see the track to go by, you could pretty near find your way west by following the trail of dead cattle here and there along the road."

"It's horrible!"

He smiled genially. "Don't blame me for it, little girl. It's not my train, and not even my West, as I told you. I just own a few sections of land out there for my ranch, and I go out now and then. But it's not my regular stamping-ground, remember."

She sat in silence tor a time, reflecting. All the old values seemed left behind. Ahead lay the path to the West, with its trail of broken bodies, its threats of storms and unknown perils, its winds that would torment her. Behind her lay the road whose shining rails led backward toward Virginia, toward home....

The afternoon was waning now, and she could see the sun beginning to sink toward the west. At this time in Virginia, the colored boys would be driving the cows home from pasture, their soft voices calling to them one by one, by name....

A wave of desolation swept over her, almost overwhelmed her. Homesickness so acute that it was physical agony possessed her. She felt she must shriek aloud for the train to stop, for the wheels to reverse, and let her go back to Virginia. She felt a mad impulse to fling herself from the train, to chance her fate by the wayside, even in that wild, lonely land, to walk back to Virginia if need be, if she could get there no other way. Home!...

Then a still crueler hurt checked her savagely—the remembrance that she had no home there any more. Strangers warmed themselves at the old hearth-fires. The household possessions were scattered, even her childhood books and toys given away. Her past had been snatched from her!...

The wheels turned on relentlessly, bearing her ever toward the West. Their sound was like a monotonous chant, "No home!—no home!—no home!—"

To be homesick for a home you didn't have any more, was the worst hurt in the world! because there wasn't any hope that you could ever win back to it in any future. It was gone forever! Thinking of it was like hearing the clods fall on the coffin of the one dearest to you....

There was no place anywhere that she could call her own now—none but the old family lot in the churchyard at home, where her mother lay under a fresh mound with a white stone at her head, beside the father who had died long ago. The cool, shadowy peace of the spot wooed her.... It would be good to lie there, at rest....

But the wheels ground on, still westward. Letty could hear the steady swish of the wind that never stopped blowing, the chant of the wheels in their mockery of her.

From time to time she saw beside the track another body, or a whitened skeleton, or perhaps but scattered bones to tell a story of what had happened....

16

The man beside her touched her arm.

"You ought to watch the sunset," he told her. "A sunset on the Texas prairie is a sight worth looking at, even if you've seen as many a one as I have."

As she looked, she saw before her a sky incredibly blue, of a clear, pure color such as she had never seen before. Far, far ahead to the west where the earth met the sky, the sun rested, a great ball of flame, its rays spreading outward and upward to the heavens it had left. In that high, clear altitude, where one can see to great distances, the sun seemed at once remote and close at hand. The wind-blown clouds above were touched to brilliant orange, rose, and gold, and all imaginable shadings of rainbow hues. There was nothing to break the view, no tree nor house nor bill, only the free sweep of the prairie, which was now a shimmering gray lit by reflected light, and at the horizon's edge the burning splendor of the sun. It seemed to Letty that the train should stop in awe to view the spectacle, that men should remove their hats before this pageant of a world on fire, with a vast desert for a stage, and no spectators save a few indifferent passengers on a train.

She caught her breath in wonder and delight, and for a while forgot her problems, feeling curiously calmed and yet exhilarated by the sight. Then she turned suddenly away.

"I won't look too long," she said in a low voice. "I can't bear to watch it fade. I'll hang that sunset in my mind as a picture and remember it always."

"You're a funny kid," the man muttered.

"It hurts to see things fade. Beautiful things should go out in a high glory."

He smiled. "A sunrise out here is grander still. Will you someday watch a sunrise on the plains and think of me?"

She nodded.

The train sped onward, bearing her straight toward the burning sunset, toward the West. Would it be a land of glory as well as a land of fear and cruelty, perhaps?...

After a while the conductor stopped to speak to Letty. "We'll have some supper at Abilene. We're runnin' late. Had a hot-box."

"Thank you, but I don't care for any," she answered. "I don't think I'm a bit hungry."

"Oh, yes, better eat a little snack," he advised. "Some time yet before we pull into Sweetwater."

And so she got off with the others at Abilene. Mr. Wirt Roddy walked along beside her, and insisted on buying ham sandwiches and fruit and little cakes, which they took back to the train to eat.

"Like a picnic, or a box supper at a church sociable," he said with a laugh, as if to make her feel that the situation was all right.

The early dark of winter came on, shutting out the world as if with a vast curtain, and the brakesman lighted the hanging lamps that swayed and flared smokily with the motion of the train.

Letty felt a strange depression which she could not analyze, a feeling as if she were hurtling through space and yet staying still. Was there any world outside this moving car? any time beyond this hour of the present? What life lay for her behind the dark curtains of the future, in this land unlike anything she had ever known? Should she be equal to it?

A strange, fluid fear enthralled her, a trembling of body and spirit, a dreamy unrest that was by turns ice and flame....

Silence had laid a stilling finger on her soul.

The man beside her sat in silence, too. She could feel his gaze upon her, but he sat with folded arms, not speaking. Of what was he thinking?...

When the train slowed up at a little town, she started up in a panic, thinking it was Sweetwater. But he laid a hand on her arm.

"Not yet. This is Merkel."

She sank back without a word.

The train moved on again, and she could hear only the ceaseless clack of the wheels, could imagine she heard the swish and shriek of the wind, and the thick, rhythmic pounding of her heart

At last the man spoke. "We're coming in to Sweetwater now. You'll have to get ready and be off *pronto*, for the train don't stop but just a few minutes."

She rose, hurriedly put on her hat and cloak, and started to pick up her old-fashioned telescope valise, but he took it from her.

"I'll bring this."

"Oh, is this your station, too?" she stammered.

"No, I go on to Colorado City, but I'll see you off."

The conductor came along, his lantern swung over his arm. "Here's where you leave us, little lady. I'll help you."

"No, I'll look after her," replied the other.

And so it was Mr. Wirt Roddy that lifted her valise off and then helped her from the car to the ground.

The wind swooped at her like a mad malevolence, so that she had to clutch her hat to keep it from being blown away. She staggered, and would have fallen before its fury, had not Mr. Wirt Roddy caught her to him for an instant to steady her. She shivered at his touch.

The night was pitch dark. Only the light from the little station-house door, and the conductor's lantern at the end of the train, and a few twinkles here and there from scattered houses gave any illumination.

Letty looked around swiftly to find Cousin Beverley. She hadn't seen him since she was a child, but she would know him, of course.

But she saw only the station agent at the door, the conductor swinging his lantern, and besides them only two rough-looking men in heavy coats and leather trousers, and broad-brimmed hats. They stared at her with curiosity. But neither was Cousin Beverley, And there was no one else there.

Cousin Beverley hadn't come to meet her!

The train bell rang its signal to depart.

"All aboard!" called the conductor at the other end of the train.

The wind caught Letty in an icy swirl, and its sound rose to a shriek.

2

LETTY GAVE A LITTLE CRY of despair. "Oh, what shall I do? Cousin Beverley didn't come to meet me!"

The night seemed waiting to swallow her like a bottomless sea, the wind ready to rend her to pieces.

One of the two lounging men stepped forward, making a gesture toward his hat. "Excuse me, ma'am, but are you Bev Mason's cousin?"

"Yes, yes! Where is he?"

"He couldn't get off for some reason or other. I don't exactly know why. But he ast me to bring you out."

Mr. Roddy called to the conductor, "Hi, hold the train a pair o' minutes, will you?"

"What fer?" was shouted back above the wind. And the bobbing lantern came down the length of the train to investigate the cause for the delay.

Letty gave a swift glance at the stranger. She could see him more plainly now by the light of the swinging lantern. He was tall, and had on high boots with spurs to them, and a heavy coat, and a broad-brimmed felt hat that shaded and partially concealed his face.

She couldn't possibly go away into the darkness and the wind with those boots and spurs, and that face that she couldn't quite see! No, not possibly! But what could she do?

Mr. Wirt Roddy stepped forward with authority. "Who might you be?" he asked, somewhat curtly.

"I might be several persons," drawled the other. "But as it happens, I'm Lige Hightower. My ranch is ten miles beyond Bev's."

"Why didn't you speak up before?" Mr. Roddy demanded.

The newcomer did not seem cowed by this masterful interrogation.

"Bev said as how the lady would be alone. So I thought this wasn't the one."

"This gentleman just helped me off the train," Letty broke in somewhat confusedly. Then she wondered instantly if that remark would offend Mr. Roddy. It was hard to deal tactfully with two men at once, when they had taken so evident a dislike to each other on sight.

She turned to the conductor. He was a fatherly man who could give her advice.

"I'm scared! Ought I to go off like this? What must I do?" Her voice rose in a frightened falsetto like a child's.

Hightower spoke up instantly, in a deep, comfortable voice. "Nothin' to be skeered of, ma'am. I'll look after you good and proper. Here's my sidekick, Newt Wortham. He'll recommend me."

The other lounger straightened up and joined the group. "Yes, ma'am. We're big bobashillies. He's all right. I been knowin' him since who laid the chunk."

The station agent strolled up to take part in the discussion. "Lige has fixed it up with my wife for you to stay all night at our house. The missis is tickled pink to see some company."

The conductor's lantern gave an upjerk of relief.

"That's all right, little lady," said the conductor heartily. "You'll be taken care of like the cat's whiskers. Good-bye and good luck to you."

He shook hands with her, made a wincing grimace of farewell to her with his eye-mustaches, waved his lantern.

"All aboard!"

Letty gazed at him in dismay. So she was really to be left like this!

Wirt Roddy took her hand. "Good-bye."

"Good-bye," said Letty, in a weak, uncertain voice. "And thank you for your courtesy."

He stooped over her and spoke softly, so that only she could hear. "I'm coming back to see you one of these days—maybe. And be sure to keep the address."

He swung onto the steps of the moving train, without waiting for her reply.

As the train rolled past her, Letty watched it through a blur of tears. It seemed like the last link between her and her old life, even though it was moving westward, instead of back toward Virginia. Trains were heartless things!

She shivered with cold, for the icy wind was at her like a great dog, leaping on her, pulling at her clothes, shaking her. She felt very small and forlorn, her heart weighted down with a sense of strangeness and apprehension.

The station agent spoke in a friendly voice, as if he read her thoughts. "If you'll wait for three shakes of a sheep's tail, while I lock up, we'll make tracks to my house."

Newt Wortham mounted a horse that had been standing unhitched, its bridle trailing on the ground, called "*Adios!* see you all later," and galloped away. The three others started off into the darkness. They plowed along through the sand of the roadway, that seemed almost ankle deep. Letty felt afraid to put her foot down into it, for it seemed like a bottomless treachery, like a trap that might catch her.

"I guess you think you need stilts for this sand," remarked Lige Hightower.

"It's not as bad now as it is sometimes," the station agent put in.

"I s'pose I'll get used to it by degrees," said Letty, in a strangled voice. She muffled her mouth with her coat to keep out the sand that the wind whirled into her face.

The station agent laughed. "They say a feller can get used to anything, just so he begins in time—even hanging. Eh, Lige?"

"Well, that's a habit I hope I never fall into," answered Lige. "Standin' on nothin' pullin' hemp ain't my idea of sport."

"Can't never tell what you're comin' to, though." The agent raised his voice above the wind, so that he was almost shouting. Letty muffled her ears now, too, to keep out the sand that was sifting in. She could feel its crawl down her neck and inside her clothes, could taste its acrid grit in her mouth, could smell it in her nostrils as she breathed, could feel its sharp sting against her face. As she stumbled along, in the darkness, tears washed sand from her half-shut eyes.

What a terrible, terrible country it was that God had sent her to! But what if it wasn't God that had sent her, but only the minister, and he had made a mistake?

The train would be miles away by now, with the conductor who was like a fatherly friend —and Mr. Wirt Roddy.

The mere thought of that strange, disturbing man troubled her pulse as his presence had done. Should she ever see him again? Who was he?—and what sort of life had he known?

The station agent led them through a gate and they came up on the porch of a little house whose windows gleamed welcoming lamplight, and whose door swung open at sound of their steps.

"Come in quick," said a cordial voice, "before the wind blows you away."

A woman in a blue gingham dress took Letty by the hand and drew her inside.

20

The station agent banged the door quickly, to shut out the riotous intrusion of the wind that tried to follow them.

His wife's eager hands were drawing off Letty's coat and hat, settling her in a rocking-chair. Her kindness, the indubitable goodness in her face, her welcome, brought tears to Letty's eyes. Not until she saw this homely, motherly woman, did she realize just how frightened and bewildered she had been, how tense with terror of the unknown. She gave a little shuddering sob and caught her breath like a child that knows it shouldn't cry, but tries in vain to keep from it.

"I'm silly," she quavered. "I guess the wind got on my nerves."

"That's all right, child. You just snub a little, if you feel like. Cryin' does you good sometimes."

But with feminine contrariety, as soon as she was bidden to cry, Letty laughed and wiped away her tears.

The station agent spoke. "She was skeered to come off with a cowboy. She'd never seed one before, and she thought a cowboy was all over horns like a horned frog."

"That's the way we grow up at first," said the cowboy gravely. "But if they ketch us early they can dehorn us an' make us safe for sassiety. And of course it don't matter about hoofs, because we always wear our boots, even to sleep in."

He smiled a wide, generous smile, and crinkled his eyes at her.

"An' out here men allus die with their boots on," added the other.

"Be ashamed to tease the little girl like that!" scolded his wife. "Never you mind 'em, honey. Men are born liars, specially in the west."

"I don't mind—now that I'm here with you," said Letty. Her cheerfulness was returning by degrees.

The room was cozy, with the open fire in the Franklin stove, the red-clothed center table, the mountainous feather bed in the corner of the room, and the carpet with its bright red roses blooming on the floor.

Letty looked shyly at the cowboy who had taken off his heavy coat and his hat and sat on the other side of the fire from her, his long frame folded up in a rocking chair. She was not afraid of him now. His eyes were kind-looking, gray, with shrewd little laughter wrinkles at the corners, and with the far-seeing gaze of one who is accustomed to look at long, unbroken distances—such a look as is in the eyes of sailors. She seemed to see the plains unroll before her in his eyes.

His hair was brown and somewhat crinkly. His face and throat were sunburned until they were almost as dark as a Mexican's, but across his forehead next to his hair, where the broad hat had shaded it, there was a band of white in startling contrast to the rest of his face. His mouth was big, and his ears stood out rather prominently. He was younger, more boyish than her acquaintance of the train, perhaps twenty-five, though she couldn't be sure.

"Well, Lige, how's tricks with you?" asked Gus Gresham, the station agent.

"All right, Gus. I wouldn't say I had the world by the tail and a downhill pull on it, but I got no kick comin' about my luck. The land I homesteaded is fair enough, though a leetle shy on water holes. An' I'm gettin' a decent bunch o' cattle started. No chance o' me bein' big rich any time soon, but I ain't askin' to have the hat passed round for me, neither."

Gus yawned comfortably in the warmth of the room. "That's good."

"Well, it ain't so bad, for a feller that hasn't had any backin'. I had to save everything I got from the wages that Old Man Wilcox paid me for cowpunchin'. An' you know what a tight-fist that old geezer was. I don't say he'd *go* to hell for a nickel, but he'd fool round the rim so long lookin' for it till he'd fall in!"

His host chuckled, as one familiar with Old Man Wilcox.

"You're in cahoots with Dave Denby, ain't you?"

"Yep. He homesteaded the land next to what I filed on, so we built our shack on the corner of the land so's he lives in his room an' I in mine. He's a good old Injun, Dave is."

"Yes, you're right, he is."

Letty leaned forward, unable to repress her curiosity. "How funny to have the house sitting on two tracts of land!"

"Yes'm, folks do that often out here. If you're taking up land, you got to live on it a certain part o' the time. But it's lonesome livin' by myself. I've known four members o' one family to go in together and build a four-room house, each one livin' in a different room on his own land."

"And you two men live by yourselves?"

"Yes'm, me and Sourdough baches it."

"What did you call him?"

"I call him old Sourdough, because he don't know how to cook no sort o' bread but sourdough biscuits when it comes his week to be biscuit-slinger. An' he calls me Saleratus, or Sal, for short, because that's the kind I make."

Letty began to show interest in this new world to which she must accommodate herself. She tried to vision the house on the ranch, with two solitary men doing all the work.

"How many cattle you got, Lige?" asked Gus.

"'Bout five hundred head, near's I can make out."

Letty opened her eyes wide in amazement. "How in the world do you manage to drive that many up every day?"

"Wha-at? Oh, I *savez*. Well, ma'am we don't drive 'em up but twict a year, spring an' fall round-ups."

She looked her astonishment. "But how do you get the milking done?"

"Calves tend to that," he replied laconically, while his lips twitched and his eyes crinkled with grave laughter.

"How funny!"

"It'd be funnier yet to try to milk one o' them wild range cows that ain't never known the customs of civilization. You couldn't do it no-ways, less'n you roped her an' throwed her an' tied her. She wouldn't consider she was born for such a lot as that."

Letty tried to see the picture of someone trying to milk a rampageous range cow.

Lige went on ruminantly. "Cattle is like humans—they is some things they jest nachelly won't stand for."

"I don't know much about the west," she answered dubiously.

"No'm—but you'll learn a heap if you stay out here long."

Silence fell on the little group for a moment or two, a comfortable, easy silence that didn't need to be broken just to make conversation.

At last Letty turned to Mrs. Gresham. "I wish it was daylight, so I could see Sweetwater."

"I wouldn't be in too much of a swivet to do that," her husband put in. "Sweetwater's no sight for sore eyes."

"But I've thought so much about it, since I got Cousin Bev's letter with this postmark."

"You don't have to live here," said Mrs. Gresham encouragingly.

"There might be worse things nor that," observed Lige, with judicial impartiality. "Women like to herd in towns, they say."

"Do you have a river here, or is it a lake?" Letty questioned.

As her three auditors looked blank, she explained, "Sweetwater, you know."

Lige chuckled throatily. "Names is like dreams—they go by contraries most times. I reckon the early settlers named this spot what they did because there ain't no water here, and the nearest is brackish, lime, you know."

"But what do you do for water?"

Mrs. Gresham spoke up. "We have cisterns. Of course, they dry up in droughts."

Her husband added his contribution of information. "Some folks that ain't got cisterns buys their water. It comes in on the train, in barrels, and you can buy it like that. They've been times when folks had to drive twenty miles for water, and bring it back in a tank and empty it into the cisterns. There's been stretches when all our drinkin' water had to be hauled in on the train. Folks learn not to be too reckless with water out in this section."

Letty lapsed into a depressed silence, trying to imagine a life where one didn't have as much water as he wanted. Why, water had been like air, taken for granted in the scheme of the universe.

Presently the warmth of the room, her fatigue, and the healthy sleepiness of youth made her drowsy, and she heard the rumble of the men's voices in talk as from a distance, caught disconnected phrases now and then, but not enough to rouse her. She found herself nodding.

Mrs. Gresham's voice roused her. "I know you're tired and sleepy after your long trip, so we'll go to bed. You're going to sleep in here with me, and Lige can bunk in the other room with Gus."

So soon Letty sank into the feather bed that billowed about her, snuggled into a warm nest and drifted off to sleep. Her dreams were a jumble of whistling winds, of sand and darkness, of wide wastes where skeleton cattle lay beside the tracks of a speeding train— and a tall stranger with black mustache, and eyes that seemed to know a great deal. She dreamed of a flaming sunrise, when all the prairies were on fire—when she stood alone and thought of Wirt Roddy....

She seemed to be buried in a mountain of sliding sand that mocked her efforts toward release—and struggled up to find herself almost smothered in the feathers....

She was blown along like a leaf in a gale, in the power of a demon wind that mocked her desperation. She screamed, but the wind shrieked louder. She struggled—but of what avail is a leaf in a tempest, a feather whirled in a cyclone? When she felt that she must die or go mad of terror, she gave a strangling cry.

Mrs. Gresham patted her shoulder. "Had a nightmare? Nothing's going to hurt you."

She shivered and lay awake for a while, remembering all that Wirt Roddy had told her of the winds and the west. Even now that she was awake, she thought she saw herself as that leaf blown fluttering helplessly over the desert sand, toward a mystery of doom. But in the end, sleep claimed her again....

· · · ·

She waked to a cheerful morning. Lige joked with the children at the breakfast table, and consumed incredible quantities of fried ham and grits and gravy, and hot biscuit. The food tasted delicious to her, too, after the irregular meals she had had in traveling.

When Lige had scraped his plate clean, he pushed his chair back and spoke to Letty. "Well, young lady, don't you think we'd better get up and dust?"

"Dust?" She looked round for a dust cloth.

"Hit the grit for the ranches. Your Cousin Bev will be honin' to see you. Leastways, he will if he ever seen you."

He smiled at his ponderous gaiety.

She rose at once.

He beckoned her toward the door. "But first—you must lamp this metropolis. View this town you've been thinkin' up fancy pictures of."

He took her by the arm and led her to the porch. He gave a wide, flourishing gesture that bade her ignore no details of the landscape spread out before her gaze.

She looked at Sweetwater, and saw a strangling collection of small houses of the rudest, simplest structure, some not even painted, some without fences around them, none softened by the protection of a tree nor made home-like by a lawn or garden. Just little bare box-like houses, naked and unbeautiful!—set down in a waste of sand.

Letty rubbed her eyes in bewilderment and dismay. Of course, there wouldn't be flowers in winter time, she told her sinking heart, she hadn't expected that. But the town obviously held no prospect of them at any season. Sand, sand, sand!

"And *this* is Sweetwater!" she faltered, in a daze.

"Yep."

"Then please take me out to a ranch as quick as possible!"

"'*Sta bueno*! We'll light a shuck!"

They started off in an antiquated buckboard that rattled alarmingly, driving a lean, wiry young horse. Mrs. Gresham had put a hot brick at Letty's feet, and Lige had wrapped a buffalo robe over her knees and tucked it in close around her.

"Thank you. That'll keep out the wind," she said gratefully.

"But the wind has gone down this morning. This ain't hardly any wind at all," he expostulated.

True, the furious blasts of the night before had abated, but there was still enough to make Letty, unused as she was to Texas weather, uncomfortable.

The driving was a slow business on account of the sand.

"This cayuse don't like to drive—hurts his pride," said Lige. "I had a time gentlin' him enough to break him in to it."

Once they were well out of the town, and on the prairies, they seemed to be going it blindly, for there was scarcely any perceptible road for their guidance. Everywhere sand, in wind-blown waves stretching out like a vast sea, the dead grass bent over in the wind like the curling foam of the waves. The sky was a cold blue today, and the atmosphere was so clear that they could see to incredible distances in all directions.

"It feels queer to be out in the open with so much space about you, and no protection at all," said Letty. "I've been used to hills and trees and houses."

He gave the horse a cut with the whip so that he jerked forward. "I like this best. Town life smothers me. A feller knows where he's at if he can see all about him. What's the use in wantin' to hide behind trees and hills and houses'?"

"This makes me think of a song old Aunt Charity used to sing, a negro spiritual:

24

> "I run to de rock for to hide my face,
> But de rock cry out, 'No hiding-place,
> No hiding-place here!'"

He listened gravely, while she sang the old song. Then he went on with the expression of his philosophy.

"When you look at it one way, a man don't amount to a pin-point. But I'm more of a man when I'm out here on the plains. Seems like I can stand up on my hind legs and look God in the face man to man, you might say, and He understands me, and I understand Him."

Letty felt vaguely shocked at what she thought might be irreverence.

"I think you can find God best in a church," she said with prim shyness.

"I ain't sayin' you can't find Him there. He must come there sometimes, anyways, to show He appreciates the trouble folks go to fix a place for Him. But I have an idea He's kind o' notionate, like me—gets fidgety if you try to pin Him in a house too long."

"I don't know," said Letty dubiously.

"When you're out on the range long stretches by yourself, when you don't hardly see a human being, you come to know how little importance folks are. And when you lie out in the open at night to sleep, with nothing between you and the earth but a blanket, and nothing between you and the sky, you get sort o' chummy with the stars."

Letty shuddered at the thought. "I'd get too lonesome!"

"Yes, I reckon there are folks that'd go loco for lonesomeness. It's accordin' to what they been used to."

They fell into a long silence, thinking their own thoughts. Letty watched the prairies stretch out before her, vast reaches of sand, covered with bunch grass growing in clumps, and curly mesquite grass, with no trees, only occasional bushes of mesquite, and sometimes tall spikes covered with sword-like growths that looked as if they could inflict sharp wounds if one ran against them. Sometimes there were cactus growth like coral formations, covered with innumerable needles, and now and then a cactus, shaped like a round little cushion stuffed with pins.

She started up presently at seeing a long, gray furred creature go leaping across the sand like a kangaroo.

"What's that?" she cried.

"Nothin' but a jackrabbit. You'll see thousands of 'em round here."

She had never seen a rabbit of such enormous size. Did the animals thrive on western air, or did the atmosphere magnify their size so that they only looked bigger?

They passed a prairie-dog town where the citizens popped out of their holes to see them, yapped saucily, as if not afraid, and dived down into their holes.

"That's a dog town," Lige explained with a wave of his whip. "When you go horseback ridin' out here you got to be careful about goin' over such a place. A horse is liable to step in a dog hole an' break his leg, or throw you a tumble."

"I wonder if I'll ever have the courage to go horseback riding out here," she said dubiously.

"Oh, yes, you will. That's maybe what you'll enjoy most. It makes you feel you own the universe to be on a horse on these prairies when the spring flowers are blooming and the Sonora doves are talkin' soft and sympathetic to each other, and the little desert wrens are flyin' round, and the field-larks are sailin' high into the sky, droppin' music down like a shower o' melody. You can see plenty o' quail with topknots, and the road runners that dash round like they was crazy, so there's always somethin' to interest you, if you like that sort o' thing."

A bird darted along in front of them, running along the ground, not using his wings at all —a black and white bird, with a long neck, that seemed to be in a prodigious hurry to get somewhere for some purpose or other.

"That's a road runner, now," said Lige. "Some calls 'em chaparral birds or paisanos. And that little cuss settin' on the limb of that mesquite bush wigglin' his forked tail is a scissor-tail."

"Even the birds out here are strangers to me. I feel like a foreigner," commented Letty.

"You'll soon get acquainted, and they'll be a heap o' company to you."

She would need companionship, she told herself. She felt oppressed by the solitude of nature, which was so different from the friendly countrysides she had known at home— these vast, distressing stretches of treeless plains, with nothing to see but a few stunted mesquite bushes, and samples of cactus that would repel the touch. No friendly intimate wild animals such as she had always been used to seeing—gossipy squirrels gray or brown, chipmunks—only these colossal jackrabbits, and these prairie dogs that yapped at you as you passed.

As if realizing her depression, and understanding its cause, the man at her side made an effort to talk to her cheerfully. He told her stories of the west of the early days, and by his easy, descriptive, jocular words, made her see something of what life had been in that region when it was even wilder and less populated than at the present- He pictured for her the great herds of buffaloes that had roamed over the unfenced pastures, till she could see the huge animals with their massive heads, their dark, shaggy hair and manes, the humps on their shoulders, as they grazed alone on the flowery plains, or as they surged in masses in their migrations. He told her of the fights the jealous bulls would have over the right to rule the herds, goring each other with their fierce, short, in-curving horns, bellowing their rage to the empty silences. He told how they would gather in thousands by the water holes, and that certain places were known as the buffalo "wallows." He pictured how the Indians used to shoot them with bows and arrows, or sometimes, when other means failed, they would drive herds of them over a precipice, down to the valley beneath, that they might have them for food. The white man, too, was fond of juicy buffalo steak, and there were no wild herds free and safe as in the old days.

Letty could shut her eyes and see those vast, moving masses of tossing manes and shaggy humps and menacing horns—buffaloes, wild, savage creatures that typified the west!

"You don't see them great herds like you used to," he said regretfully.

"I can manage to get along without them," she retorted.

He told her of the Indians that had formerly ranged on western plains, wild and free as the buffaloes—the Comanches, the Apaches, and the Kiowas—and described their battles, their marauding expeditions, when they would swoop down on some lone settler's ranch, fire his house, kill the family, perhaps, drive off the cattle and horses, and escape to the trackless plains where the white man could scarcely find them.

He told her the tragic story of Cynthia Ann Parker, into whose life despair came twice— the little white girl who was stolen from her family by the Indians, and somehow escaped the death or torture that was the usual fate. How she all but died of homesickness, when she had to resign herself to life among the Indians, while her family and friends at first made efforts to recapture her and finally gave her up as dead.

26

Letty could see the lonely little girl in the Indian wigwam, almost perishing of grief and fear, longing for death to come and set her free. She shuddered as Lige told how that when she was a beautiful young girl in her mid teens, Peta Nocona, the son of the Indian chief, took her for his wife.

"She had two Indian children," he said, "a boy, Quanah, who would be chief of the tribe, and a baby girl named Prairie Flower. She had got over grieving for her folks, and settled down to live as an Indian. But the whites came to fight the Indians after some raid the red devils had made. The Texas rangers came after them to settle up the scores."

"Oh, did they hurt her—by mistake?" cried Letty, breathlessly.

"No," he went on. "But a ranger's bullet hit Peta Nocona's side, and he knew he was done for. He was game, though, and he was bent on following the custom of his tribe in death. So he staggered to a mesquite tree, a lone tree that was growing there, and he leaned up against it and began the death song the Comanches sing when they know they face the end. It's a wild, doleful sort of chanty, enough to make your blood run cold to hear it! But that poor woman had to hear it, and know her husband was dying, killed before her eyes. True, he was an Injun, and didn't deserve no better than to be killed, but he was her man, and her children were his."

"But what became of her?" cried Letty.

"The rangers took her prisoner, and her baby that she had with her. The interpreter tried to talk to her in Comanche, but she wouldn't say nothing but one word over and over, 'Quanah! Quanah!' and they didn't know what it meant. So they told her in Comanche they'd have to take her with them, and then she told about her boy, Quanah, and begged 'em to find him. But they couldn't. They went back to the settlement with the woman, and word went round that a white woman had been took that had lived with the Indians a long time. She tried every way to get away from them, as if she was as anxious then to be an Injun as she must 'a' been to get back to her home when the redskins first took her. At last her folks recognized her for Cynthia Ann Parker."

"Poor thing, I'm glad she got home," murmured Letty.

"She broke her heart grievin' over it," he responded grimly. "She was more of an Injun then than a white person, and her child was somewhere on the plains, she didn't know where. Her folks watched her so close she didn't have no chance to get away, and, anyhow, the tribe was scattered and her man killed, so she just set and mourned, with a look on her face fit to make a stone cry, folks said. First her baby died, Prairie Flower, and then the mother went, too. She never did get reconciled. Her boy, Quanah, grew up to be the chief of his tribe, and the town of Quanah, here in the state, is named after him."

"Indians are terrible creatures, aren't they?" Letty shuddered as she thought of their savagery, and pictured a roving band of them rushing down upon some defenseless ranch house.

"Yes, the white folks had to get the best of 'em if we was to live in this country at all," he agreed.

Then he went on to tell her of old Fort Phantom Hill, where Robert E. Lee had made a stand against the Indians in the days before the Civil War—of the old, ruined structure that might yet be seen, its chimneys standing ghostlike in the gloom.

"You can see them chimneys standing there yet, with nothin' round 'em but the mesquite bushes, and the owls cryin' all night. Some folks say that at night the ghosts of the soldiers under Lee come back, and the Injun ghosts are there, too. But I ain't never seen 'em."

"This country all looks so wild, I wonder if it was worth all this trouble to take it and fight for it like this for the white folks," she commented dubiously.

"Oh, yes ma'am, it's a great country, when you come to know it," he answered heartily. "Couldn't hire me to live anywheres else."

He went on to tell her of the fights with the Mexicans, as well as the Indians, and helped her to see something of the drama of Texas history. He told her tales of the wild cattle, descendants of the cattle left by the fleeing Mexicans after their defeat, in the region between Laredo and San Antonio, and described how the early cowboys had learned from the Mexican vaqueros their skill in capturing the wild cattle, as well as the arts of roping and branding.

"Them wild cattle sure are fierce fighters when you get 'em cornered," he commented. "Folks used to hunt 'em by moonlight and try all sorts o' tricks to get the best of 'em. They're mean, but they got a lively strain in 'em that makes 'em valuable for this sort o' country."

"I don't know how anybody keeps from getting lost in this region where there aren't any roads or fences or houses to guide you."

"Oh, you get a sort o' coyote sense that helps you know directions and find the place you want."

He dramatized for her the great cattle drives twice a year when the steers were driven to the north along the famous trails—the Old Chisholm Trail, the Goodnight Trail, and others. She could see the round-ups, the stampedes, the cowboys standing night guard and all the drama of the primitive life of the west, so different from the easy, established civilization of Virginia.

Through his words she could see the early settlers, the pioneers that had come to this section, not as she had done, in a train, but in covered wagons, across prairies treacherous with Indians, scant of water, and threatened with multiple dangers—people who had lived, not as she would, in houses, but in dugouts they had fashioned for themselves. She could see cattle thieves and the swift vengeance wreaked on them when they were caught—the elemental but practical working out of law and order in a wild land. She saw quick, changing pictures of the early times, of the hardy heroic pioneers that had made possible even so much civilization as the region knew then.

"But the women—wasn't it hard on them?" she faltered.

He smiled nonchalantly. "Oh, yes, sure! But they were dead-game sports an' they stood the gaff. They didn't whine nor make life harder for their men. Of course, when you come down to brass tacks, the whole thing depended on the women folks. The women of early days could shoulder rifles and stave off Indians side by side with their husbands. And work —my stars, how they did work! Raised big families, did every lick of work, even to spinning and weaving. I take off my hat to the women of the west."

Letty felt small and unworthy at thought of them. His praise of them unconsciously rebuked her.

"But it must have been so hard on them!" she contended.

"Yep, that's right—but they didn't stop to wail over their lot. They had bigger things to think of. They fell in love an' got married, an' made homes in the wilderness for their men, an' raised children to go forward with the job. They didn't have time to think of ease or luxury, God bless 'em!"

His eyes narrowed with a far gaze, as if he were seeing a procession of the heroic women of the west, sturdy, self-reliant, unafraid—fit helpmates for pioneers.

She saw, in contrast, the women she had known, living tranquil lives, waited on by servants, keeping an exquisite daintiness of body and mind, in spacious, leisured ease and comfort. Old gardens, wide piazzas, treasured heirlooms of furniture and silver and books, traditions of gentility and family pride made life gracious and dignified for them. "Broken-down aristocracy" she heard them called, but aristocracy none the less. She felt a sudden engulfing homesickness for this familiar life, a terror of the new that she was approaching. How should she ever fit into this difficult scheme of things wherein a woman was expected to be a pioneer?

"Tell me about Cousin Bev," she said suddenly, as if to postpone as long as possible, even for a brief hour or two, the contemplation of the new necessities and obligations.

"He's a fine fellow. Hasn't had the best of luck at ranching, though. Drought caught him once and near 'bout wiped out his herd. Then he went on a note for a son of a gun that skipped the country and left him with the bag to hold. But he's a man, all right."

"I loved him when I was a little girl. I haven't seen him in years. He was so courtly and handsome and gay."

"He's changed some."

"Yes, of course. That was years ago. And tell me about his wife. Cousin Cora."

He paused as if searching for the right word. "She's not exactly the woman you'd have picked out for him. Me neither. But they's no tellin' where love nor lightnin' will strike. I've heard tell. I think she fixed her eye on him an' had him roped and branded before he knew what was happenin' to him."

"Oh!"

"I think he was too much of a gentleman to resist hard enough."

"He always was so considerate of women."

"It don't always pay to be too much so, I've heard tell."

Letty sat in apprehensive silence for a moment.

He went on. "She's the boss of that outfit, and don't you forget it. If I was you, I wouldn't go out of my way to contrary her none—if you want to live peaceable there."

A long silence fell between them, in which Letty was trying to picture what Cousin Cora would be like, and how they would get on together. She had been thinking only of Cousin Bev—remembering his lovableness, and she hadn't stopped to think that his wife was a different personality and that her welcome might be less warm than his. Had it been a mistake, after all, to come out to Texas? But the pastor had thought it best for her, and had made plans for her.

They rode for miles along the same monotony of landscape, seeing the scattered herds of long-horn cattle grazing on the sparse grass, the jackrabbits almost indistinguishable from the background of greyish grass from which they sprang up, the dwarfed mesquite bushes, the cactus, the sand.

Once Letty saw outlined against the distant slope a group of graceful creatures like gazelles.

"Them are antelope," he told her. "You can see plenty of 'em out here, though there ain't as many as used to be before the country was settled up."

"How graceful they are!"

"Yes'm, they're right pretty. They make good eatin', too. Antelope steak, now, is fine."

"I couldn't bear to see one killed!"

"Lots o' girls out here have their rifles and shoot game as good as the men. But I reckon you're too tender-hearted to kill anything. But you'll maybe learn if you stay out here."

Farther along they sighted a lone wolf-like animal that stood out clear against the sky. He lifted his nose and gave a series of quick yelps.

"That's a coyote. You'll see plenty of them round here, too. They howl round a place at night till you can't sleep good sometimes. One of 'em sounds like a half-dozen puppies in misery at once."

"Oh, I'd be scared to death to hear them!" She shivered at the thought.

"Sho—they're plumb cowards. They'd run from you. We do have wolves, though, loboes or loafers, we call 'em, big fellers that you need to look out for. And sometimes wild cats and cougars comes down from the mountains."

She turned cold at thought of those prowling creatures, and the man chuckled amiably at her cowardice.

Presently after long hours, when Letty was stiff in every muscle from sitting still in a cramped position so long, and chilled from the searching wind that not even the buffalo robe could keep out, Lige spoke encouragingly.

"We're about there now. See that house? That's Bev's outfit. This is Bev's land, an' them are some of his cattle. You can see his horses in the corral there."

Letty saw a scattered herd of thin cattle grazing in a half-hearted fashion. The house was a frame shack of apparently three or four rooms, unpainted, set in an arid waste with no fence around it—but with wire fence enclosing the corral where several horses were standing.

3

SAND MUFFLED THE SOUND of their approach. Not until Lige stopped the horse and called out, "Hello the house! Anybody home?" was the door opened. Then Cousin Bev came out quickly, hands outstretched, and face alight with welcome. In an instant Letty was over the wheels of the high buggy and in his arms—all her terrors, all her apprehensions and her woes forgotten at the sight of a home face. She trembled with ecstatic rebound of spirit, of joy, after her misery. Cousin Bev meant home, the dear past, her happy childhood brought back miraculously after a nightmare of distress.

She clutched him close with little cries of love and joy, and babbled his name over and over again.

"Oh, Cousin Bev! Cousin Bev! It's so good to see you again!"

"It's great to have you here," he ejaculated, his own voice husky, his own eyes misty with tears, as if he, too, had known homesickness and longing for a past that Texas had blotted out.

Then suddenly he seemed to remember. "Here's your Cousin Cora," he said, disengaging himself from her arms and turning her round to face his wife who stood beside them.

Letty caught her breath for an instant in admiration. Such a magnificent woman! Tall, like some goddess of the prairie, deep-bosomed, with noble, softly flowing lines like a statue; erect, instinct with vibrant, magnetic life! Her eyes were golden-brown, with slumbering fires in them, her hair was a coppery-red piled high on her head, her skin a warm cream, with a few little amber freckles, like beauty spots, across her finely shaped nose.

Letty stepped forward impulsively, then hesitated, feeling a chill of doubt.

Cousin Cora kissed her, it is true, but with reservations, coldly, as one would touch hands with a stranger. And did she imagine it, Letty asked herself, or did the gold-brown eyes have in them a look of disapproval, almost of hostility toward her?

Cousin Bev hurried them into the house. Was he merely trying to get them in out of the icy wind, or was he bridging over a difficult moment?

He helped Letty off with her coat and hat. "And the children—you haven't seen them!" he cried.

He herded them forward gaily for her inspection, like a small boy that empties his pockets of his treasures to show some loved one how rich he is.

"This is Beverly Junior, or Junior for short." He laid his hand on the shoulder of a sun-browned boy of ten, slender, wiry, with his father's dark eyes and hair and sensitive mouth.

"And this is Dan. He's eight." Dan was more like his mother, but with more freckles peppering his face.

"And here's Alice." He pushed forward a Little girl who looked as if she might be six, a child of nondescript dust-colored eyes and hair and a thin, nervous little face.

Letty put her arm around the child. "She doesn't look like either one of you," she said.

"No," said the mother. "I tell her she's a stray."

Her father cut in quickly to save the daughter's feelings. "She's more like me inside of her than any of the children."

She huddled against him with adoring eyes.

"Here's the one that's like me," Cora announced, as she went to the bed in the corner of the room and lifted up a half-awakened baby. "This is little Cora."

The child was adorable, her cheeks softly flushed with sleep, her head a mass of coppery curls that clung closely, her mouth pursed shyly, her head leaning against her mother's arm for protection from the stranger.

"Oh, what a darling!" Letty cried. "How old is she?"

"She's a yearling," answered the mother, her face softening magically as she looked down at the baby held in the curve of her arm. "She's got her daddy's dark eyes. See?"

"Bev's got a right likely bunch of young cattle here," drawled Lige, as he smilingly surveyed the group. The baby crowed and leaped with delight in her mother's arms, as if she understood the compliment, and flapped her arms toward him in invitation.

He snatched her from her mother's arms and swung her gaily toward the ceiling till she squealed with glee and clutched his hair in her hands.

"This is the only young lady that ever admired me," he announced solemnly as he extricated his hair from her tenacious fingers. "So folks, take good care of her. I aim to marry her when she grows up, before she's old enough to have sense enough to turn me down."

He returned her to her mother and began to button his coat again. He had not taken it off, merely loosed it to warm up a moment.

"But you're not going," objected Bev. "You must spend the night."

"Yes, don't snatch yourself away in the heat of the day like this," cut in Cora.

He smiled. "Nope, better get back. That pardner of mine is plumb devoured with jealousy now because I got to go for the lady instead of him. I got to get back and pacify him else he's li'ble to go into highstrikes."

"No, it's cold. You've got to stay all night," Cora ordered, flashing her imperious glance at him. "That's the word with the bark on it."

He smiled again, a broad-mouthed, white-toothed smile, that added cheer to the room. "'Sta bueno. The boss of the outfit has spoke. I didn't aim to put you out none, was all. Course I'm tickled as a box of possum heads to stay."

So that was settled, and presently Cora left the room and went into the kitchen adjoining, where the rattle of dishes, the clatter of stove-lids in preparation for supper began to be heard.

Letty wondered timidly if she should go in and offer to help. Would it be better to seem lazy and indifferent, or risk a rebuff? She finally decided to stay where she was, for she felt a certain protection in the presence of Cousin Bev, and, yes, of Lige, too.

She listened quietly as the men talked about ranch affairs, of round-ups and cattle rustlers and fall drives—matters that sounded mysterious and dramatic to her ignorant ears. This life of the west was so different from that she had known. Should she ever learn its ways, its language, its responsibilities?

She had a chance to study Cousin Bev's face at leisure now, and she found it changed from what she had remembered as a child. It had been twelve years since Cousin Bev had left Virginia to come to Texas, but her six-year-old heart had kept its picture of him. He had been tall and dark-eyed and wonderful to look at, pale and slender like a prince in a fairy tale. All the girls had been in love with him, her mother had said, because he was as good as he was handsome. But because he had a touch of lung trouble, and had had a hemorrhage, he had made up his mind to go to Texas, where the plains were high and dry and he could get well.

32

Afterward, when she was older, her mother had often told her of how hard it was for him to say goodbye to Miss Rose Douglass. But he had thought it wouldn't be fair to say a word of love or ask a promise from her that would bind her to a man that might be doomed to die in a short time. So he had gone away, without telling her he loved her, though he must have known she loved him, too.

She remembered how Miss Rose had come often to see her mother, and talked about him. But after the day when her mother had shown her the letter from him, the short note that said so little, except that he was married to Cora, she had never come again! Letty remembered, as if it had been yesterday, the look on Miss Rose's face, the stricken look in her eyes, the desperate pride with which she held her head erect. How terrible it was for a proud woman to love a man who married someone else!

Why, why had it all come about like this?

She glanced through the open door and had a swift glimpse of Cora at the kitchen stove, her face flushed and vivid, her hair tossed and glowing with life, and she felt she understood. This blinding beauty had caught him, and fettered him against his heart.

Then she remembered Miss Rose Douglass, with her quiet dignity, her slim, delicate hands that played the piano in the twilight like one dreaming of sad, beautiful things, and she wondered once more. Life was strange!

Her eyes traced the changes in Cousin Bev's face. He looked older—yes, more than twelve years older, though he was not pale now, but sun-browned as a Mexican. His face in repose was sad, though it had the look of health, and his eyes were wistful.

But one who had had lung trouble, even if he'd got over it, and who had lived twelve years in this sand desert, tormented by the wind, would not be so bright of eye, so blithe of mien as before, and a wife and four children to be responsible for were calculated to sober a man. Yes, no doubt....

But in her mind persisted the memory that a child's love had held preciously, of a gay and gallant figure, dancing, riding horseback with the girls, his steed curvetting with pride of the rider. Cousin Bev, starting off on a fox hunt in the early morning, the pack of hounds baying all about him.... Cousin Bev, dressed for a fancy-dress ball in the costume of his cavalier ancestor whose picture had hung over the mantel in the old drawing room at home....

Now he had on a dark flannel shirt, collarless, turned in at the neck, rough trousers, and heavy boots. He was only thirty-six now, and he looked older—older. How strange, how filled with awe, was life, with its time and change!

Presently, as Cora called, "Chuck's ready!" they trooped into the back room that was a combination dining room and kitchen.

The meal was rather a noisy one, for Cora was not fond of silences, her own or another's. She thumped the dishes onto the table, poured the coffee clatteringly, and did most of the talking herself, as if not trusting such an important function to anyone less experienced.

Now and then Beverly tried to draw Letty into the conversation, but she was shy, so that she found it easier to listen than to talk.

"What are we cattle men going to do if this drought keeps up?" Beverly asked Lige.

"I dunno. Looks like this section had got into a habit o' not rainin'. A regular rain, a gully-washer and toad-strangler, would be worth a fortune to this country."

"How long has it been?" asked Letty.

"A long time," he said with a shake of his head. "The cattle are beginnin' to feel it, too. Course, these here range cattle have never been used to being humored with water or grass much. Them critters can chaw a mesquite thorn or a prickly-pear leaf an' call it a hearty meal. But they're gettin' to feel abused, now, when they don't get their Fourth o' July or their Christmas drink."

"Yes," agreed Bev, soberly.

Lige grinned. "What we need is to cross those old longhorns with camels, so's they can stand the drought better."

"Don't you reckon it'll rain soon?" asked Junior.

"Well, son, I can hope louder'n anybody. But it ain't no use ribbin' myself up about it, when there ain't so much as a cloud in the sky. An' I begin to feel restless when these old Sonora reds bawl at me rebukingly, like I was the Joshua that stopped the rain."

"But what will you do if it doesn't rain?" questioned Letty. In her previous life, rain had always been taken for granted, like air.

"Well, ma'am, that I can't say. I can't read the future because I've never had much education. My mind hops round like a grasshopper with a hind leg off. Or else it travels backwards like a doodle bug. There ain't no dependence to be put in it, when it comes to the future."

His face was less homely when it was lighted by his cheerful grin. But his mouth was so wide, she told herself. It traveled back almost to his ears when he smiled—to those ears that stuck out too prominently. Why hadn't his mother smoothed down those ears when he was little? But at least, it was a kindly, good-humored face, one that you could trust. She could fancy a lost dog would take hope from that face, a child in trouble would be sure of a comforter.

Beverly spoke morosely. "I've been cleaned out once by a drought. Hope it don't happen again."

Cora spoke up with flashing vivacity. "Oh, cut out the gloom! Don't be like a turkey buzzard, flappin' round and waitin' for something to die. What will it matter if a few cow critters do die, so long as you're not the corpse?"

"A lot of difference, if they're my herd."

She tossed her russet head. "No matter what comes, be cheerful. You'll live a sight longer. If we get starved out here, we can pile the kids in a covered wagon and start out to new grass. I always did like to travel."

"I've seen a few covered wagons already," answered Lige. "Dry years brings 'em out. A lot of poor fools come out to the west and fail because they're not fit for the life here. I've seen folk try to ranch that could sca'cely tell a horned frog from a alligator."

"And when they fail, they blame it onto the west!" cried Cora with contempt. "Folks that haven't got any more backbone than a twine string had better stay in some softer place than this."

"Yes, some fellers that come out here ain't calculated to last any longer'n a clean shirt in a dog fight. There've been times when I was almost discouraged myself. Times when I thought my luck had went out like Lottie's eye. But it don't do to give up."

Lige reached a long arm across the table for the syrup pitcher.

"Well, if a drought was anything a feller could prevent by hard work or worry, I'd say worry. But when it's not, then why be mis'rable over it?" demanded Cora. "It oozes your energy away to worry and be scared of things. It just makes 'em happen, when maybe they wouldn't any other way."

34

She looked incarnate health and optimism, as if her superb body had never known a pain, or her mind a moment's anxiety over anything. The west must be a bearable place, after all, if it could produce such a magnificent creature as she was, Letty told herself. It was as if the boundless energy of the plains, the stored-up vigor of the long centuries that had waited for human life to inhabit these prairies, had expressed themselves in her. Yet was she like nature herself, contemptuous of weaklings, impatient and disregardful of others less capable than herself? Could one who had never suffered sympathize with another's pang of body or mind or soul?

On a ranch in those days, people went to bed early, because they must rise at dawn to get their work done, and so that first evening was not a long one. Letty was tired out from her ride, her eyes ached from the sting of the wind and sand, and so she was glad when Cora told her to take her place in the children's room.

She crept in beside Alice who was already curled into a ball in the middle of the bed, and listened to the breathing and the thrashing round of the two boys in another bed across the room. The air was close, as the windows were tight shut to keep out the wind and sand and cold.

Letty snuggled up to Alice for warmth, and dropped off to sleep. She was awakened later, to hear a sound outside, in the distance, it seemed, a long, lupine howl, lugubrious, dolorous, its inflections dying off into a wail—as if some lost soul stood alone on the desolate prairie and gave voice to its despair.

Then that lonely voice was answered by a series of short, quick yelps, as of half a dozen distressed puppies,—then a commingling of yelps. She shook little Alice awake.

"Alice, what is that?" she panted.

"Oh, nothin' but coyotes, and a lobo!"

Alice rolled herself into a ball again and lapsed into sleep.

Nothing but coyotes! Nothing but a pack of wolves loose on the prairie, howling, with nothing to stop their approach to the house! The sounds, at first far off, were coming nearer, nearer!...

Should she rouse the household to companion her terror? Then Cora would be contemptuous.... Better to lie quiet. Those two men in the house would not let harm come if they could prevent it. But could they?...

Her soul writhed before dark terrors, as she lay there, alone. Coyotes and wind! Wirt Roddy had told her of how terrible they were to a woman!...

The next morning Lige left early to go to his ranch, Beverly departed on horseback to see about his cattle, and Letty began to realize what would be the program for not only that day but for the days in general that stretched ahead. She comprehended that for the most part men in the west lived out of doors, as their work took them there, while she would stay in the house with Cora and the children. At least until the cold was over, she would be shut up inside the house, a prisoner hiding from the wind.

As she went about helping Cora with the morning's tasks she examined her prison. The house had four rooms, one a combination dining room and kitchen, with its cooking stove, its table covered with oilcloth, its cupboard in the corner to hold the dishes and the food, its few chairs. The room occupied by Cora and Beverly showed scant concession to beauty, but only stern, practical utility. But it was neat, with its oak bed covered with a log-cabin quilt, the dresser with its white scarf, its tidy comb and brush and various ornaments, its washstand with bowl and pitcher of heavy white ware, its enlarged pictures of Cora's father and mother, and the rag rugs on the floor.

The children's room, which now she was to share, appeared to be a place for putting everything that was crowded out from the other rooms—trunks, boxes, broken chairs, old toys. The front room used as a sitting room and as a guest chamber, had a company bed, a marble-topped center table with an ornate lamp on it, a showy red carpet, some rocking-chairs, a round stove, and a whatnot in the corner, revealing a collection of odds and ends. The front room, she discovered, was Cora's pride.

"Bev wanted me to let you have this for your room, but I told him you could just as well sleep in with the young uns. I wanted to keep this nice for company," remarked Cora.

Letty flushed. "Of course, I can just as easily sleep with the children," she murmured.

But the prospect dismayed her. Never in all her life had she habitually shared her room with another. Of course, when a girl came to spend the night with her, they had slept together in order to be sociable, but that was different. She thought of her own room at home, with its mahogany four-poster bed, its highboy and dresser, its white, ruffled curtains, its bookcase, its braided rugs, so dainty, so immaculate! A room for day-dreams and visions. Not even her mother had entered without knocking....

Cora broke in on her memories by a curt direction. "You can round up them young steers and try to teach 'em something. I'll set down to the sewing machine and run up some clothes for the baby."

So Letty began her task as governess—no easy job, for the children were restless, resentful at sitting still, and she soon learned that while their minds were quick, their training had been sketchy.

"Bev's tried to teach 'em at night, but when he rides the range all day, he's wore out. And I got to have some chance to talk to him myself," Cora explained.

So a teacher who didn't know how to teach, had to take charge of children who didn't know how to study!...

"I don't see the sense in studyin', anyhow," complained Dan, shying his arithmetic at Junior, thus precipitating a scuffle, which was settled by a cuff at both from the mother.

"I don't need to know books," he growled.

"But you will when you're a man," expostulated the inexperienced teacher.

"Naw, I won't, neither. I'm goin' to be a cowboy, like Uncle Alf. He ain't educated, an' he's got a first-class ranch."

"Alf's my oldest brother," Cora observed with pride.

Junior interrupted to express his ambitions. "I'm goin' to be sheriff an' tote a gun. You don't need learnin' for that, 'cept maybe a little, I reckon. Or maybe I'll be a Texas ranger to arrest bandits an' cattle thieves an' an' murderers. I'm a' goin to be quick on the trigger."

Alice slipped her hand shyly into Letty's. "I'll study," she said as if feeling that the teacher would be hurt by a unanimous opposition to books.

So Letty perceived that she would have need of much patience and tact and intelligence to teach these youngsters who were so full of ebullient life, and so little used to disciplined thinking. And she was so ill-fitted for such a task! Her education had been gained chiefly from desultory reading for pleasure among her father's books and those that she could borrow in the village, with no thorough drill in other branches—wobbly in arithmetic, for instance, and not to be counted on in geography or any of the sciences. Not till she faced seriously the immediate job of teaching others had she realized how little, how desperately little, she herself knew. And now there was no way that she could advance herself, out here on this desert plain away from books or schools.

But she would study hard in the children's schoolbooks, and do what she could to learn. For she must make good at teaching the children, since that was her excuse for being in Cousin Beverly's home—the home that was Cora's, too, as much as his, maybe even more. And she must do the best she could for those children who were Cousin Beverly's, whom she loved for his sake to begin with.

So the first few days wore on. Letty looked forward eagerly to the dark, when Cousin Beverly would come in; but he was generally tired from his day in the saddle and had little energy for conversation, and so they all generally went to bed early. How different from the long, delightful evenings around the fireplace in the old drawing room at home before Mother was sick—when the family and whatever company was there would sit up and talk endlessly about all manner of interesting topics, till one hated to stop for sleep at all! But in those days there had been a negro mammy to bring you breakfast in bed the next morning if you wished, and so one could indulge in late evenings without loss of energy. How far away, how long ago, that life seemed!

• • • •

On Sunday, there was a break in the routine. To begin with, they all slept later than usual and had a more leisurely breakfast. Then, in the middle of the morning, they saw two men riding up on horseback to the ranch—Lige and another.

Cora spied them through the window and threw open the door to welcome them.

"Well, if here ain't old Sourdough!" she called with loud, hearty voice. "Light and hitch and come in, boys."

The two men came in and shook hands awkwardly with Letty. Their hands seemed self-conscious, their huge boots embarrassed by a sense of social inadequacy in the presence of this strange young lady.

The newcomer announced with an attempt at casualness of manner. "Lige here said as there was a girl here as pretty as red shoes, an' prettier, too. So I had to come an' see if he was lyin'."

He paused a moment to look her over and then added: "He wasn't."

The children laughed uproariously at his wit, and Letty gave an exhibition of her blushing that did not bring a disclaimer from Sourdough as to his previous sentiments.

When Letty's color had subsided enough so that she could see clearly, she scanned the newcomer. He was shorter than Lige, but even at that he was tall, as all these western men seemed to be. What was there in the climate that made them so? The air of the west seemed to affect the men as it did the jackrabbits, so that they were elongated, yet not out of proportion, for they were not gangling at all. Maybe the little men couldn't stand the life there and quit.

Sourdough was stockier of build, and had red hair, almost the color of nasturtiums, that reached back from his forehead, and blue eyes, rather small, but bright and twinkling and alive, and roving with a gay, impudent curiosity. There wouldn't be much that would escape those two blue eyes if they were on the lookout!

But his costume was what finally chained Letty's attention, for it was different from anything she had ever seen or imagined. His shirt was a brilliant red-and-green stripe, with celluloid collar and a red crocheted tie that must surely have been the handiwork of some feminine admirer of his in the west—a tie held in place by a ring of cow's horn slipped over it. He had a belt of rattlesnake skin, and his gay blue trousers were stuffed into his boots—boots of a high, ornate character, with astonishing heels, and with spurs that jangled at each step he took, and he appeared to be fidgety as if to show off the rattle of his spurs. He still held in his hand a broad-brimmed felt hat encircled with a silver cord.

"Will you trust your fine ten-gallon hat to a nail for a while?" Cora inquired.

He grinned. "Well-um, I might, if 'twas a nail near enough for me to keep my eyes on it. I bought this here sombrero off'n a Mexicano an' I don't want to take no rash chances with it."

He hung it meticulously on a nail back of the door.

"Lige here tried to sneak away from me, to come up here by hisself, to see you," he confided to Letty. "But I was too fisty for him."

"I didn't see no sense in havin' him tag round after me everywheres I go," grumbled Lige. "So I just got on my old plug ugly and started off."

"It didn't look like no great snakes to me to stay at home by myself, as lonesome as a bed bug, so I saddled my cayuse and lit out after him. He saw me comin' hell-ter-split, and spurred his old hoss, but I poured the quirt to my clay-bank an' caught up with him."

Cora laughed and slapped him on the back. "Good enough! I bet on Sourdough risin' to the occasion!"

The talk of the morning was good-humored and noisy. Cora and Sourdough did most of it, elbowing the others out ruthlessly, to engage in their exchange of county gossip and humorous badinage, which gave them prodigious pleasure, if one might judge from their smiles and outbursts of hearty laughter. It was evident that Sourdough was a special favorite with her.

As Letty listened with interest to their talk she tried to analyze the delight it held for those two. They possessed something in kinship with each other, the same exuberant vitality of physical health and abounding spirits; the same noisy sense of humor that lay close to the surface, that broke forth in uproarious laughter at each other's jokes, and interrupted to go one better. Something of the same ego that appeared to take it for granted that the company could best be entertained by expressions of that ego.

As she listened, Letty revised her earlier impressions of Lige, who at first had seemed to her to be noisy and rough, but who now, by contrast, appeared quiet and restrained. Or had he been less restrained when he was with her alone? At least, he wasn't pushing like Sourdough—he didn't knock you down with his personality as Cora did.

Even Cora seemed to notice at last that Lige was somewhat silent. "You ain't talkin' today," she accused him. "Took a vow o' silence over anything, eh?"

"How can I talk, with this blab-mouthed pardner of mine along? I'd need a battle-axe to break into this collogue."

"To hear him tell it, you'd think I blow my head an' horns off," countered Sourdough.

"Well, I'd say there are some folks that don't know the value of silence. They opine that silence is like promises an' pie-crust, jest made to be broke," drawled Lige.

"Well, there's too goldamed much silence in my days! You go round like Mr. Tight-face, never openin' yore mouth sometimes for hours at a time; or else me ridin' the range an' nobody to talk to but jackrabbits an' steers. So when I get a chance to confab, why I jest feel like tearin' off as much talk as I can. When I'm round ladies, I ain't no oyster."

"And lockjaw's the last disease you'll die of," retorted Lige.

When dinner was ready, Cora said vivaciously, "You all come into the kitchen an' see if you've got lockjaw."

"That's a welcome sound," said Lige, as he straightened his tall form up from the rocking-chair where it had been confined. "I'm so hungry my stomach thinks my throat's cut."

38

"I'm starved too, till my belly's stickin' to my backbone," corroborated Sourdough.

"This has been Sourdough's week to cook, is why we are so famished," explained Lige gravely.

Sourdough responded with spirit. "I don't see why you got to put out that poison about me bein' a bum cook. The prairie dogs an' ground squirrels don't die like they do when you throw out yore failures!"

"Put up yore pistols, boys. It's too dark to fight," said Cora.

Late in the afternoon, when the two cowboys decided reluctantly that they must start for home, the others walked out to the road to see them depart. Sourdough swaggered up to his horse, and vaulted into the saddle like a circus performer.

Letty watched him with keen interest for the novelty of his character. His costume now—was that merely the western male's gay plumage put on to impress the visiting girl from a distance, or did he always dress like that on Sundays and holidays? And this exhibition of horsemanship—was it customary with him, or was he merely trying to show off before company?

As he caught the reins in his hands, the horse began a demonstration of rage that was indeed novel to her. He reared up on his hind legs, pawed the air with his fore feet viciously, as if determined to throw his rider. Failing in that attempt, he put his nose to the ground and threw his hind legs into the air, as if surely in that way he would unseat the vexatious rider.

He whirled and sprang high into the air with whinnies of rage, his whole body trembling. Letty caught her breath in terror of what must happen to the reckless man trying to ride the beast.

But Sourdough sat in his saddle unperturbed, laughing aloud, and taunting his horse. "So you think you can throw me, do you, yo' old bag o' bones? The hoss ain't been foaled that kin ever throw me!"

"Oh, he'll be killed!" cried Letty in a panic, to Lige, who stood beside her. "Can't you do something to save him?"

"No chance!" jeered Lige. "Don't be skeered. That's jest put on to show off before you. He's doin' it a purpose. He's goosin' his horse."

"What do you mean?" she gasped, still taut with terror at the bronco's bucking.

He laughed. "He stuck his thumb in a sensitive spot under the horse's shoulder. That sets him crazy an' makes him cut up. That's what we call goosin' a horse."

At that instant, as if to prove his perfect control of his steed. Sourdough gave a loud yell, drove his spurs into his horse's flanks, and the animal gave a wild bolt down the sandy waste. He circled and came back, to show that he could ride as he wished. He stopped his quivering horse in front of Letty, stood in his saddle and uttered a succession of yells.

"Whoopee! Who-oopee! Whoopee, ti yi yi!"

Then he yelped like a coyote, while he goosed his horse again.

At last, like a small boy that is tired of his egoistic exhibition, he cut his spurs into his horse's sides and dashed off and away, his "whoopee! whoo—oopees!" floating back, and one hand waving his silver-rimmed ten-gallon hat in wild circles round his head.

"What an extraordinary person!" ejaculated Letty.

Lige grinned. "Yep. Just bustin' full o' life, like a youngster. Consarn his hide! He ain't left a single trick for me an' old Sandstorm to pull off to impress you with!"

"Who's Sandstorm?"

"That's my horse. He's the color o' sand, you see, and he can go like a norther when he wants to. Goodbye all,"

"What's Sourdough's horse named?" Letty inquired of him.

"Marajuana. That's a Mexican weed that has intoxicatin' properties."

Lige mounted his steed nonchalantly, as if indeed unwilling to try any fancy stunts after Sourdough's performance, touched his quirt to his hat and set off in a run after his partner.

Coyote howls floated back on the wind, and Lige's voice curled round them in cowboy yells, as if not to be utterly outdistanced and outdone. "Whoopee! yipyip! ti-yi!"

4

AFTER THE SUNDAY VISIT from the two cowboys, the monotony of ranch life settled down again. Letty found the days very dull. Beverly had to be out on the range most of the waking hours, since, as he explained to her, he looked after his place unaided except for extra help at special times such as roundups and brandings. And the cattle needed to have vigilant care now, because the water holes were drying up and they had to travel farther distances on the range in order to find nourishment to keep them alive, the bunch grass and mesquite grass being scant because for so long a time there had been no rain at all in the section.

She could see that Bev was worried over the prospects, and gloomy because there was nothing he could actively do to help the situation. If only there were something she could do to help him!

She watched him with wistful eyes each morning as he buttoned his heavy coat about his throat, pulled his ear-tabs down over his ears, and started off, with a lunch in his overcoat pocket to be eaten on the range wherever he happened to be at noon.

He would be gone all day, and Letty's fancy could see him battling with the winds, those enemies never inactive, herding unruly cattle here and there, helping weak, half-starved ones stagger to their feet, all the time shivering in the cold—Beverly, who at home had known a Virginia gentleman's ease and comfort and leisure! And what did he get out of it that compensated him for the change? Though, of course, he had won back his health, by the active outdoor life he lived; and the high dry climate, while it may have been hard on herds, was good for lungs. Still—many a time Letty left her unspoken query unanswered even in her own mind.

It was not only her concern for Bev that made the hours of his absence seem long and heavy to Letty, for while he was away, she was shut up in the house with Cora and the children, with no one to serve as a buffer between her and Cora's personality. The weather was growing steadily colder as January advanced, and the wind became more boisterous and threatening than she would have believed possible when first she came to the west— so much so that she lacked courage even to take a walk outside for fresh air. The children ran in and out of doors all day like hardy little animals, and tried to entice her to follow them, but she was not daring enough. The mere thought of venturing out in it made her shiver, as she watched from the window the dead grass bent low in the wind, watched the swirls of sand blown about with purposeless energy that removed it almost as soon as it had deposited it in one spot.

She would get through the day somehow by telling herself that soon it would be dark and Bev would come home. She would watch the lazy clock that moved as slowly as a darkey snailing on an unwished errand, would long for some way by which she could speed it up and hurry Bev home the faster. When he came, there would be so much for them to talk about, so much of the old life to remember together, that the evening would wipe out the dull drag of the day, she would promise herself.

But when he did come, how different it was each time from her dreams! She would begin her carefully planned little talk, would recall Virginia, their family kin back there, the old happy times together, but Cora would spoil it all. Cora showed brusquely and plainly that she resented topics of conversation in which she could not share and glitter, memories from which she was excluded from taking the chief part.

Cousin Bev was tired at night, it was true, but the lines would seem to smooth out of his face when he thought of the old life, and his eyes would shine again in the firelight. But

41

Cora wished them to shine only for Texas!

"The quicker you forget about Virginia the better off you'll be!" she told him one night. "Those old states are back numbers. Dead, an' don't know it. Gimme a live one, like Texas."

Had Cora by any chance ever heard of Miss Rose Douglass? Or did she with her native shrewdness fancy only that there might have been such a one in Virginia? Letty once said to herself rebelliously that Cora was the sort of woman who would—if thinking could poison every other pretty woman—reduce the feminine population by large numbers instantaneously.

Cora had no intention of being ignored, even in occasional excursions of conversation. Reminiscence which did not include her was by that fact uninteresting, valueless, and not to be tolerated in her household. She had a personality that was acutely conscious of itself, that never for one moment forgot its ego, and would suffer no one about her to forget it. She had no trace of the considerate self-effacement which makes the friction of daily life less rasping, and which is considered an attribute native to woman. Cora was thoroughly a woman, though with a slashing selfishness by some considered masculine. She didn't mind work—she would cheerfully have performed all the household tasks by herself, and she would have gone hungry to feed her husband or her children or her guests—provided suitable recognition were given that sacrifice. What she was not willing to do without, what she demanded from all under her influence, was a constant awareness, a continual recognition of her personality. She wished everyone to be always aware of her existence, of her sex, of her ideas. She forced herself into the forefront of everyone's thoughts, with her overpowering personality like a battering ram of beauty and sex and self-assertiveness. It was as if she perpetually beat her breasts and cried out vaingloriously, "Here am I! Look at me. Am I not beautiful and clever and alluring? How could one take eyes or thought off of me for an instant?"

Letty noticed that her attitude was the same whoever was concerned. She commanded and commandeered notice and admiration from the children, or, if not admiration, attention and fear. Fear could serve as a substitute for approval with her, since fear signified real attentiveness.

Letty perceived that if ever the children were completely absorbed in their lessons, or listening with ardent eyes to a story she was telling, or relating to her some incident of their play or experience, their mother would inevitably recall them to awareness of herself by some interruption that affected to seem plausible, but that didn't really care overmuch about pretense, since authority was not to be questioned long. The child who was guilty of momentarily forgetting its mother's importance would be reminded by some errand that must be instantly attended to, some question that must be answered at length till the previous attention had been shattered as a bubble, or if need be, some rebuke that could be as sharp as occasion required- The interruption lasted till the interest .was gone.

If Letty were telling a fairy story, Cora might look up from her work to say, "You boys better get to your arithmetic. I don't want you to stop till you can say the multiplication table backwards as well as forwards, in yore sleep if you was called on."

And the children, as well as Letty, would be perfectly aware of Cora's sublime indifference concerning such tables.

Junior grumbled in answer one day, "Aw, shucks! You never do let us alone to have any fun!"

Cora's rage flared up like fire on tow. "Shut your mouth, boy!—if you don't want me to slap it shut! You expect me to make all these sacrifices for you to get an education and then you laze along without studying?"

Letty asked herself with silent bitterness what sacrifices were meant. Surely no salary was involved!

On another occasion, when the children were listening intently to a geography lesson, when Letty was unrolling before their minds a panorama of Africa with its elephants, its jungles, its black men and women, Dan spoke up.

"I saw a nigger in Fort Worth. Did you ever?"

"Oh, a great many!" said Letty with a smile. "Virginia is full of them, you know."

The mother spoke up shortly. "Dan, didn't I tell you not to leave your playthings round on the floor? Now you pick them up pronto!"

"Aw, Mother, lemme wait till I hear the end of this lesson!" the boy pleaded, squirming under her belligerent gaze.

"You move when I speak to you, young man! If you don't I'll wear you to a frazzle!"

And so the geography lesson was suspended for that day.

It was hard enough for an inexperienced teacher to teach at best, and try to round up undisciplined coltish young minds that would rather race off to other pastures, but when you had to do your work under the hostile gaze of an eye that was never turned completely away, what could you do? Yet she must do the best she could for Cousin Beverly's children.

• • • •

One Sunday morning when she had been there a couple of weeks, Beverly said at the breakfast table, "I've got to go over to see Lige and Sourdough about some steers. Shall I hitch up the hack and take all of you over?"

Cora's face glowed for an instant at the prospect of a jaunt, but promptly clouded with remembrance. "The baby's got a cold, and I can't take her out in this sharp wind."

Then she seemed to consider something silently for a moment, and spoke grudgingly, after an obvious struggle with her inclination.

"You can take Letty and Alice if you've a mind to. The boys can stay here with me."

"Aw, Mother, let us go!" shrilled the boys.

"No, do you want to go and leave your mother here by herself with a sick baby? Shame on you!" she cried.

"Let me stay with you and let the boys go," said Letty timidly.

"No, they'll stay home with me," she ordered. "Lige and Sourdough 'll be tickled pink to see you, so you go."

Letty dreaded the prospect of facing the wind, the bitter shouting wind that she could hear all the time, and of driving ten mules across the vacant sand to a shack to see two cowboys, but go she must. It had been nice of Cousin Bev to think of taking her, and it would never do to refuse to follow a plan that Cora had decided on.

So after a while they started off, Beverly and she and little Alice, tucked in under a buffalo robe, and bundled up with all the heaviest clothes and wraps, in a two-seated vehicle with a fringed top, which was spoken of as the "hack." The boys pressed rebellious noses against the window panes to watch them depart.

It was almost noon time when they drove up to the ranch which Beverly designated as belonging to Lige and Dave, the Cross-Bar Ranch. Letty looked at it with amazement. She had thought Bev's place unprepossessing, but this was far more so. There was a surface pond, near the house, in a "draw" or depression in which the water was low, and on the other side a wind-break—so Bev explained to her—a fence extending for a short distance to break the force of the wind from the north, so that the cattle could find shelter in a norther.

The house was of the rudest structure, with no blinds to the windows, no paint, no slightest concession to looks at all. A barbed-wire fence enclosed the corral.

At Beverly's shout to announce his arrival, the door flew open and the two men came out.

Sourdough called out in delight, "Well, dog my cats ef here ain't company!"

He swung Letty down from the high step, leaving Lige to look after little Alice. "Old Pedro said there was some good luck comin' because the bulls was bellerin' so. I thought it meant rain, but 'twas somep'n even better, to say you was comin'!"

"Old Pedro is a Mexican that lives in a dugout on our land," explained Lige, to Letty. "He's a great prophecier about weather. Everything's a sign of rain or a drought or a norther, to hear him tell it."

A wizen-faced, brown old man whose countenance had the color of metal left out in rain and sun till it has a patina over it, came forward around the corner of the house.

"Yes, senorita, when the bulls *cantar* that is a sign that we shall have rain," he said, bowing low.

"When will it be?" asked Letty, with a smile for the old man who looked as if he might be an image centuries old, dug up from the ground.

He shrugged his shoulders, under his serape. "*Quien sabe?*"

"I hope it's soon," said Beverly, "but I'd be more inclined to say those animals were bellowing because they were hungry."

As they entered the house, Letty looked about her at the rude interior. Truly it was like a place where two men kept bach alone! There was no paper on the walls, not even canvas to keep out the wind and sand, so that a coat of sand lay over everything with an impartial yellow grayness. The front room had in it a ramshackle bed—pessimistic, discouraged looking—half a dozen chairs with rawhide bottoms, across one of which lay the Navajo blanket that probably served as a spread for the bed, a plain pine table, and a box partly protruding from under the bed which might contain the wardrobe of the room's owner, save for the coat and hat hung on a nail on the door. The walls were relieved from their bareness only by a wolf skin and a couple of skunk skins stretched out for display, and a couple of crossed rifles, while several goat skins and a wildcat skin were on the floor—unmistakably a masculine dwelling!

Lige surveyed the room dubiously, as if for the first time questioning its adequacy. "This is my outfit. Sourdough bunks in the kitchen, which is on his land. If we'd 'a' knowed we was going to have company we'd 'a' cleaned up."

"Rats! what's the diffrence?" cried his partner jovially. "It's my turn to cook. Now if I'd 'a' knowed you was comin'. I'd had something fit for you to eat."

Letty put in hastily, "Oh, no. We wouldn't want you to go to any trouble. Anything you have will be all right."

"Well'um, on the plains 'tain't like you could step into a grocery store an' tote home anything you wanted. We mostly live on sow-belly an' hominy."

"He means bacon an' grits," Lige translated for Letty's benefit.

Sourdough snatched a broom from the corner, a broom that had evidently seen hard usage, and started toward the kitchen.

Lige put out a muscular arm and clutched him. "You're not aimin' to make such a large red fool of yourself as to sweep now?" he demanded. "The lady would likely ruther have sand on the floor than stirred up in her vittles."

44

Sourdough looked humiliated, like a vainglorious rooster that has suddenly been doused with dishwater, so that his proud comb droops and his feathers fall. The measure of his depression was such that for the time he was silent. He stole on tiptoe toward the kitchen, his attitude and bearing showing that he feared lest sound as well as movement might stir up objectionable sand for the lady.

Letty could hear him moving with loud stealth around in the next room, the kitchen that was also his living quarters. A chair crashed to the floor, a dish broke, a skillet clattered on the stove, and a rattle of knives and forks on a bare table announced nervous preparations for a meal.

It was too bad for him to be in there doing it all by himself. Shouldn't she offer to go and help? Her eyes indicated such a scheme to Lige, who by his dissenting brows dissuaded her. Lige sat with arms folded across his chest, and smiled in sardonic enjoyment of the situation. It must be uncommon for Sourdough to be caught at a disadvantage, when he himself recognized or admitted the fact.

It would serve them all right for the cook to sneak out of the back window and leave them to their hunger.

But he wasn't doing that, for his noise of movements gave evidence of his continued presence and energy.

Presently the red roach of hair was stuck inside the door and Sourdough hissed, with a malevolent look at his partner, "Chuck's ready! Bring yore chairs!"

As they settled themselves at the table, he observed with gloom, "I hope you've got a gonesome feelin' round yore waistband, 'cause if you ain't, this here fodder won't seem tasty."

"I'm hungry enough to swallow my tongue, as the darkeys used to say in Virginia," cried Letty gaily.

She didn't relish the idea of eating this cowboy cooking, but at least she could be polite about it. Perhaps if she talked enough she could eat less without attracting attention to the fact.

"Sorry, but you'll have to do yore own reachin'. We ain't got no waiters," said the host.

He pushed a dish of dark-brown beans toward Letty. "Take some of these Mexican frijoles. Take plenty. Take damn nigh all of 'em!"

Letty giggled as she helped herself. He was as amusing as a circus clown!

"And help yourself to the son-of-a-gun," he went on hospitably, handing her a dish of what appeared to be some sort of stew.

"Wha-at?" she faltered, her politeness for the instant forgotten.

"That's what the cowboys call this stew," Lige hastened to explain.

Sourdough snatched the conversation from him. "Yes'm, it's named that because it's got everything in it, all the innards of the calf, brains, heart, liver, lights and so on, marrow-fat an' all."

The concoction did not tempt the visitor, but she took a portion lest she show her distaste. She could keep it well to one side of her plate where it wouldn't: spoil the beans, which seemed safe enough, even if cooked by a cowboy in a sandy kitchen. She recalled an old folk-saying,

"An egg, an apple, and a nut
You may take from any slut."

45

But those safe articles were missing from the menu! There were biscuit, of a leprous complexion and heavy taste, the sourdough bread from which the cook received his name; and seeing and tasting them Letty felt that one called by such term should resent the insult with deadly weapons! She began to talk in animated fashion so that her failure to eat might go unnoticed by the cook. The coffee was strong as *aqua fortis* [nitric acid], mitigated by condensed milk poured dribblingly from the tin can.

Sourdough made conversation. "I understand Lige pretty near missed you the night you came," he observed to Letty.

"Yes. A gentleman helped me off the train and Mr. Lige was looking for me to be alone."

"Gentleman's name?" demanded Sourdough with facetious but active curiosity.

Letty blushed, and resented the fact so that she blushed more vividly.

"Face hurt you?" inquired Sourdough solicitously. "I see it gettin' red."

"No!" she snapped, putting her hand to her cheek. "His name was Mr. Wirt Roddy. Do you know him?"

"Yeah, but not much. Lives in Fort Worth. Big rich, I've heard say, but a skirt-chaser."

Letty flushed again at his crudity.

Beverly spoke. "He owns a ranch up farther north. I've met him a few times."

"He said he knew you," she commented in a tone that tried to be casual.

She felt again the old disquiet of pulse and spirit that she had known on the train. The mere sound of the man's name, the bare thought of him, shot a strange, electric thrill through her veins, fluttered her pulse, gave her a heady discompose that was half pleasurable, half painful. She saw again the envelope bearing his name that she kept hidden in an old jewel box where she treasured her few trinkets, at the bottom of her trunk. But she'd never use it, of course!...

She thought much of Wirt Roddy during the drive back to the ranch—a drive made in silence for the most part. It wasn't easy to talk, when to open the mouth for speech meant that the wind filled it with sand. Sand was an effective discourager of sociability, even though Letty was bitterly resentful of the fact, knowing, as she did, that she would not soon again be likely to have the chance for a long, uninterrupted time alone with Bev. To go back to the house that Cora filled with her dominant presence meant a spiritual smothering, but at that it wasn't so bad as to be literally smothered with sand, as might happen on the plains in the wind. There was nowhere else to go!—no friendly neighbor, no second or third cousin or aunt by virtue of a marriage a hundred years ago, as would be the case in Virginia. What a country!

By the time the ten-mile drive was over, the icy wind and the cutting sand had made Letty grateful for warmth and shelter, even without friendly welcome. To be out of that awful wind, even in another woman's house, was good! But what a life to look forward to! No companionship save with a silent, harassed man who worked all day long and was exhausted at night, a hostile woman whose antagonism was hard to understand, four restless children that had not known proper discipline!... No company to be expected save a couple of rough cowboys whose life was even more restricted, more primitive, than that at Cora's house!... and no refuge possible in nature!... No friendly woods, no quiet valleys of beauty, no healing comfort of still peace and loveliness such as one could find in any walk in the country in Virginia!... Outside, nothing but vast, desolate stretches of sand and dead grass, with a few stalks of bear grass with its spears frayed by the wind, stunted mesquite bushes, cactus, and prickly-pear!... and a demoniac wind lying in wait to torment its victims, a wind that was as knowing and as cruel as a devil or a maniac!...

Oh, for the calm and solitude of some still, woodsy nook in the country at home—some spot where she could relax and creep back into her soul's peace and happiness, if only for an hour!... To look up at benignant trees that had seen generations of human beings pass and by their silent strength could promise that even poignant griefs would pass in time! But here there were only mesquite bushes, no trees, only dwarfed, stunted shapes that said nature took a delight in cheating man of beauty.... In Virginia there were rivers, calm and life-giving, in their unhurried flow to the sea; and lakes with water lilies, and alder-fringed banks; and little, talkative brooks that gossiped of the winds that blew over them, of the birds that sang and nested, of the squirrels and chipmunks and shy forest things that come near. With a swift intolerable stab of homesickness she was aware of all these things by a vision of the heart that was more revealing than physical eye sight could have been. She saw them!... she realized them!... At home even the weather was kindly in winter, with just enough cold to be bracing, enough snow to furnish sport for the children, and ice for skating on the lakes.... While here—oh, Mr. Wirt Roddy had been right in what he said—the wind was the worst thing about the life out here on the plains!

But winter couldn't last always, and spring would come someday, so that she could go into the open and have a chance to be to herself now and then. To be alone at times was as cruel a need as hunger or thirst, she told herself. She had never known it before.

But Letty found, after all, that other visitors did come to the ranch at times. Cowboys on their way to town would stop and have dinner, casually sure of their welcome. Ranch houses were few and far between, so that almost everyone passing stopped to get warm, to chat awhile of local affairs, to take a meal or spend the night, and the boundless hospitality of the plains welcomed them all. As Letty listened to the talk of the visitors, she learned more and more of the frontier life and the western character.

One Sunday when Lige and Sourdough were there, the sheriff, Jim Hitchcock, and a deputy United States marshal stopped for dinner. They explained to Bev and the cowboys that they were on the trail of some bandits that had held up a train a few days before and managed to get away.

"Don't skeer the visitin' lady with talk o' yore violent deeds," drawled Sourdough rebukingly. "She ain't used to our rough western ways yet, an' she might think we was harsh out here."

The sheriff spoke up to reassure her. "I don't never aim to kill a man, ma'am, if I can arrest him without it. I've noticed a feller won't generally shoot as long as he'll talk to you, so I don't show a gun at first. But, ma'am, some of 'em won't talk to you..." He paused.

"And—and—then you shoot?" she faltered.

"Yes'm, if I go out to get a man, I generally bring him in, dead or alive. As long as I'm sheriff of this county, I don't humor the criminals none."

He twisted his little drooping mustaches and smiled reflectively.

Letty shuddered.

The deputy marshal laughed. "If the criminals knew old Jim as well as I do, they'd know when to look out for lightning and they could draw first. I've noticed old Jim here, just before he shoots a man, always spits right quick, and then pulls the trigger."

The sheriff grew red with embarrassment at having his little mannerisms of killing held up to ridicule. "Aw, go 'long! You're just rawhidin' me!"

Letty gazed at the mild-mannered, under-sized man with a cold fear of the perils he had faced. How did he ever come to be elected sheriff, when he didn't look brave? He looked as if he'd run from a molly cottontail, and his voice was deceptively soft and drawling. To think that he had shot men down, even if they were criminals trying to escape! She looked at his brown hands, almost expecting to see blood stains on them.

"Do you—like being sheriff?" she asked him.

He shook his head. "No, ma'am. When I serve this term of office out, I don't want no more gun-toting jobs. My wife thinks it ain't so healthy. An' I tell my boys for them never to be no officers of the peace."

"It'll shore be hard to fill yore place," averred Sourdough. "If I was to steal cattle or kill anybody or hold up a train in this county. I'd leave like a bat out of hell before old Jim got wind of it."

"At that you wouldn't be quick enough," said Lige. "Old Jim's got coyote sense, an' he's got an eye an' a ear more'n the rest of us, that tell him when a crime's goin' to be committed so he's generally on the ground before the six-shooter stops speakin'."

The sheriff smiled a slow, knowledgeable smile, and said nothing for a moment, and then he cut a look at Lige and his partner. "That extry eye of mine tell me some young squirts are studyin' 'bout getting married. I see you're gettin' red in the comb."

Sourdough growled an unintelligible expletive, and Lige reddened distressfully, till his sun-browned face became the color of brick dust, and his outstanding ears were scarlet.

Cora cut in vivaciously, "Well, you ain't got no objections, have you, Mr. Sheriff? 'T ain't no hangin' crime in this county to fall in love an' get married, is it?"

He lifted a deprecating hand. "No, nothing that I feel any call to arrest 'em for. I think it's high time they was giving thought to the matter. Folks nowadays is awful late about marryin', seems to me. 'Twas different in my young days. By the time I was old enough to vote, I had a boy big enough to get up and build the fire for me in the morning."

The dialogue gave Letty something new to think about. Until then she had not had an idea that Lige or his partner had been coming to the ranch especially to see her. She had supposed they were like all the other neighborly folk that came by to see Bev and Cora, or just to see any human face, as a relief from the oppressive vacancy of the plains. But now the significant looks that the sheriff and Cora exchanged, the teasing challenge they shot at the three concerned gave her a sudden light, as to what others might be thinking.

She blushed in distress at the thought, and then almost laughed aloud at the absurdity of it. Imagine Sourdough in love with her, or with anybody! How could he put off his clownishness long enough to woo? But what if his very buffoonery were his way of courting?—his manner of attracting attention toward himself? His roach of red hair, his tanned face, his swaggering gait were the opposite of romance, but maybe he didn't think so. Fancy coming to court in a rattlesnake belt, a gay polka-dot shirt and clattering spurs!...

And Lige—he was less comical than his partner, but certainly he wasn't the romantic figure of her dreams! She stole a glance at him, as she reflected. He had more earnestness, yes. Life was not just one guffaw after another with him, just one joke following another. He didn't care for a continual clatter of tongues, but was content to lose himself now and then in the dignity of silence. But he was homely, with his too prominent ears (poor little neglected boy; why hadn't someone smoothed them down for him early enough? But maybe his pioneer mother had had her tired hands too full of other tasks). His mouth was too big, and his browned skin made his gray eyes more vivid by contrast. He had a good face, a face anybody could trust, but he wasn't handsome, and he never could be.

Letty took a long look at him while he was listening to an anecdote Cora was relating. When Cora spoke, everybody had to pay attention to her, so that one could look without

48

being seen.

Yes, he was homely, no doubt about it. And he hadn't any education to speak of. He was just a cow-puncher, and yes, he was crude. He didn't even speak correctly. But he had a kind heart, and she must treat him politely so as not to hurt his feelings. He was sensitive, under his awkward reserve, she felt sure, not like Sourdough with his jovial impudence. But Sourdough was likable, too, in his rough way.

The two men looked so matter-of-fact, so engrossed in ranch affairs as the talk went on, while she covertly studied them, that she told herself she must have been imagining things. Or Cora and the sheriff had been having delusions, not she. No matter what Cora and the sheriff thought, these hard-headed, hard-handed cattle men were not giving any thought to romance, or to her. She could be easy on that score.

Letty's dreams had always been woven round an imagined figure, a dark-eyed, dark-haired knight of modern days, something like Beverly had been in his youth, when she had known him as a child and Miss Rose Douglass had been in love with him. Her knight must have dark hair and eyes, of course, to match her own fairness, be chivalrous of speech and courtly of manner.... A tall man, because she was so slight and slender.... But marriage was a thing far in the future, too remote to be visioned even speculatively. While no girl ever considers herself too young for romance, marriage is quite another matter.

As the days went by, Letty found that the complexity of her relations with Cora increased rather than decreased. Letty told herself that she did honestly try to do her best to get along peaceably, to placate her, to avoid giving offense. But there was an antagonism which, though she couldn't puzzle out, was very real, and it lay in the background of every moment between the two women. She would ask herself wretchedly if it was because Cora resented the burden of expense in hard times, the cost of feeding an extra member of the household. Was it that? So she would determine to eat as little as possible, to lighten the burden. But when her appetite, which at best was never hearty, began to flag in this mysterious fashion, Beverly would scold her.

"You're not eating enough to keep a hummingbird alive!" he protested, as he helped her plate generously one day.

Cora spoke up fretfully. "Yes, for pity's sake, eat! I hate to see folks mince over their vittles like they was displeased with the grub."

Then Letty ate. She would have forced down sawdust under the circumstances.

Letty told herself that maybe Cora resented having an outsider always intruding in the family life. Surely that was the reason why she disliked her. So she would make excuses to stay as much as possible away from the others. But that wasn't easy, when there was only one sitting room, and her bedroom, or the one she shared with the three children, was not heated.

If Letty stayed more than a few minutes away in the evening, Bev would call out to her, "Letty, you'll catch cold in that room without any fire. Come on in here."

Dear Bev, who was so thoughtful of everybody!

And Cora would shout to her, "Gosh, yes! Don't let's have anybody sick abed on our hands!"

So Letty would creep back to the range of warmth in the sitting room where seven people sat huddled around one stove, with no ventilation in the room, and Cora talked at Bev until he would say he was tired and must get to sleep.

When the light in the front room was put out, Letty would creep into bed beside little Alice.

There was no fire in any room except the front room, and at meal times in the kitchen, so that there was really no chance at all for privacy. No chance ever to steal away to yourself and think your own thoughts, and let your mind rest from perpetual tension and restraint. In Cora's presence she must forever be on guard, she didn't know why. But life would surely be different when spring came. Then she could steal out into the open and take walks and relieve Cora as well as herself of this perpetual rasping hostility. Spring would make everything different. Now she was only a prisoner in the house, with the wind outside to lay violent hands on her if she ventured forth, and with Cora's belligerent personality dominating her every moment inside the walls.

She told herself in her bewilderment that she didn't know how to meet the situation, because it was so different from anything she had ever known. There never had been much money, or many luxuries in her life, but always there had been love and consideration, nothing but tender care for her welfare and her wishes—even the wishes of a child. She had always been just a child, to be loved and taken care of. And now she was all of a sudden expected to be a woman! And to live in the heart-breaking position of an unwanted and resented member of another woman's home!

She would ask herself wretchedly over and over again, "Why?" Why didn't Cora like her? Cora was hospitable to everyone else. No passer-by but could be sure of a hearty welcome, a pressing invitation to eat a meal or spend the night in her home.

Night after night, as she lay awake hearing the far off howl of the coyotes that always sent a shiver of fear down her spine, and chill with the wild, instinctive terror that the sound of the high wind at night always brought to her, Letty would ask herself what was the way out. The problem seemed always more acute, more unanswerable in the dark when the wind and the coyotes were trying to howl each other down, even than it did in the day when Cora's hard egoism crowded her out.

Letty was a helpless young girl that had always been treated as a child. She had never been given responsibility, nor been expected to make decisions for herself, so that she felt bewilderingly weak and impotent. What could she do? She couldn't go back to Virginia, for there was no near relative to take her in. It would be asking charity to write to some old friend and beg to be given shelter and food. Her family pride revolted from the thought. The men of her family had always taken care of the women and so it had seemed the natural thing to turn to Cousin Bev when her mother was dead. Of course she hadn't known Cousin Bev's wife then!... And the pastor hadn't reckoned with Cora when he had felt so sure that it was the wise and right thing for her to come to Texas to live with them....

Should she write the pastor what a mistake he had made? If he knew how wretched she was, he would send her money for a ticket and tell her to come to his home. But he was poor himself, and had a house full of children. No, she couldn't impose on him. And besides, to let him know would seem to be complaining of Cousin Bev, and that she never could think of....

No, she must wait. When spring came, surely some way would open....

So she tried to make herself as silent, as inconspicuous as possible in the house, like a Little starved mouse that must not venture into notice, but must not attract suspicious glances because of its stillness, either. The little mouse waited for spring to come, but spring was far away.... And at night the coyotes slunk in packs about the place, uttering their querulous, quick yelps, and the wind wailed like all the horrors she had ever heard or read of, a banshee, a lost soul, a demon lover!...

On Sunday Lige and his partner came to spend the day at Bev's ranch. Cora was always delighted to see them, radiating welcome and good cheer and gay spirits. Cora loved company, when she had an excuse to put on her prettiest dress and arrange her shining hair with artful pains, to have the house in spotless order, to cook a good dinner that would bring praise from all who partook of it. Cora was perfectly happy on a Sunday when men visitors came in to spend the day. She would dominate the conversation as they sat together, men, women, and children grouped about the red stove in the box-like front room. Cora would be all aglow with animation, her cheeks flushed, her eyes dancing, her wonderful lustrous hair glittering with life and health and joy. Her hair was so alive that it seemed fairly to send off sparks of life and light.

Sourdough was a good match for her. He, too, was buoyantly alive, and in a gale of high spirits, with an energy as wild and limitless as the force of the wind on the prairies, as if no hint of fear or hardship or suffering had ever touched him. Letty wondered if by some sort of magic he was not immune to suffering or harm, if he were not gifted with some secret that would repel danger or heartbreak as chain armor repels bullets and sends them harmless to the ground. This climate that so terrified and dwarfed her spirits and energies, must in some way give an intoxicating stimulus and vigor to natures like Cora's and Sourdough's.

His jokes were ready, his rough wit never flagging, his laugh instantaneous at each sally his hostess made, and they played up to each other so that their minds seemed complements of each other.

Letty used sometimes to wonder how far Cora might have gone if she had had a wider training and culture, a broader opportunity, so that her native abilities might have developed more. With her beauty and her infectious spirits, she might have ruled a salon, like the women in French history, might have shaped the destinies of governments by her shrewdness and her dominance. How queer a thing was life that shut this heady creature with her wild, rich possibilities up in a little box-house on the prairie!...

On Sundays, when Cora and Sourdough led the conversation, making of it a riotous gaiety, the others were content to listen quietly, with no desire to interrupt. Beverly and Lige and Letty would sit, smiling at each other, to hear those two rattle on, in a companionable silence that left no sense of constraint.

Letty felt less unhappy on Sundays than at any other time, for then Beverly was at home, for one thing, and more rested, so that she could talk to him a little, shyly, now and then, when Cora was out of the room. Cora was always in such a good humor when company came, especially Lige and his partner, that Letty could creep out of her cranny of timidity a little and expand without fear of being hurt.

One Sunday when Letty had been at the ranch about six weeks (though it seemed to her as many years and more!) the two cowboys came as usual for their weekly visit, but this time bearing important news.

"Whoopee, ti yi yi!" Sourdough shouted as they rode up.

Cora poked her head out of the door. "What's up? Drought broke?"

"No, but next best thing."

He came into the house followed closely by Lige who was smiling his slow, comfortable smile.

"There's goin' to be a rabbit twistin' at Si Popplewell's two weeks from last Friday night— a week from next Friday. We come to let you know. Everybody invited and nobody slighted."

"Sure?" cried Cora, her eyes glittering, her face glowing with anticipation. "That's fine."

"What is a rabbit twisting?" asked Letty, curiosity getting the mastery over her shyness. It must be something pleasant to arouse such enthusiasm in these three.

Lige laughed, and as usual acted as interpreter for her. "It's no cruelty to dumb beasts. Miss Letty. That's what we call a dance in this section. If you've never been to a cowboys' ball, it'll maybe interest you."

"It will be fun. Am I invited?"

"Sure, everybody's asked. Everybody an' his chillun an' his dog will be there."

Sourdough twirled his ten-gallon hat in nervous fingers and looked at Letty. "Me an' Lige here drawed six-shooters on each other to find out which one was to ask to take you. We decided this was a bad time to kill off either one of us, with drought on an' all, so we settled it different. We 'lowed the peaceable an' fair way would be for one to take you an' t'other'n to bring you home. Agreeable to you?"

Letty flushed and gave a hesitant look at Cora. She didn't know what Cora would wish her to do, and she didn't even know what she herself cared to do. These western customs were so new to her!

Her cousin decided the matter instantly. "Sure. That's much better'n a fight between these two. Bev'll hitch up the hack an' take me an' the kids, so we'll all be there."

"Children, too?" asked Letty in amazement.

Lige answered comfortably. "Yes'm, you see so few folks live in this section, an' so few sociables happen, that everybody has to turn out to make the crowd. They send men to ride up the county an' give everybody an invite."

"All right, then, I'd hate to be the only person in the county that wasn't there," she said shyly.

Sourdough went on to explain the occasion for the festivity. "The Popplewells are so swole with pride now they got the upstairs house finished that they got to give a house-warmin'."

"The upstairs house?" queried Letty.

"Yes'm- When they first settled here they lived in a half-dugout, you know, half in the ground an' half out. But they've got two grown gals now on the carpet, an' two frying-size ones comin' on, so the old man had to build a regular house on the ground. They still live in the half-dugout, too, but they call the new part the 'upstairs house.'"

Letty laughed as she tried to picture the residence in her mind, a half-dugout combined with an upstairs house built as a separate edifice. "What a funny country!" she cried.

52

5

IN THE DAYS THAT INTERVENED before the dance, Cora showed an ebullient enthusiasm. The approaching festivity controlled everything, in one way or another. If one of the children annoyed her in any fashion, she would threaten sharply, "If you don't behave, I'll leave you home when we go to the dance." That proved instantly efficacious, and each child stepped at command, with a blithe obedience unknown in the household before, or at least since Letty's arrival. Cora had Beverly drive her the twenty-five miles to town, where she bought material to make herself a new dress for the occasion, a cheap stuff but of a lovely gold-brown tone that brought out the lights in her eyes, the live, silken sheen of her hair. She was as gay as a girl looking forward to her first dance, and Letty, looking on and thinking it all over, was touched to sympathy. She was a woman who so loved social gaiety, and life gave her so little! She, whose beauty and vivacity would attract attention in any assembly, spent her days cooped up in a shack in a remote ranch.

Cora looked over Letty's wardrobe with pursed lips and appraising eyes. From the rather scant assortment, she picked out a little last summer's frock of pale-blue china silk, with a frill of soft white lace at the throat and short sleeves.

"Wear that," she ordered.

"I'd rather not take off black just yet," said Letty, though she shook at her audacity in opposing Cora.

"Shucks and fodder! You don't want to go on looking like a crow! Don't you know that if you don't dress fine, you can't catch a beau?"

Letty cringed. "I don't know that I'm wanting to do that."

"High time you were, then. Most o' the girls round here are married by your age. You don't want to be an old maid, do you?"

Letty couldn't truthfully assert that she did, and so the discussion ended by her consenting to wear the blue dress. On the whole, it was easier to give in than to argue.

Cora tried to spur Beverly to more enthusiasm in anticipation of the event. "Old slow poke!" she called him. "Needs a little touch of high life to make him go."

One day after he had left the house, Cora said to Letty. "That man don't honestly care whether he goes to that dance or not. But then he never does know what's good for him. I always have to make up my mind for him."

"Do you?"

"Yeah. He'd 'a' been dead of the doldrums as well as of the lung-woe by this time, if it hadn't been for me."

Letty looked up with unfeigned interest. "What did you do?"

Cora wrung out her dishcloth and spoke succinctly. "I married him."

Letty laughed. "But you didn't make up his mind about that, did you?" she asked, for the moment forgetting the confidence Lige had given her on their drive from Sweetwater, regarding the manner of Bev's wooing as he imagined it.

Cora put her hands on her hips and surveyed her questioner. "Sure as shooting. He was gettin' worse instead of better of his consumption. He was bachin', so he wasn't getting the sort o' food he ought to have. He was blue, and sick, and discouraged. He looked like a motherless calf! He was goin' to give up and go back to Virginia to die—and he would have, too 1"

"Poor thing!" cried Letty, with quick sympathy. She could just see him! And he hadn't written her mother how bad he felt at all, but had sent her only cheerful letters!

Cora went on. "I went to his ranch one day with my brother, and we had a talk while Bud was projecting round by hisself. Bev told me he was quittin'. I told him he wasn't. I'd been in love with him like a prairie fire, ever since the first time I set eyes on him. He didn't know what he wanted, but I knew dam well what I wanted!... I wanted Bev.... So we was married."

Letty made an inarticulate sound in her throat. Her mind flashed back to Miss Rose Douglass, who had never known how her heartbreak had come about. Would it comfort her to know?

Cora continued, pride swelling her voice. "I nursed him, and saw that he got the right grub, and my oldest brother helped him get a start with his herd—and look at him now!—cured of his consumption, got this ranch homesteaded and clear, and a good herd started!"

Her tone softened as she lived back through those struggles. "That's better than coffin space in one of your old Virginia graveyards, huh?"

"Yes, indeed! I should say so!" ejaculated her listener.

As Letty thought over the matter, unwilling admiration for Cora seized her. Those capable hands, had nursed Bev back to health, had fed him, had slaved for him. That magnificent body had borne him four fine children. That driving energy and optimism had rescued him from hopelessness and compelled him back to health and a measure of success. And there was no question of her love for him. Cora loved her man with a fierce, protecting devotion that had something elemental in it, something divine. She might love to laugh and joke with her visitors, but no one who knew her could doubt for an instant that her whole heart was Bev's. She was passionately, exultingly in love with him.

She went on. "I guess there's not many women as crazy over their husbands as I am over Bev." She was talking more to herself than to Letty. "I've heard women say they loved their children more than their men. Well, all I got to say is—if I had to choose between losing Bev, and giving up all them four young uns, I'd chuck the four quicker'n a cat can wink its eye."

She gazed out of the window, a far look in her eyes. "Bev's the whole world to me. I love him like a cyclone. And I love him, too, the way the prairie feels when it's still and calm at night, when the wind don't blow an' the spring flowers are in bloom and the stars shine soft."

Her voice became husky, and she passed a hand across her eyes. "There ain't any way of loving that I don't love Bev!"

Letty's heart twisted sharply with envy. Would life ever grant to her a love like that? Beside that burning reality, her shy, maiden dreams of romance seemed pallid, remote, unsubstantial....

What was love? she asked herself. Something more than the fantasy she had imagined it—more than an ardent vow, a kiss in the moonlight, more than a shimmer of white satin and orange blossoms, an array of bridal presents. Love could mean scrubbing of floors and washing of dishes, and going without things that girls longed for—it could mean struggle and sacrifice and suspense. If two people rightly loved, their love could glorify all common tasks and hardships beyond the fairy dreams of romance....

But then—her knight would lift her above the need for toil and hardship, and life would somehow, somewhere, be ideal.... She must wait!

• • • •

The day of the dance came at last, clear and cold.

"Good we got a drought on, so's the rain can't spoil the fun," Cora tendered opinion, as she surveyed the heavens that showed no clouds.

The Si Popplewells lived about fifteen miles away, and so the family made preparations to start soon after noon, to be sure of arriving before the festivities began. Sourdough and Lige came by in a buggy with a lead horse behind, for the use of the discarded swain to ride after Letty was picked up.

Sourdough took the lead in plans and conversation. "I claim first chance. Old Lige can fetch you home, because maybe I'll be so blowed from dancing that I couldn't talk."

"No such luck!" growled Lige. "Your tongue is calculated to travel faster'n a jackrabbit could run if he had as many legs as a thousand-leg."

Beverly and Cora and all the children, even to the baby, piled into the two-seated hack, with a basket of food to be eaten on the way. They were bundled up like … to keep out the cold, but their cheeks were red and their eyes bright. Even the baby seemed infected with the general enthusiasm, for she leaped and crowed with pleasure at being taken out for a drive. And on Bev's sober face was a companionable smile.

For a mile or so Lige rode along by the buggy that held Letty and his partner, and then with a wave of his hat, he spurred his horse and caught up with Beverly. Evidently he would not encroach on his partner's right of escort, since the division had been made according to agreement. He would play fair.

They reached the Popplewell ranch before dark and found a number of vehicles standing in the road, the horses having been unhitched and turned into the corral. As a cowboys' dance lasted most of the night, there was no need to keep the animals hitched.

Letty was curious to see the "half-dugout" and the "upstairs house," whose novelty of architecture had tickled her imagination when she had heard of them. She perceived that the half-dugout, as its name implied, was a domicile the upper part only of which was wood, the lower being an excavation like a cellar.

"A regular dugout would be too dark," Sourdough explained to her. "You got to have some wall above if you're going to have any window light. Of course, some o' the real old-timers did live in regular dugouts at first for a time till they could do better. But they generally made out to have part of it up, anyhow."

He swaggered back with Letty on a tour of inspection. The dugout was behind the upstairs house, and separated from it. The upstairs house was merely an ordinary ranch structure, with a porch across the front, and four rooms arranged much as in Bev's house. The dugout, he told her, was used as a kitchen and dining room now, and the other for living and sleeping quarters.

All of the furniture had been moved from the house and was in full view, piled in the yard outside, the family evidently sure that no damage from rain was likely to come to it. Or perhaps they had counted on the presence of so many healthy men that it could be quickly restored to place in the event of a threatened downpour. The furniture, of itself, Letty decided after viewing it, was not of an elegance to occasion much concern, even if it did get rained on. Though, as the value of any article increases with the distance from the possibility of replacing it, the Popplewells might have conceivably suffered much inconvenience in getting a new outfit.

The Popplewells were cordial hosts. Old Man Si, as the younger folks called him, was a short, stubby person with a grizzly goatee, which he plucked at nervously. Perhaps he would have felt more at home at a round-up or branding than at a dance, but he was determined to neglect none of his duties. His wife was a tall, thin woman, who looked as if

55

she might have borne most of the responsibilities as well as the children for the family. The offspring were noisily in evidence, heard as well as seen on all sides.

Letty tried to count them. There were the twins, the oldest girls, Maude and Gertie, high-bosomed, high-colored girls much alike, their black hair done up in knots at the nape of the neck and banged across the forehead, their black eyes flashing with gaiety. They wore dresses of red cheesecloth, made with ruffles whose exuberance would have attracted attention anywhere. Letty had never seen so many ruffles nor such full ones. The Popplewell girls would have been upborne like balloons had a high gale caught them!

Sourdough pointed out the "frying-size" girls to her, not so resplendent of costume, because they were not yet "out on the carpet"—that is of an age and inclination to marry, but equally exhilarated in their greetings to the arriving guests, and in their enjoyment of the occasion. Perhaps they would like to shove their elder sisters into quick matrimony, to leave the "carpet" and the upstairs house with its elegance in their undisputed possession.

Then there were several boys, whose relative ages were hard to appraise, since they seemed simultaneous.

"Where do you come in?" Letty asked one of the boys who seemed a trifle smaller than the others.

"Him? Oh, he's the runty pig of the lot," explained the father.

He laid his hand on the bobbing head of a bashful little girl of about four. "And here's the mean 'un." But his look and tone of affection removed the sting from the adjective. He guffawed as she scooted toward the rear in her embarrassment at having attention called to her.

Letty scanned the crowd. It appeared that every family had brought all the children, even to the babies in arms. And, indeed, who would have been left at home to mind them? Surely the tired mothers needed the change and recreation more than anybody else.

But the babies presented a slight problem, for they were put to sleep on the floor of the half-dugout before the dance actually began. The older children "milled around," as Lige expressed it, in the party, enjoying it as much as their elders did. They could hardly have endured the grief of banishment, but no one contemplated such cruel and unnecessary punishment. Small boys stalked around in brand-new boots, in swaggering imitation of the cowboys.

Letty's eyes were bright with interest as she observed the guests. The girls and women were dressed in all sorts of garbs, some as handsome as would have been worn at a dance in Virginia, while others showed less adherence to current styles. It was clear that the lack of suitable apparel had kept no female at home!

The men were likewise varied in their attire. Some were brave in "store clothes," while others were decked out in exaggerated cowboy costumes. The master of ceremonies, "the caller," as Letty learned he was titled, wore leggings of fringed leather, ornate boots into which his trousers were stuffed, blue flannel shirt with collar turned back, and a red silk bandana draped coyly round his throat. He was fully aware of his impressive costume and swaggered a bit to be sure that others were noticing.

This leader it was who finally called the assembly to order and announced that the dance would begin. He took his stand in the middle of the floor in the main front room, called stentoriously, "Choose your partners. Get in the ring."

He signaled to the fiddler to tune up. That important figure was a wizened little man who might have been seventy-five years old, whose face was brown and gnarled as a walnut, and whose twinkling blue eyes needed no glasses to aid their vision. He waved his fiddle in gay salute to the crowd.

"What is that he's got on his fiddle?" Letty asked her escort.

"Snake rattles," he informed her.

"What in the world for?"

"To keep dampness from the fiddle. Folks say a rattler never lets his rattles get wet no matter if he swims a river. He holds his rattles out of the water. So it's considered a good thing to keep the damp out of fiddle strings."

She looked about fearfully. "Are there many rattlesnakes round here?"

"Worlds of 'em. But they're in winter quarters now. In old prairie-dog holes and such like."

She shivered. "Then I'll never take a walk!"

He chuckled. "Folks don't walk here. Too far from anywheres to anywheres. But you'll learn to ride horseback when spring comes on. I'll teach you how to shoot rattlers—it's fun."

"Everybody's telling me to learn how to shoot!" She shook her head vehemently. "I don't want to know."

The fiddler had warmed up to his task now, and the tune made the guests' feet dance expectantly, as the caller gave directions.

"We'll do-se-do, now.

"Gentlemen to the center, ladies hands all.
Sashay to your partners, do-se-do!
Put on airs, go upstairs,
Gentlemen advance, all promenade slow!"

As the dancers moved through the figures of the old-fashioned square dance, Letty felt a lightness of heart she had not known since she had left Virginia. There was a carefree gaiety about the assembly, a neighborly joviality that softened the crudities of the costumes, that made the bare room attractive because of the hospitality that had brought them all there. Everybody was having a good time.

As she went lightly through the movements of the dance, obeying the directions of the fantastic "caller," Letty's mind could busy itself with thoughts remote from the scene, even while her interested eyes saw everything about her, and her ears caught every rhythm of the fiddler's tunes. Would it happen, by any chance, that her train acquaintance would come to the dance? It wasn't likely, since he lived in Fort Worth, and must have gone back long ago. But maybe he was in this section on business. Oh, by a mere remote chance!

So every time the door opened to admit a late arrival, she would look up quickly to see if it were Mr. Wirt Roddy. Each time, when the newcomer proved to be someone else, she felt a slight disappointment, a grievance not to be analyzed. It would have been interesting to see him again, she carefully explained to her mind. And perhaps he'd be good fun at a dance. She had guessed that beneath his look of rather bored indifference he had a strong capacity for enjoyment, if a thing appealed to his tastes. Yes, the dance would be gayer if he were there. But he wasn't there!...

She had almost forgotten her faint, mysterious fear of him, or put it down as only her silly shyness, and she remembered only the man's attractiveness, his cordiality to her....

While she danced with Lige or Sourdough, or some other of the cowboys, she was thinking of Wirt Roddy. It would be nice to see again that ironic smile at her naive ignorance of the west. Oh, she was wiser now, and knew better how well-informed he was about things than she had that day on the train.... If she ever saw him again, she'd tell him he was right in all he said about the wind.... She could see his slow smile as she told him....

There was no man on the floor as handsome as he. The cowboy's swaggering would seem crude beside his calm arrogance, his assurance of superiority.... She could see him as vividly as on that day, twisting his black mustache in aloof amusement, his dark eyes bright with mirth that she hadn't quite understood.

If he came into the room the fiddler would stop, the dance would break up for a moment, and then the gaiety would begin again, the livelier because he was there.

But he didn't come!

Briskly the "caller" promoted the gaiety. He would clap his hands together or make vehement gestures as he shouted directions, leading the song which the others sang with him, to the fiddler's blithe accompaniment.

They were dancing a square dance to the tune of "Skip-to-my-Lou."

"Gone again, skip-to-my-Lou.
Gone again, skip-to-my-Lou,
Gone again, skip-to-my-Lou,
Skip-to-my-Loula, my darling!"

His directions for the movements of the dance figures formed the theme for new stanzas when the familiar ones had given out.

"Can't get a red bird, blue bird'll do.
Can't get a red bird, blue bird'll do,
Can't get a red bird, blue bird'll do,
Skip-to-my-Loula, my darling!"

Stanzas of that song and others were improvised, commenting on conspicuous guests, to be caught up by the crowd in spontaneous folk-singing.

Presently the riotous tune of "Shoot the Buffalo" was begun, and they danced to its measures with laughing eyes.

"Oh, the hawk he shot the buzzard,
And the buzzard shot the crow;
And we'll rally round the cane-brake
And shoot the buffalo!"

Letty never lacked for partners Young men crowded round her petitioning for dances and she had to choose diplomatically to avoid giving offense. Lige and Sourdough naturally claimed the preference, but they were only two among many. Oh, these young men were different from those she had known at home, but they were young and she was young, and tonight she would be gay, no matter what the morrow might be.

The pounding of heavy boots on the floor raised a haze of sand that blurred the features of the throng, as Letty watched them....

As the dance progressed the children one by one succumbed to sleep, and were dragged off the floor to be laid beside the babies in the dugout, thus leaving more space for the adults. The dancers would rest for a brief lull, retire to the rear for a drink of black coffee and a piece of cake or pie, and then would begin another song. Some of the men sampled the contents of a keg of whiskey. The fiddler would rolic away on the old favorites among the tunes, "Guinea in the Low Ground," "Turkey in the Straw," "Sugar in the Coffee," and "Arkansas Traveler."

The hilarity went on all night. Dawn showed a haggard crowd with sleep-bleared eyes, disheveled hair, cheeks flushed from the exertion and the close air of the rooms. The fiddler's arm was stiff, the caller's voice was hoarse as a foghorn or a bull-frog's basso, and Letty felt ready to collapse from fatigue. But Sourdough and Cora looked as if they could have gone on for another day without stopping.

As the last dance was finished. Sourdough looked straight into Letty's eyes as he sang with the others,

"Many a lass have I let pass
Because I wanted you!"

Then the tune broke out gaily,

"Hell Among the Yearlings!"

As the guests gathered to drink more black coffee before starting the long ride home, Letty heard a cowboy say to Si Popplewell, "I saw Wirt Roddy a couple o' days ago."

"Why in heck didn't ye tell him to come tonight?" the host growled.

"Did. Give a cordial invite, but I couldn't get him to stay over. Said he was gettin' back to go to a dance in Fort Worth."

"I'll be bound for Wirt Roddy to be headed for some fandango or other," grunted Si.

And so he had been near her, in the neighborhood, and hadn't come to see her! That night on the train, as he said good-bye, he had whispered that he would come—maybe; but he hadn't even sent her a line! He could have come to this dance instead of the other if he had wanted to. But he hadn't wanted to!...

The coffee was bitter and nauseating to her, the crowd, of a sudden, uncouth. She wanted to hurry home.... But Cora's house wasn't home!...

Cora, looking as rosy and fresh as the sunrise, hustled her husband and children into their wraps and into the hack to go to the ranch....

Lige took his place in the buggy with Letty going home, and Sourdough rode on his restive horse beside them for a time. The sun was just rising, and the prairie was a dim golden-gray from the sand and the dead grass, now flooded with unearthly radiance, while the sky became gorgeous with streamers of clouds like trailing flames. Into Letty's mind flashed a whimsical request that the man on- the train had made of her.

"Won't you sometime watch a sunrise on the plains—and think of me?"

But she wouldn't think of him! She wouldn't—not ever again! Why should she?

6

ON THE DAY FOLLOWING the dance, Cora went about with a teasing mystery in her eyes, her smile. She was fondling some secret, as a woman will, dangling it in every gesture, laughing at it through lowered eye lashes, caressing it with every tone of her voice. The curve of her lovely lips, the twinkling of her dimples spoke of a secret she could tell if she would. But she wouldn't! She showed that she wished all beholders to know that she was concealing something, but she meant to keep on concealing it.

On Sunday morning as she was dusting the front room, Beverly laid an admiring arm about her shoulder.

"You're looking mighty pretty and set up over something today and yesterday. What is it?"

But she gave him only a quick, possessive kiss, a flick of the dust cloth and a toss of her lustrous head.

"Never you mind! You just don't trash up this room any more than you can help today. It's Sunday, you know."

"We have a Sunday every week."

But she danced away from him in silence, the very crinkles in her shining hair suggestive of mystery.

To the children she said, "You got to take a bath all round before this evening. We're going to have the big meal at night 'stead of in the middle of the day today."

"Why?" they chorused.

But they got no illuminating reply. Cora was not versed in subtleties of dissimulation, having scarcely ever had, in her forthright existence, an emotion she had felt inclined to hide. She was as naively transparent as a glass of water. Letty knew that soon the explanation would appear, and so she tried to wait in patience. She wondered what was in the air, but she would not ask. Maybe Cora wanted her to tease with the others, but she kept a silence that may have been discreet or may have been only stubborn.

But at any rate, she felt lighter of heart because she noticed that Cora was in high good humor over something, for a cowboy ballad sounded from the kitchen during her bustlings about in there. She was indulgent with the children's protests over being bathed, even while she soaped them firmly, and she even persuaded Letty to lie down in the afternoon for a nap, "so's to look pretty when the company comes," she said.

Letty, kindling a little with the excitement she felt but did not understand, took special pains with her toilet as she dressed in the afternoon. She brushed her yellow hair until it was tinglingly alive, and shone like a nimbus about her head when she had arranged it. She put on a little-girlish dress of a dull sort of bluish-green that made her eyes look bluer and brought out the fairness of her skin. She decided that she was too pale, after a critical examination of her reflection in the leprous mirror over the dresser, so she plucked a pink petal from a flower on Alice's summer hat and gave herself a little color. She blushed in guilt as she did so, and looked fearfully around at every sound. The knowledge that she had "painted her face" gave her a sense of high, intoxicating excitement that of itself imparted to her cheeks the most charming color imaginable.

Who could be coming that day? And why was Cora so pleased over the prospect?

It was hard for her and the children to wait until the middle of the afternoon to find out anything, but Cora was inexorable in her refusal to divulge her secret.

When, about three o'clock, she heard the sound of galloping horses, Letty ran to the window and peeped out in palpitating suspense to see who the visitors were. But she jerked her palms outward with a gesture of disappointment as she saw.

"Who is it?" asked Cora, with a crafty smile. Cora, who usually ran first to the window or the door to discover an arriving visitor and greet him!

"Just Lige and Sourdough!" cried Letty, a slight frown creasing her forehead, and her red mouth in a moue of disappointment.

"Huh!"

Letty was never sure of all that Cora's "Huh!" conveyed. It usually expressed contempt for ignorance, and disapproval, and mirth not always tactful, but she could not be positive about what else it might hold. Letty tried to analyze it now, while the riders dismounted and came in, but she was unable to decide all its nuances and suggestions.

Sourdough entered with a swaggering slink, and with gusty greetings that filled the room so that Lige had scant chance to say a word. But his slow, awkward smile told Letty that he was glad to be there.

Sourdough was full of ebullient spirits, prancing about the room with his hands flouncing the tails of his store coat. His red hair looked excited and the very freckles on his face were fidgety. He was nervous enough for four people, Letty said to herself.

Lige smiled his slow, wide smile as he watched his partner.

The talk was brisk and jovial, for the most part about the dance, which had gone down in county history as a distinct success. Such pessimistic topics as drought were pushed to the background of everybody's thoughts.

At last, when it appeared that the children could not possibly wait any longer, Cora called them into the kitchen to supper. Sunday night supper was generally a cold "hand-out" from the "safe," or cupboard, comprising the leftovers from dinner, with not even the trouble of setting the table. But tonight there was a white cloth, Cora had some of her peach preserves in a glass dish in the center of the table, and her supper was a festive affair.

Letty was deep in speculation all during the meal. No one had come besides Lige and Sourdough, who came every Sunday, and so why the excitement of preparation and suspense? No one else had been expected, that was plain, for Cora could not have hidden her disappointment or annoyance if that had been the case.

Supper was a gay meal, with Cora and Sourdough more hilarious and amused than usual, their sparkles and crackles of wit evoking smiles from Lige and Bev.

When the food had been consumed, and Sourdough leaned back with a vasty breath, Letty began as usual to help clear away the dishes, but Cora stopped her.

"Bev'll help me tonight. You young folks go on sit in the front room by the fire and enjoy yourselves."

Why this sudden self-effacement on Cora's part?

"But I'll help you first."

Cora took her by the shoulders and gave her a playful push that propelled her toward the door, the while she winked at Sourdough. "Scat out o' here!"

That worthy laughed strangely and bolted for the front room.

As Letty and Lige followed, she heard Cora call sharply to one of the children, "Come here now, you! You young uns are going to bed in a pair o' minutes."

Then the kitchen door was closed.

What did it all mean? The elaborate casualness with which Cora had planned for Letty to go with the two young men would have been embarrassing, she told herself, if there had been only one. But there were two!

Sourdough self-consciously stoked the stove, pokered the coals with noisy vigor, and then tiptoed over to close the door that led into the children's room.

Lige shook with silent laughter. "Skeered o' drafts?" he jeered.

"Naw. Ears."

Sourdough stood with his back to the stove, his feet wide apart, his hands thrust under his coat at the back—obviously struggling with some emotion. But what? Letty puzzled over the queerness of the situation, and Lige sat with arms folded, a knowing smile on his lips. He knew all about it!

"What's the joke?" asked Letty, unable longer to conceal her curiosity.

Lige wiped the smile from his face, though his eyes still twinkled, but he said nothing.

"Damn you! Why can't you say something?" jerked Sourdough. "'Stead o' settin' there with a grin on yore mouth like a catfish?"

Lige answered him with respectful gravity that was enough of itself to arouse suspicion in the mind of anyone who knew the relations between the two.

"You have the floor. This plan was yours, remember, old scout. I'll speak up when my time comes. I've got my little piece prepared."

Sourdough swallowed vehemently. The room throbbed with silence.

Letty sat on a footstool, the glow from the open door of the stove shining on her yellow hair, her hands clasped about her knees, as she looked up at him expectantly.

He gazed down at her and his eyes softened, though his hands still twitched nervously at his coat tails.

He began as if he were rehearsing a prepared speech. "I maybe can't say it as it ought to be said. I got to pick my words like a feller picks his steps when he's walkin' barefoot through a bed o' prickly pear..."

He paused, unable to proceed.

"Yes?" she said. "What is it, Sourdough? I'm wild to know! Don't tease me so!"

He gulped, and began again. "Generally, I reckon a girl knows when men is in love with her. Mebbe she knows it afore they do. Mebbe sometimes by just knowin' it, she makes it come to pass when it wouldn't a' been so otherwise. I can't say. But you—now you're such a little girl, and so young—mebbe perhaps you don't know?"

His voice rose in interrogative. Her blue eyes widened, and their look of surprise gave him his answer.

"You see. Miss Letty, Lige an' me are both in love with you. No, don't say nothing," he interposed as she made an inarticulate sound of denial. "It ain't yore turn to talk yet. Take my word for it, it's so. Now Lige an' me have been side-pardners for a long time, an' we didn't want to do nothin' that wasn't square to each other. I said to him if I asked you first, mebbe it wouldn't be totin' fair with him An' if he asked you first, mebbe I wouldn't have no more chance than a hoot owl in hell. So I made a proposition to him that if we talked to you together an' told you to take yore pick, that way, there couldn't be no hard feelin's."

He wiped his forehead, as one who has paused in a prodigious physical exertion.

Letty gave a little hysterical giggle. "Do you usually propose in a duet like this?"

He glared at her and snorted like an astonished and indignant horse. "Good gosh, no! We don't usually propose at all! Why, Lige here, is so girl-shy that hithertofore you couldn't drag him round where calico was. But one look at you got him locoed."

Letty shot a quick, surreptitious look at Lige, who flickered a whimsical smile at her and nodded bashfully. His turn hadn't come to speak, then!

Sourdough went on with his rehearsed oration. "We'd like you to choose an' put us out of our misery. Otherwise, we can't be no manner of use for the spring work, round-up and branding and such."

So, they took it for granted that she must choose one of them! How funny, how deliciously amusing!

"I—" she began, but Sourdough again cut her short.

"Here we are." His thumb gestured first at himself and then at his partner. "Proud but pore. Either of us'd lick a million wild cats to protect you—but you'll likely have to do yore own washin' for a spell if you marry either of us. But we don't aim to always be pore. Someday we can put diamonds on you and build you a fine house. That is, if it ever rains again in this God-forgotten country!"

Letty's face crinkled with laughter. It was impossible to take this seriously, when Sourdough was so funny. "But I—" she began, only to be interrupted again by Sourdough.

He turned on Lige ferociously. "Now you spit out *yore* little speech, you dumb son-of-a-gun! You'd let me give myself the thumps doin' all the talkin', would you?"

Lige leaned forward in his chair and clasped his hands between his knees. When he spoke there was a jocose tenderness in his voice and in his face.

"Miss Letty, I reckon Sourdough has put it about right for both of us. You maybe couldn't see anything to cotton to in either of us rough fellows. But we sure do love you! and we'd do our durndest to make you happy."

Her laughter bubbled over in confusion, and her eyes were bright as she said teasingly, "You talk like you expected me to marry both of you at once!"

"No'm, just one," he answered her gravely. "If you just say which one, that un'll hit the ceilin' and t'other un'll hit the grit."

Two pairs of eyes gazed straight at her expectantly, without a wink or a flicker of an eyelash, so intent were they.

She pulled herself together to answer. They really were serious then, and this wasn't one of Sourdough's jokes.

"But I'm sorry—but I don't love either one of you—like that!" she cried impetuously.

"No?" questioned Lige softly, his unwavering gaze on hers.

She shook her head. "Not with the—marrying kind of love!"

Sourdough kicked the leg of the stove to release his emotions. "Gosh dam it! By gatlings, I knew nothing so good as that could happen to one of my fambly."

She tried earnestly to explain her position. "You see, I like you both—oh, lots! I couldn't choose between you, and I want you to keep on coming to see me. But I'm not in love with either one of you, and so of course I couldn't marry you."

Sourdough gulped mournfully, his Adam's apple almost overcome with emotion. "Just as you say, Miss Letty."

"I'm so sorry," she went on quickly. "You've both been so good to me. I don't know how I could have got along without you, but I—well, being in love is a different thing, isn't it?"

"It shore is," agreed Sourdough. "If you ain't never been in love, you don't know what it is to be livin' in a rainbow one minute, and all gormed with gloom the next."

63

Lige spoke up gently, considerate of her feelings, rather than of his own, as usual. Kind, thoughtful Lige! "Maybe we rushed you too much. Maybe if we'd waited a while you could learn to like one of us." His tone was hopeful, questioning.

But she couldn't, of course, and so the kind and fair thing was to tell him so frankly, and let him think of someone else.

"No, I'm afraid not. I'm not thinking about marrying at all, not for years and years yet."

Silence pulsed and throbbed in the Little room. Through the open door of the stove, the fire smiled and chuckled at these absurd young human beings, while outside the wind *whooed* at them, but except for that there was stillness for a time.

Sourdough gave thought to Letty's statement for a few moments, mulling it over in his mind, and then he roused to protest. He brought his palms together with a whack.

"If you're not thinkin' o' gettin' married, why, you're wrong, then. It's natural for girls to marry, come yore age—not that you are so all-fired old at that," he apologized hastily.

She smiled to show that she held no grudge against him.

He went on with emphasis. "And it'd be pleasanter to have yore own home, 'stead o' washin' dishes in some other woman's dump."

Letty murmured, "Yes." How true that was, how very true! But not in the pitiful little shack on the plains, where either of those rough cowboys would take her! Romance wasn't dead in the world, and her knight would come riding up someday to rescue her. She would wait for him, she must wait!

Sourdough's jaw set sternly. "If you can't favor either of us, we don't hold it against you. Fact is, it only shows the sense you've got. But you'd ought to marry."

She shook her head, smilingly.

"Yes, you'd ought to. An' all o' these young fellers in the county'll be hitchin' their horses at front of here soon. Now we better help you pick somebody else, if you're certain sure you won't have us."

"I don't want anybody," she cut in.

"Excuse me, but you do—only you just don't know it yet." He turned to Lige. "Now who you reckon she *might* come to like?"

"I dunno," said Lige shortly, as if he did not relish the turn the discussion was taking.

"How about Rufe Weaver?"

"No," snapped Lige. "He's crooked. Crooked as a dog's hind leg. She mustn't think of him."

"'Sta bueno, then." Sourdough accepted the rebuff but did not relinquish his idea of providing for Letty. "There's Alec Rountree. He's got a good ranch."

Lige reared up in resentment. "He got it from his dad. He'll never make anything of his own. Too lazy to grow fast, even when he was a boy."

"Yeah, you're right. No get up and get to him." Sourdough nodded as in satisfaction at seeing one more possible rival put out of the way. "He hasn't got the sprawl of a louse!"

Letty smiled and smoothed her dress over her knees. Men were so funny—like little boys!

But she didn't need to say anything now, for she had not been invited to share this part of the confab.

Sourdough reluctantly dragged forth another name from the pit of his acquaintance. "There's Alf Anderson. He's thrifty and saving. He got his own ranch, without any help."

"You said it. He's so stingy he'd crawl under the fence to save wearing out the hinges by opening the gate!"

Sourdough snorted. "You don't seem to think much of yore friends here in the county."

"You're doin' the pickin'. They aren't my choice," was the imperturbable answer. "You ast for my advice, and I give it to you."

"'Twan't nothing to call forth no great amount of gratitude, I'd say!"

Lige smiled in serene silence.

"Well, all right then, old hoss," went on his partner. "How about Jack Newton? He ain't crooked, an' he ain't lazy, nor yet so stingy."

Lige sniffed contempt. "She'd as well marry a rag doll. No spunk to him at all. I could take a corn cob with a lightnin' bug on the end of it an' chase him out o' the county!"

Letty laughed bubblingly at the evoked picture. She had danced with Jack Newton at the ball, and she remembered him, a tall and timorous young fellow who had stumbled over her feet and been in an agony of confusion over it. She was glad they hadn't picked Jack Newton for her!

"I believe you're picking out the ones you don't like," she accused Sourdough.

He blushed a brick-red in guilt. "Come to think of it, I don't choose any of 'em as a husband for you, neither. When it comes to that, ain't nary one of 'em worth the scrapin's of yore boot heel."

"Well, then, don't you think you might let the matter rest as it is for a while?" Her tone was deceptively serious, but her eyes were dancing, and her dimples twinkled back and forth. "Maybe some more young men will come to the country. Or maybe I didn't see them all that night."

"Maybe." His tone was pessimistic.

Lige spoke up, as he straightened his tall form in his chair. "I don't know as I'm encouraging that kind of immigration to this section. I'd ruther build barbwire fences to keep 'em out of this neck o' the woods."

Sourdough sighed dolorously. "Well, tell you what. Miss Letty. I think you better not say the yes to any feller till Lige an' me have give him the once-over. There's some curious cattle on the range here sometimes, an' you might not understand the brands."

She laughed and blushed and spread her palms out prettily before the blaze of the fire. "All right. I'll ask advice from you two before I fall in love with anybody."

"That's as much as we'd ought to expect now," he said resignedly.

Lige smiled his slow, tranquil smile.

Silence fell over the little group, a curious, pulsing silence that was companionable, and yet self-conscious. Since the topic of main importance had been discussed and disposed of, the two men seemed to have nothing further to say, and Letty was a bit afraid of starting an argument over anything just then.

At last she turned impulsively to Lige. "I wish you'd tell me some more stories of the west —like the ones you told me the day we drove from Sweetwater."

His eyes lighted up with an inner satisfaction. "Did they interest you? I was just tryin' to make you forget the miles an' the hours an' the sand. You seemed so little an' pitiful-like."

"Tell me a fairy story of the plains," she said dreamily, her half-closed eyes gazing at the flames.

"Well now, we haven't got any fairy stories of the prairies that I know of. Perhaps we settlers came too late to catch up with the fairies. Or maybe we're too soon and had ought to sit round an' wait a spell until they show up."

"Haven't you got a single fairy story?" Her jesting tone rebuked and challenged him. "Not one? Haven't you ever seen a fairy?"

"Well, I couldn't say as I've seen one. But then again I wouldn't swear I haven't. Maybe I have seen one, and didn't have gumption enough to know it. Thought it was a ball of thistledown blowin' in the wind. Or a flower, in the years when we had rain and the spring prairies bloomed like a bouquet. Or an antelope fadin' out of sight. Or a ground squirrel, so little an' graceful, dartin' away into the ground. You know you make me think of a ground squirrel. Miss Letty? Maybe us rough cowpunchers just ain't acquainted with fairies. Of course I'd take my hat off to one anywheres I met it, if I only knowed what it was."

She nodded at him imperiously. "Tell me something pretty, anyhow."

His face brightened as an idea came to him. "I can tell you a wild horse story," he offered, but with certain dubiousness of tone.

Sourdough gave a whinnying laugh. "She asks for a fairy an' all he can give her is a wild hoss! I'll say that's a hoss on me!"

Letty laughed a little tinkle of a laugh that had not sounded out so gaily or so spontaneously since long before she left Virginia. "Tell me about it," she commanded.

Lige cleared his throat self-consciously, and moved his barge-like boots about on the floor, as he sought words in which to begin.

"Well, you know there's a raft of wild horses on these western plains, all the way from Mexico to Canada—though not as many as there used to be."

"Where do they come from?" she questioned. "T didn't know horses were wild."

"When the Spanish settled Texas long and long ago—you know, don't you, that Texas has been under six flags, one of 'em Spain's?—they brought Arabian horses with them. Some of 'em got away an' got lost. An' when the Spanish left, they stayed on. That's how the wild horses got started in the west."

His eyes took on the far-seeing look that she had come to recognize in them when he was thinking. "There were herds of 'em roaming the prairies when this section began to be settled up. Each herd had its leader, a stallion that could scent danger, that could find a way of escape for his herd when they were about to be cornered.

"The cowboys wanted good horses, you see, and every cowboy would like to have a horse better'n the rest. So they all tried to catch the stallion leadin' the herd. It was a great sight in the old days, they tell me, to see these herds of wild horses go racing across the plains—Arabian stock, you know, that was beauties to look at and like the wind for speed. All over the west you can hear old cowmen tell about these wild horses! Many of 'em was caught, and they've got a lot of tales about them. But they'll always tell you of a horse that nobody could catch. One that was too fast to be caught up with, too clever to be cornered, too game to be tired out."

Her eyes were shining with interest as she listened.

"They say some of these stallions weren't just flesh and blood, weren't living horses, but something that did not die," he went on musingly. "Spirits, you might say they were; maybe devils. You'll often hear of a pacing white stallion that couldn't never be taken, that laughed at your lasso. They'll tell you of a big black horse that no man living could come near to. You could see him racing over the prairies, when dusk began to come, going as fast as the wind. You could see his mane floating back like a black banner, you could hear him neighing. But no lariat was ever made that could capture him."

"Is he hereabout now?" Letty asked, thrilled, but a bit fearful.

66

"Maybe. He hasn't been caught, at any rate. If you see him you can know him, because his hoofs are like fire, they say, and his mane and tail stream in the wind, and he neighs at night, as he goes like the norther when it sweeps over the plain."

He gestured with free motions of his hands, to show the stallion's speed and ease of motion.

Letty listened, her head cocked to one side a little, in a way she had when she was deep in thought.

The wind gave a whistling shriek outside, and she shivered as she imagined a demon steed, racing like a black shadow across the plain, a lonely, terrible figure, neighing in the night!

Sourdough spoke up. "Some folks say he comes ahead of a storm. An' maybe that's the reason they've thought they've seed him about here so much."

"Do you have storms often here?" Letty trembled and leaned closer to the fire. She felt as if the black wing of a storm even then had come near to her.

Sourdough was roused to his usual braggadocio. "Gosh, yes! These winds come off'n the Cap Rock so that this section is a sort of pocket for storms. Folks have cellars an' dugouts to go to when cyclones come."

She paled and shuddered. So it had been true, then, what Mr. Wirt Roddy had told her!

"I'll dream of cyclones and demon horses!"

Lige's big hands stretched themselves deprecatingly to her as if to shield her from even a thought of harm.

"Sho, now, Miss Letty, we didn't go to scare you. We wouldn't scare you for the world. Nothin's goin' to hurt you, so long as me an' Sourdough has got our senses an' our six-shooters. Why, we'd rope an' bulldog old Nick hisself if he so much as batted an eye winker to let on he was aimin' to hurt you."

"I'm afraid of storms," she confessed. Then she hummed softly the old spiritual she had learned from her black mammy in Virginia:

"Lord, I don't want to die in a storm, in a storm!
Lord, I don't want to die in a storm, in a storm!
When de wind blows east, an' de wind blows west.
Lord, I don't want to die in a storm!"

7

CORA MOVED BRISKLY about the Monday morning kitchen like a nature goddess in a blue-gingham dress, repairing the ravages of visitors' appetites and the muss which Sunday leisure brings about in a house where men and children spend the hours. Letty reflected on the futility of cleaning up—for look how hard she and Cora had worked the day before to put the house in shining order, and now everything was upset again! But the house was so little, and so many people had to live in it that it was impossible to keep it straight.

Beverly sat by the window mending a piece of harness. The baby was perched in her highchair beside the stove and pounded on her tin breakfast plate with a spoon, the noise giving her keen delight. The energy of her gesture occasionally brought the spoon up at a wrong angle, to strike her head with its coppery curls, and made her blink and catch her breath from the shock. But she was spirited and determined, hence would not give over her orchestral attempts. She looked at her father now and then to win a smile from him.

Cora was cleaning the kitchen with an equal vigor. She broomed the older children out of the room with emphatic gesture.

"You young uns get in the front room an' get to your books."

Letty was drying the dishes and putting them away in the bottom part of the "safe" to keep them from the sand. She could never, never get used to the sight and touch and smell of sand everywhere all the time! The smooth oilcloth on the table was gritty again a moment after you had wiped it off with a damp cloth. There wasn't any use in dusting the furniture, for the sand followed your every movement. A yellowish-gray film was over everything you saw or touched. When you woke up in the morning the sand was on your cheeks and in your eyes and nostrils, and gritting down inside your clothes against your body! Ugh! what a country!…

Then she smiled as she thought of the night before. How funny and friendly those cowboys had been! Their antiphonal proposal struck her suddenly as so comical that she chuckled to herself with amusement. Of course, she couldn't ever think of marrying either one of them, but they were jolly and good-hearted, and she liked them both.…

Wasn't Sourdough a regular cut-up! He could make a hit as a clown in a circus if he wanted to. He had a native wit and humor that could have meant a good deal to him if he had had a chance at an education. But just to be a cowpuncher didn't give a man any chance at all.…

Lige was more serious, more of a man, but he was pretty much of a boy at heart himself, with his awkward dignity, his shy, big-mouthed smile. He talked less than Sourdough, but he thought more.…

How delicious for Sourdough to think they must rustle her a husband! And Lige's finding fault with every man his partner proposed!…

She giggled at the remembrance, as she stooped to put away the plates.

Cora smiled in a pleased fashion. "Tell us what's the joke."

Letty blushed, as if she had been overheard in her thoughts. "Oh, nothing!"

Cora was scouring the stove with a blackened cloth, but she paused in her task to turn a significant look upon her.

"Haven't you got no news to tell us?—after last night?"

Letty's blush deepened. "No, not a thing."

Cora dropped her cloth in indignation. "Do you mean to tell me that those boys didn't pop the question last night, after Sourdough asking me to give 'em a good chance, an' me goin' to so much trouble to do it?"

Letty's face was burning now, and her heart aghast. "Oh, they—they did!" she stammered. "But—but—that was all there was to it!"

Cora looked astounded. "And you didn't take either of 'em?" Her tone was menacing.

Letty shrank from her look and voice, so cold, so hard. "No."

"And why, pray?"

"Oh, come now, Cora," Beverly interposed. "Don't embarrass the child."

"Keep your tongue off of this, Bev," she warned him. Then she turned again to Letty, with a relentless, "Why?"

Letty's knees were wobbling and her muscles felt like water, but she plucked up spirit to defend herself. "Because I don't love either of them. Because I'm not ready to think of marrying."

It was as if she took up a cudgel to protect her chance of far-off romance, her right to love when and whom she chose.

But Cora recognized no reserves of thought or speech, no privilege of privacy even in one's secret heart!

"And why ain't you in love with 'em? There ain't two better boys in this county than them two."

"I know they're good—and I like them. But—" Letty faltered, feeling a sense of loyalty to her friends. She couldn't voice the thought that these two kind men were rough and uncouth and common, not to be considered as remotely possible lovers. To laugh and talk with them was good fun, yes … to dance with them, yes … But to marry? Her whole being gave a shuddering *no!*

But Cora with clairvoyant malice read her thoughts. "Oh, so they ain't good enough for you—huh?" she sneered.

"Cora!" Beverly's voice was sharp. And then he smiled one of his rare smiles at her in attempt to placate her and bring peace between her and Letty. "You must have said 'no' to a lot of likely young men, my girl, before you married me. Girls have to have their freedom to choose. You wouldn't have let anybody else pick for you, would you?"

She turned on him like an iceberg afire.

"Yes, but I was livin' in my own home, with men of my own to support me an' take care of me. I wasn't livin' in some other woman's house … where I wasn't wanted!"

Letty gave a sharp little cry.

Beverly sprang to his feet, and his chair crashed backward to the floor. "Cora!—be careful!" he grated.

But Cora's fury, long controlled, was unleashed now. Not even for Bev would she restrain herself.

"Oh—so I've got to be careful, huh? I've got to walk soft an' talk pleasant an' cover up my feelings at seein' you treat another woman better than you do me!"

"Cora—hush!" he cried, towering over her. "You know she's just like my little sister!"

"Oh, you think I haven't got eyes in my head, to see how she honeyfuggles round you—an' how you think she's so pretty an' sweet an' *refined*? You think she hung the moon in the sky, because she's your cousin, an' came from Virginia. An' I'm nothin' but your wife—no better'n a coyote!"

She looked like a flame of jealous fury, her eyes glittering, her cheeks burning, her hair seeming to send out sparks of light.

"For God's sake, Cora!" Beverly clutched at her wrist, but she flung him off.

Letty shrank huddled against the table, the dish towel pressed close against her mouth to stifle her sobs. Her body shook. Terror poured its poison through her veins.

"I didn't know! I didn't know!" Her bitter voice wailed out at last. "I wish I'd have died before I came!"

"And I—" began Cora, but a look at Beverly's face, so white and stern, so awesome in its look of scorn, silenced her.

"Stop right there, Cora!" he said in a tone of ice and flint.

He stared for a moment at the two women, petrified in their attitudes, one of wrath and one of terror.

"Letty, I think you'd better go into the front room with the children," he said.

Then he turned to his wife. "Cora, I'm goin' out for a while, to give you time to think—and come to yourself."

He snatched his coat and hat from their nail behind the door.

The door opened, closed, the wind swallowed him.

Letty fled to the children's room, to flung herself face downward on the bed. Her body writhed and jerked with sobs. The room was icy cold, and she shook with a nervous chill, so that presently she crept under the covers, terrified lest she be sick and bring more annoyance to Cora, more trouble to Bev....

She tried to think, but she could only feel, a devouring shame, a heartache that swelled and pulsed through her whole body, a despair....

If only she might die, quickly, and be out of it all!...

How life had tricked and cheated her!... To have to live a dependent, in another woman's home—where she was hated! To know that her being there made life hard for Bev—poor Bev, who had had so much to bear!... That was the hardest of all. She remembered something her black mammy had said once, "Motherless chilluns are better off dead." Ah, dear God, yes!... But they didn't die!...

She was exhausted from crying, her head throbbed like a hot drum, but she tried to think of some way out. She must think ... Surely there was some way out of this ... What could she do? She hadn't any money to take her anywhere—and there was nowhere for her to go ... Virginia seemed as far away as another planet she might have lived on in an earlier existence, its people like figures in a dim dream. She smiled ironically as she remembered that the pastor had thought he was doing the kind thing for her when he had written that letter to Cousin Bev asking if he wouldn't take her in to live with his family. Heartbreak could come about through people's mistakes as well as through their sins. Who had sinned here? yet three people were wretched....

She couldn't think of staying on here—and yet, where could she go? She wasn't trained to make her living, for Virginia girls didn't go outside the home..... But what if you didn't have any home?... To whom could you turn?...

Should she marry one of the cowboys? She writhed away from the thought. To marry one of those rough, uncouth men, even if they were good and kind?... and without love? She'd rather die!...

Should she appeal to Mr. Wirt Roddy for advice and help? That thought stayed longer in her mind. She had forgotten her faint fear of him that she had known on the train, and she

70

visioned him now as a knightly figure that might come riding to her rescue—not her prince of romance, but an older man who might help her. He had emerged into chivalry in her remembrance now.... But he had been in the county and hadn't come to see her! He had forgotten all about her, and wouldn't even recall her name if she wrote to him. No, she couldn't do that!... Shame harried her, but pride blocked every way of escape.... Her pride must be crucified, whichever way she turned!...

At last she fell asleep from sheer physical and emotional exhaustion, and lay in a sort of stupor until evening. She had no realization of time—whether die had lain there for hours or for days. All she knew was that the thought of lifting her head from the pillow was intolerable, that any exertion was an effort impossible to make.

She was awakened to see Bev standing beside her bed, and Cora behind him, with a lighted lamp in her hand.

"Wake up, Letty, and come have some supper," he said gently.

She shook her head, her throat closing at thought of food eaten at Cora's table. She would rather starve.

"I don't want anything."

"You'll get sick if you don't eat," said Cora dully.

Letty sat up in submission, though every movement was an intolerable exertion. What matter what she did, anyhow?

Beverly stood looking first at one and then the other of the two women. He spoke in a voice that was gentle but had a tired deadness in it.

"I can't bear for you two girls to misunderstand each other. Cora, can't you see that Letty is no more in love with me nor I with her than—than my own little Alice? She's just like my young sister that died when I was a boy. And I'm the nearest to a father or brother or uncle that she has now. Don't you see that?"

Cora nodded sullenly. What coercion of spirit had Bev put on her to bring her even to this outward show of submission?

He turned to Letty. "And I don't want you to misjudge Cora. She's got one of the kindest hearts in ...the world. She'd take in any old hobo or tramp Mexican and nurse him through small-pox. She would deprive herself of food to give to a dog. And I wouldn't be alive myself tonight if it hadn't been for her."

"Yes," whispered Letty, clasping her cold hands together, and looking up at him with eyes that had a dull glaze over them, like a sick mockingbird's.

He went on. "But she just can't stand the thought of my looking at another woman. She ought to know by this time that I never do."

Letty realized that he was talking more to his wife than to her, and her heart beat thickly as she waited for Cora to answer. But the sullen silence was maintained. Letty felt as if the three were in a dialogue of the dead.

"And why should I even wish to think of anybody else?" His face wore a bleak look, but his voice was tender. "When a fellow's married to the prettiest girl in the county, he hasn't got eyes for anybody else."

Cora flung her head up haughtily, but her eyes swam with tears. "Bev, you never hurt me before, like you did this morning!"

His gaze met hers squarely. "You never gave me cause—before."

Letty looked wretchedly up at them. Was another quarrel going to start between them, over her. She must rouse herself, say something to prevent it.

71

"I think I'll just undress and go to sleep," she stammered. "I'll—feel better in the morning."

So they put the lamp down on the table and went into the kitchen.

The little house was silent earlier than usual that night, and the children were asleep. But outside, the night was wide awake and full of menace. The coyotes yelped all through the dark hours, their yapping, lugubrious cries prowling about the plains, and the wind uttered unearthly sounds. She could hear it wailing like a lost soul, like a banshee, like a demon lover....

· · · ·

The next morning Letty moved about the house like the little gray wraith of a girl long dead. A strange constraint lay over the whole household, and even the children were quieter, under the spell of it. Only the baby was untroubled by it, and high on her throne she struck her tin cymbal with indifferent delight.

Soon after breakfast Beverly spoke to his wife. "Cora, I've got to go over to see Hube Henderson about some steers. How about you going with me?"

Letty read his considerate thought. He would keep the two women apart as much as possible for a while, till the bitterness and hurt could heal somewhat.

"Sure, I'll go with you," said Cora.

He would know, Letty told herself, that Cora would be glad to go off alone with him, without even the children to come between them. And *she* could have the unwonted freedom of a day to herself—except for the youngsters, who didn't count. Children were companions, but not intruders in one's privacy of thought. One could suffer without shame in the presence of children.

"You want to wrap up well," he told Cora. "The cattle have been acting a little like we might have a norther before long."

"You think today?"

"No, not this soon, I guess."

When they had driven away, after directions to the children to be good, Letty felt as if a steel trap that had held her heart constricted had been released. Hube Henderson, she knew, lived five miles beyond Lige and Sourdough, which meant that Bev and Cora would be gone all day. They couldn't get back until late afternoon. She had the blessing of a whole day in which to think. Maybe by the time they came home, she could know what to do. To stay on meant that she would keep upsetting the peace of Beverly's home—that she'd make life hard for him. She could bear the humiliation for herself, if there were no other way, but she couldn't bring strife and hard feeling into his home....

Perhaps if she prayed hard enough God would show her a way out. He ought to, honestly, she thought—because it was the pastor that had got her into this fix.

She had sorely missed the church life since she had come to the ranch; but with the nearest church twenty-five miles away, so that one couldn't drive there and back in a day through the wind and sand, they couldn't go. There was talk of a camp-meeting in the summer time, but summer was a million years away....

All through the day, a prayer for guidance, for a way of escape, fluttered round and through all Letty's thoughts. In the past, prayer had been a somewhat perfunctory business with her, a matter of saying her childish prayers at night and morning, more as a ritual than anything else, though she had not been insincere. But now, she felt that for the first time in her life she actually prayed. Her thoughts strained upward in an agony of appeal. Surely if she prayed hard enough, and *believed*, God would open a way for her, would show her what to do!...

72

All the while she was busy with household tasks, cooking and washing dishes, her heart was uttering its petitions for help. Even while she was talking to the children, behind her words, behind her surface thoughts, her prayers were live things, wild, formless, intense, beating the air like wings....

In the mid-afternoon Letty stood at the window looking out over the prairie, so that her eyes might have at least temporary rest from the prison of the house. She saw a number of gaunt cattle bunched together in groups here and there, their heads put together, their backs to the north. Their mournful continuous lowing had a note of fear in it.

The boys came and stood beside her to see them.

Junior said casually, "The old-timers say when cattle act thataway, there's goin' to be a norther."

"I wonder will it be a blue norther or a cross-eyed norther?" conjectured Dan. "They's all sort, you know."

"I dunno," answered Junior.

Alice shyly slipped her hand in Letty's, as if for protection from marauding winds. "I don't like northers!"

Letty's heart fluttered wildly, like a prisoned bird. Neither did she! oh, neither did she! To face another of these terrible winds, whose cold chilled you to the marrow of your bones, whose violence battered at you, bruised you in body and mind, whose unknown terrors made you sick!... But maybe it wouldn't come. Maybe the children were wrong in their prophecy. Then she remembered what Bev had said, and shivered. And the cattle knew, they must know! Poor things, out defenseless on the plains, how they must suffer when the northers came!...

There came a strange stillness for a time, when the wind seemed to have gathered its forces together and withdrawn for a while. Ah, the cattle had been mistaken, after all, for the wind was not blowing at all! "All signs fail in Texas!"

The sky was blue, with a golden gauze of sand over it, and no clouds were anywhere to be seen—the heavens as empty as the prairies themselves, that stretched out to infinity, with no sign of human life on them.... In Virginia there would be someone passing almost any time that you looked out, and so you never got lonesome, with a neighborly road to look at. But here there weren't even what you could call roads to be seen, just stretches of sand everywhere the same....

Presently she watched the sun slip toward the horizon. A naked, uncovered sun moving across a vacant sky, to join an empty plain! But he shot a fiery glow athwart the heavens and the earth, and the gauzy sand became more luminous, more dazzling, as if it must show all the radiance that sunset clouds usually reflected. The earth itself seemed to give forth light, a yellow, cosmic light, and the golden glow overspread all the sky in an effect such as Letty had never seen before. She thought of the sunset she had witnessed from the train, when Mr. Wirt Roddy had called her attention to the splendor of the scene. Sunset and sunrise were marvelous in this land—but, oh, the hours between!...

As she turned toward the north, she saw a puny cloud, slight and fragile, touching the prairie's rim, a white, feathery nothing, like a ball of thistledown floating along the ground. But as she looked, it grew and darkened. Swiftly it spread over the sky until it blotted out the blue, till it hung, a black pall, over the wide heavens. It happened so quickly, with such incredible rapidity that Letty could scarcely believe it, even while her eyes watched it.

Letty, with the children close behind her, stepped to the door and opened it, that she might have a better look at this amazing cloud transformation like a necromancer's magic, like the effects the Indian magician? work deluding the physical eyesight. As she met the outer air, she felt the icy chill of a sudden drop in temperature. She heard the norther as it came roaring over the plains.

"It sure is a rip-snorter of a one!" cried Junior, as they darted back into the house and slammed the door to shut out the wind.

Night was on them almost immediately, for the clouds had blotted out the daylight, wiping out even the brief wintry dusk that usually obtained.... And Bev and Cora hadn't come home!...

To still her terror of the wind, and to keep the children from being panicky, Letty bustled about in the kitchen, making a brave show of fearless activity, in preparation of supper for the children. She could not eat anything herself, but the youngsters made a meal in apprehensive silence, very unlike their usual noise.

When she had washed and dried the supper dishes and put them away, she gathered the children together in the front room to wait for Bev and Cora to come home. She mustn't let the children see her panic, she told herself. She must control herself, for their sake, so they wouldn't be scared.... They were game youngsters and tried to seem unconcerned, in order to keep her from being uneasy, but she could feel their fear, and they hers.

The boys built up a red fire in the stove, and its glow lit the room with cheer they did not feel. Outside, the wind on the plains roared like a thousand devils let loose from the pit.... Where were Bev and Cora? Could they make it home?...

"Do you reckon Papa an' Mamma will get home all right," quavered Alice, as she huddled against Letty.

"Oh, yes, I'm sure they will," she lied consolingly.

"Sing to us," said Dan.

And so Letty sang song after song to keep them from thinking of their danger and of their parents, out on the wild plains. Old ballads, nursery jungles, negro folk-songs, she sang, until her voice was tired and her body drooped.

But each time that silence came, the children moved uneasily and the wind outside let her hear the menace of its sounds. She mustn't hear the wind, if she could help it!...

At last, without realizing what she was doing, she drifted into the strains of the old spiritual she had heard her black mammy sing when storms threatened. She remembered how Mammy had rebuked her once for making fun of her fear of the lightning, "Hush, chile! Don't you know we mustn't talk when de Lawd's speakin' in His thunder an' His winds?"

So, thinking of the comfort of those loving black arms, and longing for it now, she sang:

"Lord, I don't want to die in a storm, in a storm.
Lord, I don't want to die in a storm, in a storm!
When the wind blows east, an' the wind blows west.
Lord, I don't want to die in a storm!"

Still Bev and Cora hadn't come!...

Presently Letty noticed that the children were becoming drowsy from the warmth of the fire, and were nodding. Oh, she couldn't let them go to sleep and leave her alone! But it would be cruel to rouse them. Poor little things, they were scared, too!

Junior slumped back in a rocking-chair, his head lolling to one side, Dan put his head on his arms on the table by which he was sitting, and made no concealment of his slumber, while Alice crept over to the bed and lay down. Letty held the sleeping baby in her arms as

74

she rocked back and forth. The warmth, the companionship of the little unconscious body gave her comfort, as she held it close.

Would Bev and Cora be able to make their way home through this gale? Were they lost on the plains, perhaps freezing to death? Would a night like this bring back Bev's old trouble with his lungs and maybe be the death of him?... And he had invented that errand today in order to contrive a way to keep her and Cora apart for a time!... His death would be on her hands!...

How could any horse find its way in such a storm and blackness? Surely all sense of direction would be lost, even the coyote sense that plainsmen were said to have.... And in that lonely wilderness there were no neighbor lights to guide a traveler to safety. And even if there were, wouldn't this swirling sand hide them from view?...

Urged by an uncontrollable restlessness, she laid the baby down on the bed beside Alice, covered the two with a blanket, and fell to pacing the floor like a wild thing trapped. She felt an utter desolation of loneliness such as she had never conceived of. She started to rouse the sleeping children, but pity stayed her. Why wake them to suffer as she was suffering!

She fancied she could see a lost horse staggering futilely in a desert of sand, mocked by the winds, while two stiff and frozen figures in the hack were still forever—and because of her!...

The wind was a demon that had driven them all crazy; that had put false thoughts in Cora's mind, making her stir up this trouble; that had made Bev speak harshly to his wife and bring bitterness between them. It was the wind that had sent him on this errand, in order to lure him and Cora to their deaths! And all because of her!—The wind was determined to destroy her, because she feared it so! It was after her, and she couldn't escape it!...

She saw the wind as a black stallion with mane a-stream, and hoofs of fire, speeding across the trackless plains, deathless, defiant!... What if she were out on this prairie this night? He would trample her down to her death with his fiery hoofs.... A phantom, riderless horse, whom no mortal would ever ride—that no lariat flung by human hands could capture! His proud neck arching, his eyes glancing flames, he raced toward her across the sand— supernatural, Satanic, the wind of the North!...

But this was folly, she told herself. She mustn't let her fancy run away with her reason. The wind was not a demon horse—it was only the gale! It might have power to sweep the house from its foundations and tear it into splinters, but a wind could do that! It might kill her, yes, but it was *only the wind!*

People went crazy, if they let false ideas get possession of their minds. What had made her so deathly afraid of the wind? Ah, yes, it was the man on the train, Mr. Wirt Roddy, who had put the fear of the wind on her like a spell!... Cruel, cruel!... He wouldn't have done it, surely, if he had known all it would mean. But now that she understood it, it wouldn't scare her so!... It was the something you didn't understand that froze you with terror....

She was calmer for a moment, and then she sprang up in frantic terror. She could hear unmistakably the sound of a horse running at full speed. It was coming, nearer and nearer!... A long shrill neigh sounded—just outside the door!...

She gave a shivering scream and huddled against the wall, her senses swooning from stark terror.

In an instant the door was flung open, and the muffled figure of a man entered, and slammed the door behind him.

75

Silent, stiff as a statue of ice, Letty stood there, unable to speak, unable to breathe. *Who was it?*

Then as a broad hat was swept off, and a muffler was removed from his throat, Lige stood revealed.

"Did I skeer you?" he asked, with his comfortable smile.

"You? You?" she choked, her fingers twisting.

Then she began to sob, in the ecstasy of her relief.

He took off his overcoat and came to spread his fingers out before the blaze of the stove.

"Thought you might be skeered o' the wind, an' so I come to look after you."

Her mind struggled with the mystery of it. "How did you know—was by myself?" she babbled almost incoherently.

"Bev an' Cora stopped by my place. Had started home from Hube's when the norther caught 'em. I made 'em stay there an' let me come on to take care of you an' the kids."

He paused a moment, to give her time to take it in, much in the way one would dole out morsels of nourishment to one starving. Too much at once would not be wise.

Then he continued. "A woman would freeze to death drivin' ten miles in this wind—an' Bev's old trouble would be almost sure to come back on him if he got exposed too bad."

"And you rode ten miles in this storm to look after me?" She could not believe it!

He nodded and smiled. "Sure. They're at my place now, as snug as bugs in a rug—an' here I am with you all. So there ain't nothin' to worry about at all."

His tone and gesture seemed to wave away her fears visibly. She wiped her eyes and checked her sobbing, but she couldn't stop the shuddering catch of breath, such as a child makes when it tries hard to stop crying but cannot, all at once.

"What's all these here tears about?" he wanted to know.

They broke out afresh at his reminder. "Oh, Lige, I've been so mis'rable! Cora hates me, an' don't want me to stay here! An' it makes everything so hard for Bev for me to stay! An' I've been scared half crazy of the wind!"

"Huh! the wind's just a big blowhard! You'll get used to it after a while, if you stay long enough." Then he drew his brows together in thought. "But the other matter's different. I *savez*. If you could be willing maybe to marry me, an' let me take you away from here?"

She shook her head without speaking, as if instinctively.

"No?" he said softly.

"No—I'm sorry, Lige!"

Tears trickled down her cheeks, and her shoulders heaved.

He patted her arm with big, awkward hand: "That's all right. I understand. Maybe someday—"

They stood in silence for a few moments, while the wind ceased its clamor for a time, as if to hear their thoughts....

Oh, how blessed not to be alone with the night and the storm! And, oh, how good that the wind was not blowing so hard!...

Then, with a roar of released tension, the gale struck the house, its fearful impact threatening to sweep the structure from its foundations, to blow it to splinters!...

Letty gave a shriek of mad terror, and flung herself into Lige's arms. *"The wind! The wind! Oh! save me—don't let the wind get me!"*

He gathered her close with rough tenderness.

"There, there, honey, I won't let nothing hurt you! Wind nor women nor nothin' else!"

He kissed her tear-wet cheeks, he smoothed her hair, he murmured soothing words to her as a mother would comfort a child—while the wind shook the house and its roaring filled their ears.

She clung to him, babbling disconnected words, just as she had used to cling to her black mammy when anything frightened her in the night. She heard herself promise that she would marry Lige the next day—not because she loved him, not because she was ready for marriage—but because she must spare Bev—and because she was afraid of the wind!

8

WHEN THE STORM HAD ABATED, and Bev and Cora had come home, Lige and Letty drove to the county seat and were married by the justice of the peace. As Letty stood mechanically saying her "I do," she saw, as on a stage before her eyes, the wedding she had always envisioned for herself—the home church made beautiful with flowers, and filled with friends who had known and loved her from her babyhood, the pastor saying a prayer for her happiness, the gallant figure with dark and splendid eyes who was to have stood beside her.

She must put away her hope of romance, as one lays away the garments of the dead. Dreams as yet unbodied must be given up. The knightly figure, which the wand of time and place was to have summoned up for her, must fade into nothingness before ever he had a shape or a name. The future as well as the past must be put behind her! Her youth was over, before it had begun....

But she made no protest, she shed no tear—but still and chill she stood to accept her fate. The wind had decreed it so.

While many girls are women at eighteen, Letty was scarcely more than a child in physical development or in knowledge of the world. Only a short while before she had reluctantly given up playing with dolls because she thought she was too old for such childishness, and she had merely dreamed her girlish dreams, with no experience of life's actualities. Hence, in spite of her dull unhappiness, she was not prepared to realize what she had undertaken. Her own ignorance mercifully anesthetized her to a knowledge of the pain that might be possible for her. She mourned over what she was giving up, rather than what she was going forward to.

The drive to her new home was made in silence for the most part, and this time Lige put forth no effort to entertain her with stories of the west, but left her to her thoughts. Perhaps he had his own thoughts to engage him, or perhaps he saw that she was not inclined to talk. So he merely saw to it that she was well covered by the buffalo robe to keep her warm, and addressed a remark now and then to the horse.

As she rode up to Lige's house, Letty experienced a queer remoteness from reality, as if only her body were there, and she herself were far away. All this could not be true! It could not be that life was bringing her to that rude shack set in a bleak expanse of sand, to spend her days! This was some other girl, who had borrowed her face and form, and who was to go through this experience of pioneer struggle, of strife with the wind, of a loveless marriage; not she herself, Letty Mason! It was like a picture on a lantern slide, with all the appearance of reality, but soon it would vanish and its place be taken by another.

She gazed at the house, which had a bald and naked look, with its shutterless windows, its unpainted walls set up on a few rocks, just a box-house, with no clapboards. Set up in makeshift fashion with a rock at each corner, and an occasional one along the walls, it looked as if it might blow away in a strong wind, to go bouncing across the plains like, a leaf. No trees about it, no flowers, no grass! This was to be her home!

Lige called out "Whoopee!" to apprize his partner of their arrival.

Sourdough stuck his head out of the door to shout in response. "Blast yore hide, you old sun of a gun! What you mean stayin' away so long? Where you been all day last night?"

Then as he caught a glimpse of Letty, he fell against the door casing in a state of collapse not altogether pretense.

"By gatlins! See who's come!" he whooped.

Letty laughed at his embarrassment. "Might as well get used to the sight of me. Sourdough. I've come to stay."

"What in heck?—" he began, his mouth wide open, his jaw dropping.

"Meet my wife," Lige spoke succinctly, as he led her in.

Sourdough slumped down on a chair and put his hands to his head in a gesture of bewilderment. "No!" he contended, challenging first one and then the other with his glance.

They nodded.

"You old sly possum!" he mournfully accused Lige. "I might 'a' knowed you had somethin' in yore head when you tore off the other night an' made me stay at home. If I'd 'a' went, maybe she'd 'a' married me!"

"Nope, you didn't have no chanct at all," said Lige, in an effort to console him.

He turned his reproachful gaze on Letty. "An' I ast you first!"

She dimpled and blushed, though she felt a pang of pity for his disappointment. "Just about five minutes first, wasn't it?"

He roused indignantly. "'Twas me thought of the whole thing, an' drug him round there by the ear. He never could 'a' proposed to no girl by hisself."

Lige's chest expanded in pride. "You don't know me. You can't buffalo me like this. You'd ought to have heard me when the storm was goin' on. The norther loosened my tongue, you might say. If they was givin' medals for the prize proposals, I'd have one pinned on me right now."

Sourdough regarded him with a heavy glance. "You got the prize all right," he conceded morosely.

"Yeah, just think of it!" bragged Lige.

"What I'm thinkin' about is *me*. This sure knocks me off the Christmas tree!"

Lige hastened to make his tone cordial. "This needn't make no difference at all, old scout. As soon as we get time to turn round, we'll run up another room here an' use your kitchen just for the chuck department."

Sourdough waggled his hand in a gesture of negation. "Not on yore tintype. I ain't stayin' round to be second fiddle. If I can't be tablecloth, I won't be dishrag! I'll bust out of here an' set me up a one-room shack further over on my land."

Letty spoke up heartily, "Build it close. Sourdough, so you can come over here for your meals."

"I dunno. I dunno," he growled. "I'm mighty particular about my cookin'."

"Well, I haven't had much experience, that's the truth," she admitted.

"An' when a pusson of no experience comes up again an outfit that is short on material to work with, it's a pore showin', I'd say."

He went into the kitchen and slammed the door heavily behind him.

It was plain that he was hard smitten with disappointment, since he had no wish to talk, since he wouldn't even stay in the same room with the newcomer. Letty felt more wretched still, seeing Sourdough's unhappiness in her marriage. Life was a strange, queer, twisted thing, that left you no choice at all!...

. . . .

In the days that followed, she was often to think of Sourdough's comment, in relation to other things as well as cooking. Truly she had had no experience. In Virginia she had been given no training in household affairs, because "Mammy" had allowed her only to play at tasks, never to do anything worthwhile, for she took the lead in management, especially after the mother's illness set in. Mammy liked to run things in her own way, and turned out work as swiftly and as efficiently as a machine—a machine with capacious arms and a turbaned head, and a mouth full of negro melodies. Letty had dusted a little, when she cared to, and had arranged flowers for the vases in the various rooms, when she felt the inclination. Here she found those talents of slight avail, since there were no flowers, and since it was a futile exertion to dust, when the sand covered everything again immediately afterward.

True, she had had some slight experience at Cora's house, but that capable person had managed her own household affairs herself, for the most part, assigning to the guest—who was obviously to be regarded, and to regard herself, as temporary—only such minor tasks as drying dishes, making beds and so forth. The cooking and the planning Cora had jealously reserved for herself. In consequence Letty must learn almost everything from the beginning—how to make bread without milk, how to prepare and plan meals without the pantry supplies she had always looked on as simple necessities. Bricks without clay or straw, she discovered!

So deep was her bitterness against Cora that she would almost have longed to forget any useful knowledge she had learned from her. For she would forget Cora, she told herself —would put her out of her mind as completely as possible—because thinking of her was a pain and a shame, a reminder of that humiliation she had suffered—a reminder that she had taken the only way of escape from her—a marriage without love! The thought of her cousin's wife scorched her soul, and made her aware of latent emotions she had never guessed were in her nature. She mustn't hate Cora, she told herself, for that was a sin. The only way to keep from it was to forget her, quickly, completely, to rinse her mind of her.

Yet she loved Bev, and couldn't bear to forget him!

She wouldn't let herself think of what Bev must have suffered in letting her go as he had. But he had been helpless. A look almost of death had been in his eyes as he stooped to kiss her good-bye that day. How often must he have asked himself in laceration of spirit if he had done all that he could, if he might not have saved her in some way!

But the wind had willed it otherwise.

Yet the work was about all she had to break the monotony of the days, she learned. Life at Bev's house had been exciting and vivid, by contrast, with the children to interest her and make constant appeals to her.

No books, no magazines, no music, no outside companionship!

But what afflicted her most in the new life was the lack of privacy in the little two-room shack. She thought of her upstairs room at home in Virginia, where no one had entered without her invitation, not even her mother—her dainty room, white-curtained, immaculate, inviolate....

The intrusions, the intimacies of married life appalled her. Fastidious, passionless, unwon, she felt desperately at times as if she must run away from the house, flee blindly across the prairies! If only by some magic she could win her way back to her girlhood!... She hadn't been ready for marriage—for this marriage without love!... If only life had let her wait awhile, perhaps she might have come to love Lige, after all. Perhaps she could have someday married him of her own accord—for he was kind and good and honest and loyal, she told herself. But Cora and the wind hadn't let her wait! Or was it that the wind hadn't let Cora allow her to wait?...

She who had felt sympathy with Sourdough because he hadn't married her, now felt sorry for Lige because he had. She tried to keep him from knowing how she felt, to conceal from him the fact that he had married a girl who didn't love him. True, she had told him, even on that night of the storm, before her surrender, that she didn't love him—but she knew that he had afterwards thought of that as maiden shyness. A married woman loved her husband, in his simple creed of life. She read his mind, his clean and candid mind, and knew that he believed she cared for him as he did for her.

She had read novels, wherein women had married without love, and where invariably they fell in love with their husbands afterward, dutifully and passionately. But life, she discovered, differed from romances in various aspects....

But she would try not to let Lige know how she felt....

When he came in from riding the range, tired and dusty, and clasped her in eager arms to greet her, she never pushed him away as she felt an almost uncontrollable impulse to do —but stood, still and chill, to receive his kiss. She even tried to kiss him in response—but the attempt was not successful.

"You ain't much of a kisser, are you?" Lige inquired ruefully one day.

She flushed. "No—but I'll try to learn," she replied. Perhaps it was practice that counted, as in making bread.

He looked at her thoughtfully. "Now, me—give a hearty smack, with a noise like a steer drawing his hoof out of the mud."

He did, indeed!...

She felt a sense of unreality with regard to her life, that lessened her wretchedness in some degree. This was not actual, she would tell herself—in the midst of the rawest realism of her experience. This was a dreadful dream, from which she would presently waken, to find herself in her little white room at home. Dreams lasted a long time, it is true, or seemed to, but when you woke, you found that it had been only a few minutes or so. Soon she would hear the chime of the old clock in the downstairs hall at home, and wake to listen to a mockingbird's song in the night, to the musical baying of a fox hound. Soon Mammy would come to bring her hot water for her morning bath, and tell her to, "Hurry up, honey, if you wants yore waffles good an' hot."

Of some trivial detail, such as the inescapable Mexican beans, she would say to herself, "I'll remember this when I wake up." Or perhaps of something else, she would say, "I'll try to forget this, after I am awake." But the wind and the sand, she knew, she could never forget. Heaven was a place where there was no wind nor sand. Hell was where there was nothing else!...

She had impulses of ambition to improve the looks of her habitation. If only she had material to work with, she could make the two rooms of the shack more presentable—at least, less repellantly crude and bare than at present. But when she was a day's journey from even the cheap store of the plains, what could she do? And Lige was hard up for money now, and worried over the continued drought, though he tried to hide his despondency from her.

She spoke aloud to herself one day, when Lige was out on the range. "If the church at home knew how poor I am, they'd send me a missionary box!" Should she write them? But no, "I wouldn't have them know for the world!"

One day she spoke timidly to Lige. "If we could canvas and paper the walls, the room would look a lot better, and the sand wouldn't come in so bad."

"That's so, honey," he said, rubbing his chin reflectively and smiling. Then his smile became rueful. "But we ain't got no canvas nor paper. When times are better, you can have anything in the world you want. Just make out your order—don't care what it is. But right now, we got to go slow on expenses. I wish it was different, I sure do."

A life in which canvas and wallpaper were unattainable luxuries!...

But she found in a box under the bed, a stack of old newspapers and she decided to use them as a substitute. She made paste of flour and water, and one day when Lige came home, he found the lower part of the walls of the front room covered—rather unevenly, it is true—with newspapers.

"I left the tall reaching for you to do," she told him.

He reached first for her, to give her one of his heartiest hugs, one of his most resounding kisses.

"Well, you sure are a smart little trick!" he cried.

"I put the papers right side up, so we can stand by the wall and read," she told him.

She received another kiss as reward.

When he had finished the papering job, he rearranged the decorations on the wall—the skins, the polished longhorns, the crossed rifles. On the floor, which she had scrubbed vehemently, she placed again the goat skins, the wolf skin. She covered the bed with the Navajo blanket. She contrived a dressing table from an old goods box, over which she draped the skirt of a white muslin dress of hers, and placed on it her simple toilet articles. Lige beamed with admiration of the results of her efforts.

"You sure are some little fixer!" he cried.

She moved aside to straighten a rug quickly, just in time to escape another kiss. Perhaps it was not judicious to attempt improvements, after all....

When she waked from this long dream, she would laugh over the memory of her house on the plains! But now she couldn't laugh, much, over anything. There was a heaviness in her throat, a tightness about her head, a constriction about her heart that never left her. In the mornings, when she waked, before she was fully conscious of her surroundings, before memory had taken possession of her mind, she would feel a dull oppression of spirit which she could not define or explain. She would ask herself the cause of her distress, before the flash of remembrance came to tell her—she was married, and this was her home!... Just so, on the days right after her mother's death, she had wakened with a woe which she could not at first understand, until she became roused enough to remember.

She saw very few people, save Lige and Sourdough—who had as quickly as possible erected his one-room house and taken up his separate life—and old Pedro, the Mexican, who lived in a dugout, and who came occasionally to talk to her in his broken dialect. She felt for him something of the same affectionate familiarity she had felt for the darkeys at home in Virginia. He was simple and childlike of heart, and yet wise, because he was old.

Occasionally a cowboy stopped for a meal, or a ranchman and his wife came in to break their journey to town. The women of the plains were philosophic souls that had learned to bear their hardships with fortitude, and they showed that they expected Letty to do the same. Yet in their faces she read strange secrets without their knowing it, stories of their struggles and adjustments and their longings.

Gran'ma Powers, a wizened little old woman who looked as if Time had found her indestructible and retired in defeat from his attacks on her, stopped by with her son one day. She gazed at the front room admiringly. "You got yore house fixed up real purty, ain't you?"

Letty gave a rebellious sigh, as she thought of the dream house which her bridal days were to have brought her.

"Well, it's a roof over our heads, at least," she conceded.

"Huh!" mumbled the old woman, with toothless sarcasm. "You better be thankful you got a house to live in. When me an' my Jim homesteaded we lived in a dugout a long spell. You don't know nothin' about hard times, if you haven't had to do for a man an' three babies in a dugout."

Letty shuddered. There were depths to which she hadn't yet descended.

"I can't imagine how you did it!" she cried.

"I didn't have no time to imagine. It's what folks imagines that gen'rally ruins 'em. It's like maggots in the brain. My hands and feet had to keep movin' so fast that my head didn't have no chance to contradict em."

"But why did you come out here, if you didn't have a house to come to?" Letty questioned. Curiosity was unmannerly, yes, but she had to ask.

Gran'ma didn't mind, for she chuckled, as one looking back on prehistoric jokes.

"There wasn't a house nor a tree nor a Lord's blessed thing on these bald-headed prairies when we got here, 'cept wild cattle an' wild horses an' Injuns an' buffaloes. Jim an' me had hove everything we had into a covered wagon an' we started out. We lived in the wagon till Jim got the dugout ready for us."

"But how did you *live*?"

"We lived on game, mostly. Buffalo steak is pretty good, an' antelope is fine. An' when folks is pore an' hongry, they ain't noways choosey."

Letty considered a moment. "I think you were awfully brave."

"If you got chillun, you got to strike out to give 'em a chanct. But it ain't been allus easy, I can tell you. Two o' my babies was born while I was by myself in the house, except for the other babies, an' Jim was out ridin' the range. But I got through all right, an' eight out o' the twelve chillun are livin' today. I got one boy in the state legislature, an' one a preacher."

Her head lifted with pioneer pride. Her dim blue eyes that had looked life and death in the face, unafraid, were filled with wise and quiet victory.

Admiration for her surged up in Letty's young heart. "You deserve to have one President of the United States!" she cried.

Gran'ma cackled enjoyingly, "Maybe I will."

Letty faced her with sudden determination for knowledge. Here was a woman who had grown old and wise on the plains, who had lived through long experiences with pioneer hardships, and the problems that a woman has to wrestle with in the west. Surely she could be able to give her some wisp of advice, of encouragement.

"How did you ever get used to the wind?" she demanded.

A shrewd look came into the far-seeing old eyes that even yet disdained the use of spectacles.

"Honey, that's the hardest thing a woman is up against on the plains. Men don't know what it means to us. Their nerves ain't like our'n. They're made so they can stand some things better nor we can, while agin they're weak as babies about something we don't think enough of to be skeered about."

Gran'ma paused a moment, to remember the winds that had harassed her. "I near 'bout fashed myself out over the wind at fust. When I see my complexion bein' ruint, an' my eyes near 'bout put out with sand, an' my nerves wore to a frazzle, I wanted to holler whenever the wind begin to rise."

"That's the way I feel," muttered Letty, her hands involuntarily clenching with nervousness at the thought.

"Then I certain sure could agree with the old sayin', 'Never mind the weather, so the wind don't blow.' But I got over all that. I saw that other things in life was more vallyble than my pink skin—an' it used to be pink as a peach-bloom in them days, honey, though you wouldn't think it to look at it now. An' I say to myself, 'Let God's leather take His weather!' An' I got over hatin' it so. But I had to stop lookin' in the lookin' glass."

Letty gave a shiver. "I can stand everything better than I can the wind. The lonesomeness, the lack of anything, the work, nothing's so bad as the wind!"

"Better not think too much about it," cautioned the old woman. "In a storm country like this, if I was you, I wouldn't *remind* the Lord of wind so much!"

"I guess you're right," faltered Letty. "I'll try to remember about it."

Yes, that was wisdom, and she must heed it. If she stopped thinking about the wind, maybe it would stop blowing.

But she couldn't, and it didn't!

Her restless thoughts prowled like coyotes round the Cap Rock that made a gathering place for storms. "The worst in the state," Lige had said. And it was so close! And their little shack had no cyclone cellar to flee to!...

Many a night she shivered with fear, listening to the wind rush and shriek, as she pictured a cyclone from the vision Mr. Wirt Roddy had given her. A vast cloud of sand that spiraled to the sky, sweeping with a roar over the plains toward her, inescapable, resistless, remorseless!...

And Lige slept heavily beside her, unaware of her terrors.

Many a time she told herself that she would face the facts and be rational. What if a cyclone came? At least it would sweep her away from this prisoning shack. What if it killed her? Then she would be free from marriage, because the Bible said there was no marrying nor giving in marriage in Heaven. Death had its desirable aspects....

Perhaps it was because she thought so continually of wind, that the sandstorm came. Who knows the power of nervous suggestion to stir up wind and sand? She had thought she knew all the possibilities of this dual torment, but she had much yet to learn.

When she had been married about a month—though it seemed like a cycle of eternity to her—a fierce wind arose, a wind that circled and seemed to come from all directions at once. It caught up the sand from the plains that were dry as powder, and drove it with whirling motions across the wide spaces that offered no obstacle to break its force. The impact of the wind against the house was terrific. Letty shuddered with every creak and tremor of the frail structure, expecting to see it blown to pieces.

The sand was hurled against the house with a violence that seemed hellishly malevolent, vindictive. The wind had gathered to itself seven other devils of sand to torment the helpless inmates of the lonely house. Sand streamed in through the cracks in the walls, and slit the newspapers into ribbons. It seeped in at the edges of doors and windows that were shut as tight as possible. It came down from the ceiling, it blew upward through cracks in the flooring. It hung like a yellow fog in the room.

Letty looked out of the window to see the sky. The sun rode aloft in a pageantry of clouds, casting a yellow glow over a strange world. Whirling curtains of dust, veils that writhed and twisted, hung like cloth of gold from the heavens, as high as she could see. The wind was no longer naked and invisible. It had clothed itself with those swirling veils that revealed its obscene antics, its horrific gestures. It was a thing unbearable to *see* the wind!

Letty turned from the window and averted her eyes.

But she could not escape the sand. Her eyes smarted with it, her face stung with it, her nostrils were clogged when she breathed, and her throat choked with it. Whatever her hand touched felt its harshness that gave her a nervous shiver. When she lay down at night, her pillow was scratchy with its covering of sand, she could feel the grains crawling inside her clothing like vermin. When she waked from snatches of sleep, nervous and wretched, it was to find her eyes filled with sand so that she could scarcely open them, her cheeks were rough with it. Not even her tears could cleanse her eyes completely.

When she set the table for a meal, she would turn the plates and cups downward, so that they might remain clean as long as possible. She did the cooking in covered vessels, and served portions hastily, then put the covers back. But even so, despite all her efforts, they ate sand with every mouthful of food they took.

The sand came in at the doors and windows to collect in such piles that it could not easily be swept out by the broom. Lige removed it with a shovel.

Lige and Letty moved about the house like silent, stumbling victims of torture.

Once he called her to the window. "Look how that sand has piled like snowdrifts there by the wind-break. You could bury a steer and never tell there was anything there."

She looked in amazement. "I never dreamed of anything like this!" she choked.

"I've seen it bad in town, when it has drifted over picket fences till you could walk right over and not know they was any fence there," he told her.

"Oh, I wouldn't walk on it!" she cried passionately, her hands twisting. "I wouldn't trust it. I'd be afraid it would catch me in a trap like quicksand and smother me!"

"I dunno about that," he said, coughing.

"This sand is—is wicked!" she said shrilly.

Oh, sand was treacherous, more treacherous than anything else in the world, save wind! No human being, no wild beast even, could be so tricky and so crafty and so cruel as the wind and the sand!... But the wind controlled the sand ... The wind was behind all the evil that the sand did, it was the evil mind. The wind was a will, a force, a pitiless intelligence, as well as a power....

If you listened right, you could hear it laugh and shriek at you. You could see its footsteps in the bending grass—when there was any grass, before starving cattle had eaten it down to the roots—you could see it twisting the mesquite bushes, and blowing the clouds away that had come to bring rain, and lashing the clothes hung on the line. But you couldn't see the wind, except when it drew the sand up over itself ... Then you saw a mad, elemental thing that you couldn't bear to look at....

The sandstorm lasted for three days....

Just when a wild look was coming into Letty's eyes, when she had begun to mutter to herself much of the time, but in an undertone so that Lige would not hear and ask, "What did you say, honey?" the wind subsided.

The calm was like that after a flood, when the waters have receded, and the eye sees only the wreckage, the perverse devastation that it has wrought.

The ground in some places was swept so bare that it looked as if the whole top surface had been blown away, while in other places against the house, by the wind-break, wherever any slight obstruction had made possible a nucleus for the sand to collect, great drifts were piled. It was fantastic, incredible.

This was in the last days of March.

In March in Virginia the hepaticas would be coming out. There would be anemones, too, and windflowers fair and frail, and trillium, small like a baby cyclamen, painted, and with its whorl of deep-green leaves. And the dog-tooth violets, and other flowers of the woods.... The trees would be misting with young green, and a green flush would have stolen over the grass and the meadows. The birds that had gone south for the winter would be winging their way back to the north.... Spring, in Virginia!...

As Letty fed dried cow-chips picked from the range into the round iron stove, she could shut her eyes and see the great old fireplaces at home, with their leaping rainbowed flames, and their beds of brilliant coals where visions lay, whence dreams stole forth....

Did dreams ever wake again, once they were dead?...

Yet underneath her deadness, Letty felt always a sense of curious, still expectancy of something that was to come. She asked herself, "What is it?" She searched the realms of possibility, though even the unquenchable optimism of youth gave her no promise of change. Still she questioned—but the answer eluded her.

— 9 —

I**T SEEMED IMPOSSIBLE** to Letty to meet the demands of realty, to adjust herself to the world in which she found herself,—as if a stranger should obstinately refuse or be unable to learn the language of the country he had been exiled to, or to adapt himself to the customs of the place. The whole situation was so overpoweringly strange and displeasing that she was bewildered, thrown back upon herself. Her body ate and slept and walked around in the performance of household tasks, but it was not she herself. Where was she?—she often asked herself. She could not find the answer.

It seemed to her that an abyss of time as well as of space separated her from her old life. Yet in her dreams she crossed back to it, and in her waking thoughts she bridged the chasm, sometimes involuntarily, sometimes by urging her reluctant will. She crossed off each day on her calender, not as a prisoner eager for the visioned end of his captivity (for what end could come to hers?) not as one that looked forward to the coming of a certain joy (what could the future hold for her?), but with a dull inertness that must occupy itself in some way.

Her calendar told her it was well on in April.

It would be April in Virginia, too!… She saw the woods, all softly green with their varying shades, the dark, steadfast tones of the cedars and pine trees that even in winter had held out immutable hope of spring; the young tenderness of leaf on countless others, the willows beside the streams, the shimmering bodies of the birches, the rich glow of copper beeches. The dogwood would be white on the hillsides, with now and then the rarer pink beside it. The flowering of the dogwood had always been to her the efflorescence of spring and youth and joy. The dogwood was blossoming in Virginia,—but should she ever see it again?…

The wild flowers would be coming on now, the violets, the wood pansies, the wild azaleas with their delicate colors, and many another flower she had loved and looked for each spring…. Did the dead feel as she did—a torturing homesickness to be back among the scenes and people one had always known?

One day Letty said to Lige as they sat in enforced idleness, looking out of the window. "How queer it seems to think that it's April, with no grass, no trees, no flowers, nor anything!"

"That's right, honey, it does," he agreed, shoving his hands deep in his pockets. "But you mustn't think it's always like this out here. We haven't got no flowers now, on account of the drought, you know, and the sandstorms."

"Do you have them, other springs?" she asked listlessly.

"Oh, sure! The purtiest you ever saw. Why, this time in ordinary years the plains would be like one great flower-bed. The whole prairies is decked out with 'em. Looks like you was ridin' over a rainbow as you lope along. And sweet, my, how they do smell!" He gave a reminiscent whiff.

"Tell me about them." She leaned her head on her hand and gazed out across the stretch of sand, a dead, greyish-yellow in the sunlight.

"We got all sorts o' flowers. I ain't no botanist, an' I can't tell you about the right entitlements for 'em. But if you could see 'em, maybe you'd know the names to call 'em by. Women knows more about such things than men. There's bear-grass, of course—you've seen it about. It's got sharp pointed leaves, an' has spikes of blooms standin' up tall an' creamy-white. Like the yucca, or what some folks call Spanish Dagger, on account of its

87

sword spikes. You can see them plants scattered here and there, but they ain't nothin' to look at till they bloom."

"And what else?"

"There's all sorts of cactus—some that grows up tall an' straight, an' some that's sprangly. There's one they call the pin-cushion, because it's like a little round squatty pin-cushion settin' on the ground, full o' pins. They got purty blooms, red an' yellow. Then there's the prickly pear, with its flat leaves an' its yellow blooms. But you got to watch out that you don't touch it, account o' the stickers."

Even the flowers here on the plains seemed to hold menace!

"Do you reckon there'll be any flowers next spring, Lige?"

"Oh, sure!" he promised grandiosely. "An' I bet you a steer you'll say they got Virginia beat all hollow. We got some here I guess you never heard of up there."

"What would they be?"

"Well," he cleared his throat to meet her challenge. "There's tumbleweed, for instance. When it's dry it goes tumblin' across the plains like a little ghost of a plant. In spring it has goldy blossoms that grow in clusters, somep'n like wisteria. Then there's the wild onion. That don't sound pretty, but I've heard Yankees say it was considerable like the trailing arbutus that they set a lot o' store by."

"It must be pretty," she cried, her eyes brightening at the thought.

"Then we got buttercups, an' all sorts o' daisies, yellow an' red and blue. I reckon they're all daisies. Then there's somep'n that looks like larkspurs I saw in my grandma's garden in East Texas. Wild larkspur, I guess it is. There's somep'n like honeysuckle, too, pink an' white. An' there's horsemint, tall an' sort o' pinkish-lavender, in stalks like. Oh, there must be hundreds o' flowers I don't know the names to call 'em by. There's a plant that runs along the ground, that has a strong yellow bloom, an' smells like musk. I disremember the name if I ever knowed it."

"I'll just shut my eyes and see next spring," she said softly.

"I'm sorry I'm such a ignorant galoot as not to know the names. But I'll ask everybody I see an' learn 'em for you before they bloom again."

"That'll be nice, Lige." She managed a smile for him.

"But, honest, you never saw anything purtier than these plains in the spring. Everything comes green an' blooms all at once, as if it knowed that 'twouldn't be long before the hot winds burned it up. The ground is like a gay-colored quilt, with all sorts o' flowers smilin' up at you. Makes you forget the cussed hard times of the winter, an' the northers an' the sandstorms an' everything you been through. Makes you glad you're a cowpuncher to be ridin' the range, when you have all that to look at."

"It won't be such a terrible long time till next spring, will it, Lige?"

His big-mouthed smile was cheerful. "Sure not. Just the matter of a year now. Springs come round pretty regular every year. Guess you think it slipped a cog this time, but it'll make it up to you, next year—you see if it don't. You wait."

It seemed incredible that spring's flowered footstep could ever touch that dead expanse of sand that her eyes looked at—but Letty told herself that miracles had happened in Bible times, and maybe they would again. She would wait, with what patience she could muster.

It was hard to wait, when one was young, especially when the cloaked and hooded years held out no certain promise of relief. Youth lasted such a little time at best! Letty felt as she sometimes imagined a corpse might feel—dead, but quiveringly alive to expectancy; dead to delight, but alive to pain. She went about her daily tasks, passive but rebellious, at once relaxed and tense. Six months before she had never known the alphabet of pain, and now it seemed to her that she had gone through all its possible changes and combinations. But surely life had done its worst to her—and any change would mean an easement....

The wind, which seemed all powerful, perhaps was a weakling, if one only knew the magic word or gesture to compel it to submission and retreat. She thought of all the folk tales she had ever heard, the lore of the old volumes in her father's library that she had read but half comprehendingly. Perhaps if she thought hard enough, she could divine the abracadabra that controlled the wind, could hit upon the mystic waving of hands that could overawe it, the cabalistic command that could send it forever from her. Words and gestures were magical things, that had more power than one could know, and human thoughts were terrible in their might.... What if the warning that Gran'ma Powers had given her were right? —that one mustn't remind God of the wind? Maybe by just thinking about it she brought it on herself. Maybe by thinking hard the other way she could ward it off. Who knew the awesome might of human will? Who knew the force of the wind's will?

So she consciously practiced gestures that might by chance reveal themselves as mystic, that might disclose to her the hidden secret of command over the wind. She whispered to herself phrases that came into her thoughts, that might be runic rhymes that could bind the wind by a spell. Someday, out of the unknown or forgotten lore, would come to her the inspiration that would save her....

"Who hath gathered the winds in his fists?"

In her fear, she would clench her fists, as if to overmaster the wind.

As her eyes were rested and soothed by the mirages which the desert plain at times held shimmeringly before her gaze, so her spirit was given an unreal gratification by the mental mirages which she called up for herself, pleasure pictures that she drew out of the past, scenes of beauty and joy in which she moved. She recognized dimly that this was a false pleasure, which made the pain of the present more acute when she saw them fade, as fade they must, before the harsh realities of her present. But she could not resist. It was as if she administered some drug to her soul, by which she could at will ignore the ugly facts of her existence, and project herself into a life that was not altogether of the past, but of the happy past blended with a future wherein all would be miraculously well with her. Her sense of truth made her scorn herself for these subterfuges, but she writhed away from a facing of facts.

When Lige was not in the house to overhear, she held long dialogues with persons imagined or actual, wherein she dramatized her dreams of ease and joy.

These fantasies sometimes carried over into her dreams at night, changed, intensified, distorted, so that now and then she would awake from the shock of finding herself traveling strange routes unknown to her conscious thoughts. Fear would startle her into wakefulness, so that she would tremble, baffled and perplexed.

One day, toward the end of April, when Lige was out on the range, Letty lay down to sleep a while in the afternoon. She might as well sleep, she told herself—since there was nothing else to do—no book to read, no magazine, no piano to keep her company as at home in Virginia. How long she had lain there she did not know—when she was awakened by a knocking on the door.

She sprang up hastily, straightened the tumbled covers on the bed, smoothed her hair with nervous hands, and went to open the door. Who could it be? Some cowboy, probably, stopping on his way to town.

A tall figure stood there. The broad-brimmed Stetson hat shaded the man's face so that for an instant she did not recognize him. And then a shock that was half pain, half pleasure, a wild leap of the pulse, a tremor of the body told her who it was. Her companion of the train trip, Wirt Roddy, stood before her.

Her eyes, wide open, stared at him, as if not believing their vision, her lips were glued together so that she couldn't speak, and a sudden impulse to run away swiftly impelled her.

"This is not what I'd call a hearty welcome." His voice jeered lightly at her, while his eyes held a challenge, half humorous, half stern. "Aren't you glad to see me?"

"Yes, yes." She forced her tongue to speak, though it seemed to clatter in her mouth. "Will you come in?"

"Sure."

"I was surprised at seeing anyone. We have so few visitors," she said in apology for her discomfiture. "Lige is off on the range."

He stretched out his hand to take hers, though she had not offered to shake hands with him, because hers were so cold and trembling. But there was no escape without seeming rude.

"Will you have a seat?"

She pushed forward one of the old ladder-backed chairs with its cowhide bottom.

He sat down and looked at her a moment in silence, caressing his black mustache thoughtfully. "And so you're married?" he mentioned at last.

"Yes." What comments was one expected to make about one's marriage?

"I was surprised to hear it. Kinder sudden, wasn't it?"

"Yes. life is sudden, I've found out lately. I was surprised myself." Her tone tried to be calm and casual.

His eyes roved over the bare, crude room, taking in each detail of its shabbiness. She resented his appraisal of it, but no appropriate way of showing it occurred to her at the moment. This man had the knack of making her feel that he was well aware of his superiority and rather expected everyone else to be equally awake to it.

He shot a long, keen look at her from half-closed eyes that looked thoughtful but full of tricky impulse, too. "I didn't know you were thinking about marrying."

"No?" she said curtly, angry that the little pulse in her throat should throb so, afraid that he would notice it.

"No," came his antiphonal response, grave and unhumorous. "I didn't know any of these fellows out here would suit you."

"Did you know *anything* of me?" She turned her palms outward in a gesture of negation, of defense.

"Pretty much." He leaned his elbow on the table, and crossed his long legs comfortably.

"And how?" she shot at him.

"Plenty o' ways," he answered easily, as if insouciantly aware of and yet ignoring her resentment. "I own a ranch out here, as I told you, and I come out this way pretty regular."

So it had been, not once but many times, that he had been in the section and had not come to see her! Anger surged within her. He hadn't come when she needed help, when he might have shown her a way out of her impossible situation. What right had he to come now, when it was too late to do any good? Oh, she hated him! She seemed to live over again in concentrated bitterness all that she had suffered since she saw this man first, all the agony and bewilderment he might have saved her from if he had come to see her as he promised. To promise so lightly, and then forget!

"I didn't know you were interested in what happened to me. I thought you had forgotten," she said coldly.

"Not by a long shot! I've known everything you've done, everywhere you've gone since I saw you. I could 'most tell you every fellow you danced with that night at the cowboy ball."

Surprise widened her eyes. "You weren't there!"

"No, I wasn't there." He gave no elaboration to his answer to satisfy her curiosity.

She told herself that she wouldn't ask, but she did. "Why didn't you come, then, if you were so close?"

A guarded look came into his dark eyes. "I wanted to, but I reckoned I'd better not."

What could he mean by that? Perhaps he had been afraid that she would ask some favor of him; impose on his casual politeness of the train trip.

"And how do you like the west?" he asked with grim jocoseness.

She gave a quick turn of her palms upward, as if to say, "How can you ask? What answer but one is there?"

"And the wind?" he jeered softly.

She shuddered involuntarily. "I hate it!" she jerked. Then instantly she caught her lip between her teeth. She hadn't meant to betray herself, to give him the satisfaction of knowing he had been right, the pleasure of saying, "I told you so."

"I did tell you so, didn't I?" he mocked, as if reading her thoughts. He studied her face that she half turned from him in annoyance.

"Your skin is still soft and white, but not so much so as it was the last time I saw you. Your cheeks aren't quite so pink as they used to be—though they're blushing now that I call attention to them. Your hair isn't quite so yellow and shiny as that other day. Looks like it has faded a little—No?"

She flared up, till her cheeks were bright enough to refute his charges. "You've got no call to say such things to me!"

He went on as if she had not spoken. "And your eyes aren't so blue and clear—look like they've been having tears as well as sand in them—No?"

"They haven't!" she lied hotly. "Just the wind and sand!"

"Well, I reckon that's about enough, anyhow," he conceded gravely.

She looked past him out through the window. Maybe Lige would be coming home soon.

She gave no answer to the man beside her. Why didn't he go? Why had he ever come—just to tease and torment her? If he knew all that she had to bear, he wouldn't be so mocking. He must be a cruel man. Again her old, throbbing fear of him arose—the fear that she had felt on the train without being able to analyze, but that had disappeared as memory glossed over the happenings of that day.

Again he ignored her disdain, her timorous tremors. He began to hum softly to himself again, as that day on the train—and yes, it was the same tune, that mournful tune!

"But they buried him there, on the lone prai-rie.
Where the buzzards wait, and the winds blow free.
In a narrow grave, just six by three;
They buried him there, on the lone prai-rie!"

She seemed to see a desolate plain stretching out before her, a vast waste of sand, and of years, with a solitary mound in the wilderness. Would it be her fate to live here till she died, and be buried on this desolate plain? Her soul shuddered away from the picture.

"*But they buried him there, on the lone -prai-rie!*" His song gave answer to her protest.

"Stop!" she shrilled, almost hysterically. "I—I don't like that song!"

"It isn't cheerful," he conceded. "But then life isn't so damned cheerful, I've found, anyhow."

"Why make it worse, then, for yourself, or for anybody else?" she challenged.

His eyes narrowed as they looked at her reflectively. "I often wonder. Some devil within me drives me on, I guess."

She stared at his brooding face, his languorous, melancholy eyes, that looked out with longing, and with sad, bitter mockery. "And does nothing drive you the other way?" she asked, almost in a whisper.

The mockery diminished and the sadness increased. "Yes. Yes. There are angels, too. But they mostly have flaming swords to bar me from what I once had—or might have had—and lost."

His face softened curiously, grew gentler, younger, under her gaze, as if unknown to himself, some gracious touch had erased the cynicism, the hardness, the unworthiness, and had shown for an instant the man he might have been.

She was not afraid of this man!—nor did she hate him.

"We generally keep the things we really want, don't we, or do we?" she asked simply.

He shook his head. "No, no, not always … Sometimes we give a thing up because we are cowards, or set in our selfishness—or maybe, for conscience's sake—because we know we're not fit to take care of it tight. There's lot of reasons, if you look for 'em."

She looked for the reason which had kept him from coming to see her when he was so close, but she could not find it.

Suddenly his face cleared, the moroseness disappeared, and a boyish smile came out.

"I brought you a present," he said gaily.

"A present—for me?"

"Yes." He reached for the new target rifle he had laid on the table when he came into the room, and held it out to her.

She drew back, bewildered. "But I don't know how to use a gun. I never touched one in my life," she protested. "But it was nice of you to think of me, and thank you just the same."

"Lige will teach you how to shoot. All the girls out here have rifles and go hunting just like the men. You ought to have a little gun."

"I couldn't bear to kill anything! If I saw a rabbit or a squirrel I had shot, or a little bird fluttering round with a broken wing, I'd cry my eyes out. I think it's cruel to shoot things."

"It's likely you eat game that other folks shoot," he mocked her lightly.

"But that's different."

He smiled cajolingly, as at a foolish child. "And there are other things to shoot—rattlesnakes and coyotes, for instance. You can't say you love them."

"Somebody else will have to do the killing," she said, her hands stubbornly behind her, refusing to touch the toy gun.

He laughed, looked about him, and before she knew what he was doing, he had put it up on the wall beside the crossed rifles Lige had there.

That brought her a sudden memory of her husband. "Lige mightn't like me to take it, anyway," she said dubiously.

He laughed lightly. "Call it a wedding present. Nobody ever refuses a wedding present, for that would be an insult."

She flushed, and her skin felt prickly all over. "You are making fun of me!"

He sobered at once. "No, truly," he affirmed.

She writhed under the sense of her inadequacy to deal with the situation properly. If only she were older, and had more poise she could deftly put this man in his place, could dismiss him at once if she liked, could banish him definitely. He must go before Lige came in, because Lige wouldn't understand his being there. But how could she tell him, this cool stranger, that her husband might be jealous of his presence? Wouldn't he laugh at her all the more, silently, exultingly?

He stroked his black, silky mustache, and looked as if he read her thoughts.

"Lige, my husband, will be here soon," she stammered. "He and Sourdough are out looking after some steers."

"That so?"

But he made no movement to leave.

She stirred nervously, longing for him to go. And yet, and yet, the room would seem duller and lonelier than ever when he had gone. For of course he would never come back.

Why had he come this time? Her perplexed eyes tried to plumb his ironic smile, but in vain.

Could he hear the muffled pounding of her heart? Could he see the flutter of the frightened pulse in her throat, or note the trembling of her body? Perhaps he saw, and was gloating over her weakness....

So tranced with excitement over the thought was she, so thralled with the spell of those tragical, humorous eyes, that she failed to hear the hoofbeats of horses outside.

Her eyes fixed on the man beside her, her cheeks flushed, her lips parted, her slight frame trembling, so she stood, one hand over her wildly beating heart, when the door was flung open and Lige entered, with Sourdough behind him.

She started back with an exclamation, and then tried to recover her composure.

"Lige, this is Mr. Wirt Roddy, that came up on the train with me, you remember."

"Yes, I remember. How d'ye do?"

She presented Sourdough to him, but he showed no trace of his usual blithe humor or cordiality. Contrary to his characteristic heartiness, he failed to extend a hand of greeting to the stranger. But the guest did not appear to notice, unless a flicker of black eyelashes might be so interpreted.

"Have a chair," Lige said.

"I can't stay long," was the answer. "I'm on my way to town. I aim to spend the night at Bev's and get an early start."

But he dropped back into his chair and lighted his pipe, looking more at home than either of the other two men.

Sourdough leaned against the door casing, his arms crossed over his chest, and eyed the visitor coolly. He held his unlighted pipe in his mouth.

Lige crossed the room to another chair, his spurs clattering as he walked.

"How you makin' out at your ranch?" he asked the visitor politely.

"Pretty poorly. I shipped most of my cattle before the worst hit me. I had a hunch that there was goin' to be a drop in cattle prices, and I kinder felt this drought was going to last longer than we thought. So I got from under the best I could. But the critters I kept are looking bad. It would cost such a hell of a lot to haul feed for 'em that there's no profit in doing that."

"You said it," was Lige's gloomy rejoinder. "I dunno how us little ranchers is goin' to hold out if this keeps up."

"It's the worst dry spell I ever saw, an' I been living in this section all my life," said Sourdough. "The sun stalks across the sky as impudent as if he was thumbing his nose at you. Clouds don't mean nothin' no more when you see 'em."

"But they are beautiful, anyhow," put in Letty timidly. "When my eyes get tired of looking at the sand, I look up at the sky to rest them. I never saw such wonderful colors as there are here some days."

"Yes, the altitude and the clear atmosphere make you see things better than anywhere else," said Wirt Roddy. "The sunsets and sunrises here are some of the prettiest shows on earth, I reckon."

She thought of the sunset they had witnessed together on the train—how long ago! And of his telling her to watch a sunrise someday and think of him. How often had she done that! It was as if he had put his signature on the sky at sunrise and sunset, had placed his mark, his "brand," indelibly on her memory at such hours. But this was foolish, and she must forget—for wasn't she married now?

Sourdough removed his pipe from his mouth and gazed reflectively into its bowl. "Old-timers hereabouts say that the clouds deck themselves out purtiest in dry weather, so I ain't glad to see them gay colors now. They spell ska'se' o' rain."

"But if you've got to take the hardships, why not have the beauty along with it?" argued Letty, to make conversation.

"I don't calculate them starvin' cow-critters take much comfort out o' rainbows an' cloud pretties now," he said grimly. "Leastways, they haven't said nothing to me about 'em if they have, an' they talk aplenty to me about the drought as I ride by 'em."

"There's no countin' on what cattle or women will find to complain of," commented the visitor.

Letty gave him a quick look. "If women complain more than men do, maybe it's because they have the men to complain of," she retorted with sudden spirit.

Lige gave a darting glance of surprise.

"Oh, I'm not talking about me," she said to reassure him. "But women in general have a pretty hard time."

Sourdough maintained a stoic calm, his pipe held bias in his mouth, his teeth clenching down on it.

The stranger was the only one of the group that appeared to be really at ease. Lige, usually so kindly, so hospitable, seemed stiffened into a frozen formality that was as strange to him as if he had put on an alien garb. Sourdough's bantering tongue that had usually a friendly gibe for everyone he met, man or woman, friend or stranger, now was uncommunicative. Letty saw a new being in him, a man on guard, defensively hostile. But against what?

She glanced at her husband and his partner furtively, fearful, feeling a queer sense of guilt, as if she had done or thought something that had wounded them. Then she told herself with reassuring pride that Lige and Sourdough could never be angry or offended with her—those two men that loved her loyally in their rough way.

They would protect her from any danger that threatened her, using fists or pistols according to the need. They would lay down their lives to defend her, if that were necessary, she knew. What was it Sourdough had said on the night the two had proposed to her? "Either of us'd lick a million wildcats to protect you." And Lige said, "Why, we'd rope an' bulldog old Nick hisself if he so much as batted an eye winker to let on he was thinkin' o' hurting you." On the night of the storm, he had said, "I won't let nothin' hurt you!"

And they wouldn't, if they could help it.

A silence fell upon the group, a clamorous silence that seemed filled with magnetic menace. In it seemed to be gathered up all threatening sounds imaginable—of angry voices, violent winds, the crack of pistol shots. To Letty's dramatic imagination the room was tense with struggle, ravaged by desperate emotions.

Involuntarily she sat on the edge of her chair, her fingers clenched tight.

Wirt Roddy sat nonchalantly smoking his pipe, and saying no word. Yet a psychic instinct told her that he read her thoughts, that he was pleased by her tumult, gratified by the hubbub in her heart—that he was feeling his superiority over these two cowpunchers beside him.

What if he and Lige should ever come to conflict over anything? Which would be the stronger man, the better fighter? Yet it would be two against one, for Sourdough would side with his partner, no matter what the issue was. And something told her that Sourdough if once thoroughly roused would be as quick to shoot as he was to laugh.

She shivered, as if a norther had suddenly blown its icy breath upon her.

Then a mist seemed to clear away from before her eyes, and she saw the room in another light, the situation in another aspect. Here was merely a transient stranger whom she had met once on the train—who had stopped for a few minutes on his way to town. That was but simple and natural, for didn't other cattlemen do the same? Soon he would be gone, and life would go on as before. She had been light-headed with nervousness and had imagined foolish things.

Her eyes asked him to go, without knowing that they did so.

She felt a thrill of superstitious alarm at seeing him instantly respond to her wish.... What power did he have, to read her secret thoughts?... Did he feel regret over having teased and disturbed her? He was considerate, after all, and she had been silly to feel afraid of him.

She did not offer to shake hands with him in parting, since to do so might be to call attention to the failure of the men to do so. Her eyes apologized for the slight, for their remissness, and his lashes flickered understandingly. It was uncanny how he could tell what she was thinking and feeling.

When he said good-bye and moved toward the door, she felt an indescribable pang of regret. Was everything interesting to go out of her life—to leave only the dull days, the lonely monotony?

He sprang into his saddle and waved a hand back at her. Her hand fluttered in answer, and then she watched him gallop down the sand in the direction of town.

Her gaze followed him until her eyes ached, till presently the speck that had been rider and horse was out of sight and there was nothing to look at but a stretch of yellow sand, with a sun beginning to sink toward the west.

95

As she turned back to the room, she saw that the eyes of the two men were fixed on her, eyes farseeing but inscrutable. She realized anew that the eyes of plainsmen have a far look in them, an expression that comes only to those whose vision is used to long distances, to vast reaches of desert or sea, that men whose gaze is habitually cut off by trees or houses never come to have. That far look had vision in it, and was not simple to read.

Had she betrayed her nervousness? Was she too easy to read? Could these men, too, as well as the stranger, see with clairvoyant eyes into her soul? Wirt Roddy had known her thoughts effortlessly. Could Lige and Sourdough do the same?

She flushed and tingled and shrank back, shamed and frightened as if her naked body were exposed to their gaze.

Yet, after all, what had she done? she asked herself hotly.

Lige glanced at the wall where the guns were crossed.

"Whose target rifle is that?" he asked.

"It's mine. Mr. Roddy brought it to me," she stammered. Oh, why had the man persisted in leaving it when she hadn't wanted it?

He cleared his throat. "Humph! How come him to do that?"

"I told him I didn't want it," she hastened to exculpate herself. "I told him I didn't know how to shoot and didn't care to learn. But he said it was a wedding present, and so he put it up there with the others."

Lige turned away and said nothing.

Sourdough spoke up dryly. "If you was to ask me. I'd say he had his nerve!"

But then nobody had asked him, she thought angrily. Why did he have to thrust himself into hers and Lige's affairs?

"I don't reckon there's any harm done," she said with elaborate casualness.

"Me an' Lige can make out to keep you supplied with game enough, I reckon," said Sourdough uncompromisingly.

She laughed shortly. "There's not much left round here for anybody to shoot. Looks like the birds and the rabbits have been killed by the drought, or have gone somewhere else where they can find green things growing."

"They'll come back soon as it rains," said Lige. "These prairies will be working alive with life. Jackrabbits, molly-cottontails, ground squirrels, and all sorts o' things. And birds that near 'bout bust their throats a-singing."

The tension at her heart released. So Lige wasn't angry with her, after all. Perhaps he would be if he knew all her unhappy thoughts, but she would try to keep them to herself. He had enough to bother him, with the drought and losing so many of his cattle.

Sourdough rose to go.

"I don't like that hombre," he said, his hand on the doorknob. He turned to Letty. "Is he comin' back again?"

She turned red with confusion and anger. "How do I know, Sourdough?" she flashed. "I didn't know he was coming this time. I didn't ask him his plans."

Sourdough wiped his mouth with his hand. "He's one white man I don't cotton to. He's too doggoned stuck on hisself. And he gives me a queasy feeling, like a rattler does."

Tears of anger rose in her eyes. "I think you're hard to say such things. Sourdough!—like you was blaming me for something. Mr. Roddy was kind to me on the train, and I was glad to see him stop by. It's plenty lonesome for me, with you and Lige gone most of the time." Her voice broke on a sob.

Lige laid a hand on Letty's arm, and his gaze rebuked his partner. With his wisdom, he said no word.

Letty trembled. Was she to bring hard feeling between her husband and his best friend— these two that had meant everything to each other before she came?

10

AFTER WIRT RODDY'S VISIT, Letty's nervous lethargy deepened. It was as if some long-anticipated event had taken place, leaving a queer emptiness in the world, because now nothing was to be expected. Ever since Letty had said good-bye to him that night at the station in Sweetwater, and watched the train vanish in a swirl of wind, she had looked for him to return. Consciously or unconsciously she had expected him. Up to the time of her marriage, she had counted on his dashing up as a figure of romance, to relieve her of the unhappiness that Cora's tyranny imposed on her. Somehow, he would change things. Would he not have power even over the wind? She had not definitely thought of him as a wooer, had not pictured marriage, but had merely dazzled her dull environment with romantic imagery of rescue and change. He would open the door of her prison and show her a way of flight.

Since her marriage she had been too inert to be actively interested in him, or in anything, but she had made an effort, according to her ideals of wifehood that must be dutiful, even though unwilling, to put him out of her conscious mind. A married woman shouldn't be thinking of any other man.

But he had not gone, for frequently he had risen to the surface of her languid musings, electrifying them to life, had given a tingling color to hours that otherwise were as empty as the gray sand.

He was a man that would not be forgotten. The very thought of him seemed, with casual insolence, to dare one to ignore him. She could see his lip curl with amused scorn at the idea, could catch the flicker of his black eyelashes over ironic eyes as he challenged her to forget him, if she could. He was always aware of himself, in much the same way that Cora was of herself, though with more subtlety, more suavity, more worldly poise instead of her forthright methods. His egoism was a rapier thrust while Cora's knocked you down with a stick of stove-wood if you got in her way.

Well, she hadn't forgotten him, but she must, she told herself. Thinking about him upset her. That was bad enough, but the thought of him might cause disturbance between her and Lige, or between him and Lige, or between her husband and his partner. The situation held a danger, any way you looked at it. Thinking was a mental ferment that might lead to explosions—and wreckage, if you didn't watch out. She would forget him, if she had to remember to remind herself every hour of the day!

She spoke no more to her husband, nor he to her, of Wirt Roddy or his visit, but often as she looked at Lige she wondered what was in his thoughts. She scarcely knew this calm and quiet man she lived with. She didn't know him—she was only married to him. She realized the steady strength of him, his sure wisdom in everyday practicality, his sane justice; but she felt that there might be passions, swift and vehement, to which he could be roused that as yet she knew nothing about. She had never heard his voice raised in anger or impatience, yet she dimly comprehended that there were in his nature possibilities of wrath as resistless as a cyclone. Only some extraordinary occasion would call forth rage in him, she felt sure, as he probably would live his placid life out without any such disturbance. He would never seek trouble.

She watched him often, as the spring days passed into summer. He might be good-looking if he shaved oftener, and took better care of himself and of his clothes, like the men she had known in Virginia. But his hard life made him too careless. She shivered with repulsion when she saw him unshaved, with a dirty shirt on, covered with dust from the range, with his heavy boots that scarcely knew what a polishing meant. And the repulsion deepened when she had to wash his dirty shirts—she, who had never had to wash so much as a pocket handkerchief in her girlhood at home....

And he seemed to take her drudgery too much for granted, as if it were natural that a woman should wash and cook and clean up for her man. Such things were expected of pioneer wives—but she wasn't a pioneer, and she hadn't wanted to be a wife. Life had compelled her against her will—life and Cora and the relentless wind....

· · · ·

One Sunday, Bev and Cora and the children drove over to spend the day with her. She hadn't seen Cora since her marriage, and had almost hoped never to see her again. She knew, with a woman's sure intuitiveness, that Cora still blamed her for her quarrel with Bev, and she on her side had felt too bitterly resentful to make any advances toward reconciliation. The fact that she was not happy had shut a door between them. If hers had been a love marriage, if she had been happy and content, she could joyously have gone all the way to be friends again. But when she remembered how Cora's hardness and fiery jealousy without cause had driven her into this uncongenial environment, this blind alley from which she could not hope to escape, she felt a surge of anger, almost of hatred. If Cora had not in her selfish egotism misjudged her, she might have had time to find herself, to work out a better way from her problems.

She had seen Bev a few times for brief glimpses since her marriage, when neither had dared speak of what was in their hearts, or do more than hint sympathy and encouragement.

Now, she told herself, she must be more distant to him, for fear Cora would misunderstand and be jealous again.

"I'm so glad to see you all," she said. "But, Cora, I'm ashamed for you to see my house so cluttered up."

Cora's housewifely eye swept the shack and passed judgment on the sand and disorder she saw, but her tongue withheld criticism. "Oh, with this terrible wind blowing sand everywhere, nobody can keep a clean house," she said formally.

But Letty read in her look, "You ought to do better than this."

And the truth hurt, for she realized her shortcomings as a housekeeper. She couldn't put any heart into the work, and then, too she had never had any training to fit her for it. At home Mammy had treated her like a child that couldn't even wait on herself properly, for she dearly loved to wait on her "baby." If Mammy could see her in her present life, cooking and washing and scrubbing, even picking up cow-chips from the prairies sometimes to use as fuel—and cooking in that stingy way, without the things to do with, or the food to cook! How Mammy would curl her lip in pitying scorn at her baby's Sunday dinner—and company come in, too!

As she bustled about preparing dinner for her guests, Letty told herself for the hundredth time that girls ought to be trained to work, to support themselves, so that misfortune couldn't overwhelm them as it had her. To be expected to be a competent pioneer heroine and wife without warning or preparation was like being drowned suddenly, or smothered in an avalanche of sand!

Little Alice shyly trotted everywhere after Letty, but with cautious glances at her mother, obviously realizing her fiery jealousy and fearful of kindling it, but adoring Letty as ever.

"I don't like you to be married," the child said to Letty, as she stood by the stove frying ham.

Letty almost flashed back, "Neither do I!" but she caught her words in time, horrified at the instinctive impulse of revelation.

She smiled at Alice and said, "I miss you little folks a lot."

"Since you been gone, I don't have nobody to play with," mourned Alice.

Ironically Letty thought, "Neither do I." She held up her hand to protect her face from the sputtering hot grease, and it served as a shield for her eyes as well, to hide them from the child.

"The boys think they're smarter'n me an' they don't let me know how to play their games."

"Boys don't know much about girls, do they, little Alice?" asked Letty, with a twisting, fugitive smile.

"Not much," said Alice, proudly passing the fork for her to turn the ham with, her face lighted with love, so that for a moment it was actually pretty.

Letty felt a sudden ache of pity for the child. Someday she would be a woman, with her sensitive soul athrill with dreams, with ideals of life and love that perhaps the plain face would render futile. What would life do to little Alice? Would it fling her unready into the arms of a husband she didn't love? Would it break her heart in loneliness, or send her to serve as a patient drudge in some other woman's house?

If only she could snatch little Alice in her arms, and run away from the cruel world with her!

"Papa used to play with me, but he's mos' gen'rally too tired now of nights," went on Alice.

"Don't he feel well?" asked Letty, with quick anxiety.

"I dunno. He's just tired, I reckon. Mother says he's mopey."

"Maybe he's worried about the drought," suggested Letty. "Men have a lot of things to worry them, come to think of it. They've got the living to make, you know."

"I'm goin' to make a living myself when I'm grown," boasted the child.

"That'll be fine. I hope you will."

"Big Buddy says I ain't pretty, so nobody'll ever want to marry me. Do you think I ain't pretty—a bit?" She peered wistfully at the woman.

Letty gave her a quick hug. "To me you're the sweetest, prettiest little girl I know! And all sorts of lovely things are going to happen to you when you're grown. You can make them happen, little Alice, if only you don't get in a hurry about life—or let anybody push you too fast. Take your time!"

The small face brightened as if someone had lighted rose candles within her breast. "I will—I won't," she declared joyously.

Letty sent a defiant adjuration to fate to be kind to little Alice. For a moment she felt that it didn't matter what happened to her, if only little Alice could be happy. And ordinary happiness wouldn't do for Alice, any more than for herself. Each was an idealist, sensitive, too easily hurt....

From the other room came the sound of high, boyish laughter and Cora's chatter with Sourdough.

Lige poked a face in the doorway. "Chuck most ready?"

"Pretty soon," she said.

"I'll set the table for you."

"No—me!" cut in Alice.

"All right. *'Sta bueno*—but get a shove on, 'cause I'm most ready to pass out with hunger."

He withdrew to the other room to talk with Bev.

Presently Letty summoned them in to dinner. It was a tight squeeze to get them all seated round the table in the small kitchen, but the feat was accomplished with laughter which helped to ease the social strain. Letty, her face flushed from the heat of the stove, presided, and urged upon her guests the plain fare, fried ham, grits, the eternal frijoles, biscuit that had too much soda in them, and canned peaches for dessert.

Even if she had known the guests were coming, she told herself, she had no materials to serve a better meal—but, oh, she might have had her house shining clean! She writhed as she read Cora's contemptuous thoughts.

The men chatted on, unaware of what the women were thinking.

"How your cattle holding out in the drought?" Lige asked Bev.

Cora rushed in to answer for him. "I got my brothers to drive most of his herd to free lands northeast when they took theirs."

"That was a good hunch," said Lige soberly. "Sourdough is aimin' to start right soon with as many of ours as can stand the trip. But there's a lot of 'em that are so poor they couldn't make it. They'll have to take their chances here. Slim chances they are, too, with feed so high, and costing so much to haul it that it would break a man to try to do it."

"Bev wanted to go 'long with his cattle, but I knew he wasn't strong enough to stand the trip," said Cora. "Hard ridin' an' campin' out nights is no job for a man that's had lung trouble. You never know when you'll start something again."

"He looks well now," said Letty. She felt that perhaps Bev was sensitive about his ailment —his disability—and resented Cora's lack of tact in parading it.

Bev smiled indulgently. "Cora keeps a sharp eye out for me, and a good thing that she does, too, I guess."

"Yep, I watch him like a hawk. I ain't ambitious to be a widow, for I don't think crepe would be becomin' to my style of beauty at all," said his wife emphatically.

"When are you goin' to start your bunch off, Lige?" asked Bev.

"Sourdough is aimin' to go with 'em in a couple o' days now. I'll start with him, an' go a little piece, and then I'll come back to stay with Letty an' look after the ones that are left here."

· · · ·

It was, in fact, the next day that Lige and Sourdough began to round up the cattle in preparation for taking them to the free lands in sections where rain had fallen and where there was grazing. The plan was for him to go, in company with two other men, to drive the cattle to the neighborhood of Devil's River, about one hundred fifty miles southwest of them, and try their chances there. The other man who had gone scouting had reported that the grass was better there, and there was water for the cattle.

It was a hard task to gather the cattle together, scattered as they were over the vast, unfenced pastures, mixed in with cattle of many other ranchmen. The creatures were not only wild, according to their nature, but they were nervous and frightened and high-strung on account of their famished condition.

They seemed to realize that this round-up was unusual, out of time, not a regular affair like the spring and fall round-up, and so they were suspicious and hard to manage. Lige and Sourdough "worked the range" for miles and miles, closing in on groups of cattle here and there, and heading them toward a central point not far from the ranch house, from which they planned to make a start for the drive to Devil's River. But the animals would break away from their control, and scatter, to run back in all directions. Full of tricky impulses, nervous from fear, and wild and intractable as well as stubborn, they made the task of collecting them very hard for the two men.

From the window, as she watched, Letty tried to see what was happening, since the day was clear and windless, so that no sand was blown to obscure the vision, and the extraordinary clearness of the atmosphere made it possible to see objects on the rolling plains for long distances. She was moved with pity alike for the struggling men and for the scared beasts that could not understand what was being attempted.

Two days they worked at the seemingly hopeless task, but by nightfall of the second day, they had succeeded in bunching about half of the herd, and would start the drive next morning.

Lige came in exhausted.

"We've had a hell of a time gettin' these cow brutes herded," he said, as he slumped down into a chair and leaned his arms on the table. "They been starved so long, that they're more'n half mad. We didn't get more'n half of 'em together, work as hard as we could. I'm wore out."

His face was streaked with dirt and sweat, his hair disheveled, his attitude one of fatigue and dejection.

He went on to explain the situation to her. "I got to stand night guard over the bunch tonight, so Sourdough can be fresh to start tomorrow morning early. Would you be scared to stay here at the house by yourself?"

"Oh, yes, I would!" she quavered.

"I could get old Pedro to sleep in the kitchen, though I was aimin' to have him help me with the cattle," he offered.

"I'd rather go with you. Let me do that, Lige."

He smiled a tired smile. "You never sat up all night on the plains with a bunch of wild cattle that's liable to stampede any time. Don't take nothin' to start a bunch when it's restless an' suspicious as these are now."

"Let me try it this once," she pleaded. "I'm afraid to stay here without you. An' I wouldn't be so scared on the plains tonight, because the wind's not blowing. Please, Lige!"

"All right," he said slowly, too tired to argue with her. "I reckon there ain't no real danger with me an' Pedro both on the job. It'll be something different from anything you've ever done."

And so it was, she found out. It was an experience that she would never forget, she told herself often during the night. Lige made a fire on the ground to keep her warm, and spread a bed of blankets for her, a little distance away from the cattle which he had at last succeeded in "bedding down," or getting settled to rest and sleep. He and old Pedro took turns staying with her and circling round and round the herd on horseback, to keep them in place. It was a weird and impressive picture, the flaring firelight, where she sat huddled in blankets, the vast empty plains silver-gray with the unearthly radiance of moonlight, the cattle bunched together in a mass of dark bodies and long horns like polished spears in the moonlight.

At the least sign of restlessness in the cattle, Lige would begin to circle round them, singing to them, some cowboy song, dolorous, monotonous, soothing in its sad strains.

The cattle, tired from their two days' struggle, at last became quiet and slept. Then Letty rested, too, with Pedro keeping guard over her, and Lige a silent watcher by the cattle. She felt like some being in another world, in a life alien to anything she had ever known, as she lay, half awake, half asleep, there on the hard ground, under the white tent of the sky, with the wind blowing on her face. Would the wild cattle stampede suddenly and trample her to death? But Lige was watching over her and them…. And so she slept.

The next morning by daybreak Lige and Sourdough were making preparations for the start for their "drive." Letty gave them breakfast by lamplight and watched them mount their horses before the first streak of color came in the sky, and called out her "good-bye and good luck" to them.

But the cattle, rested from the night's sleep, were more active than ever, and seemed suspicious of danger. As the dark, moving mass came nearer the ranch house, when the drive begun, they were showing signs of panic. Would the men be able to control them? Would they stampede in spite of what could be done?

Long horns tossed wildly in the air, bodies lunged and plunged against each other, and the brutes began a mad bellowing. The fear of each intensified the fear of the others, and the mass surged forward, uncontrollable with rage and fright.

The stampede that Lige had been afraid of had come!

Thrilled by the sight, so novel and strange to her, yet terrified of what might happen to the two men, Letty watched from the door. Lige and Sourdough were riding desperately to try to keep the herd together, to keep the cattle from scattering all over the range again, and rendering their hard toil of no avail. She could see them circling round and round the lunging, plunging mass, and above the lowing and bellowing of the beasts their voices rose in shouts and calls to quiet them.

The stampede swept on, till the dark mass was hid in the cloud of sand it raised about it, so that the woman, waiting at the door, could not see what was happening. Would the men be able to hold the herd? And turn them, circle them till they wore them out and get them under control again? Or would the maddened beasts trample them underfoot to their death?

All day Letty walked the floor in a fever of fear. She pictured the bodies of the men lying face downward in the sand, while the avalanche of cattle that had swept over them passed on. Who would be left to bear her the news? She felt as never before the desolation of this lonely land, where human habitations, human faces were so few, so few, so far away. What would happen to her there helpless, if Lige and Sourdough never came back? She could not walk the ten miles to the nearest ranch. Perhaps no passerby might come for days on days….

Perhaps the men had not been killed, but were lying wounded and helpless, in need of aid, with no one nigh to give it!…

Night came, and Lige had not returned. Would he ever come back? Letty lighted the lamp and set it in the window, so that he could see its glimmer from afar if he should be on his way home. She had supper ready, in case he should be there to eat it…. Then she folded her hands in an agony of helplessness, and waited….

The wind was mercifully still, so that she did not suffer tortures of fear of it, as she had that night of the storm at Bev's house, but she imagined that it was quiet with some purpose in view. Was it stealing up on tiptoe, to peer into the window at her? to listen to hear if she cried aloud, to eavesdrop her heartbeats and her thoughts? That would be just like the evil, treacherous wind….

As her terror began to mount unbearably because of the wind's crafty stillness, she heard the sound of galloping hoofs in the sand, and she hushed her very breathing.

Then the door sprang open and Lige staggered in, dropping with fatigue. She had never seen a man look so worn out, so completely used up. His eyes were bleared and bloodshot, and half closed for lack of sleep, his face was lined with exhaustion and covered with dirt and sweat, and his whole body sagged as if the backbone had been taken from it.

He dropped into a chair, too spent to speak at first. She ran to him, brought water to bathe his face, eased off his heavy boots from his swollen feet, and held a cup of coffee to his parched lips. "Poor fellow, so tired!" she murmured, with tears in her eyes for his sufferings.

When he had recovered enough so that he could eat the food she had prepared for him, she waited on him with eager solicitude for his every wish, and then turned the covers of the bed back for him so that he might drag himself to rest.

"How did you stop the stampede?" she asked.

"Oh, we kept circlin' round an' round 'em till we got 'em wore out, but it pretty nigh wore us out first. But we caught up with the rest o' the bunch that are goin' an' Sourdough ought not have any more trouble much with 'em now."

"How long will it take Sourdough to get to where they're going?"

"About ten days or so to get to Devil's River. The critters are so weak they can't travel more'n about a dozen miles a day. Trail drivers usually can make fifteen, but these beasts are too feeble."

After that, for a time, from day to day would come rumors to Lige that some of the cattle were in various places. He would go out and work the range to bring them in, in the effort to collect them near the last water hole that had any water in it. That was near the ranch house. Gradually he got a fair number of them rounded up, almost as many as the herd that Sourdough had driven away with him. Some had died from starvation and thirst, and some were so weak that they seemed on their last legs, but maybe they could hold out till it rained, Lige said. But rain would have to come soon.

The weeks that should have been late spring passed into summer, and still no rain came —a strange cycle of days that mocked their name—May!...

As in a stupor of pain, Letty visioned May at home in Virginia, saw with reminiscent eyes each aspect of its loveliness; felt with aching physical senses each forest odor, each vagrant breeze, smoothness of leaf and fern, coolness of water; heard each bird song, each woodland sound. She lived a divided life, one of the body—there on the prairie desert in the drought,—the other of the spirit where she was back at home in the country in Virginia. Sometimes she asked herself in perturbation and fright if her homesickness and sufferings were making her a little flighty.

Back in Virginia the birds would be singing and building their nests. Here no birds sang, for there were none! They had perished of hunger or had flown away to greener, kindlier climes. The wrens in the boxes by the old side porch would be starting their households anew, with twitterings and flutterings and soft calls to each other. Such tiny gray birds, vocal with love and delight! There would be song sparrows making their nests low, near the ground in tangles of rose vines, in blackberry clumps. They would stop in their toil now and then to teeter on some swaying vine and practice their sweet, soft song, the same each spring, but with subtle variations to express each little love story. The catbirds would be wrangling at each other across the old lawn, their voices shrill in objurgations, their funny, flat tails quivering and jerking with wrath. They would dance across the grass with mincing, finical steps, then make a sudden swoop at some enemy or some insect. Catbirds were amusing things!

There would be cardinals, flashing like sudden gay thoughts of beauty through the green stillness, uttering their wild, sweet trills. Here the sand stretched lifeless and grayish-yellow, with never blade of green. Oh, for a cardinal's wing to flit over its deadness!

She could see the hummingbirds on wings as swift and as invisible as light, dart among the blossoms of the honeysuckles, their bodies poised for an instant over the cream or coral chalices, their wings whirring rapturously, as their needle-sharp beaks pierced into the cups to drink of the nectar spring had distilled for them. She could hear their sharp, almost inaudible cries of delight.

There would be bluebirds like flashing hints of heaven, through the woods' greenness. Her eyes ached to see the pure, healing color of a bluebird once again! She thought of the flocks of indigo buntings she used sometimes to see in the fields about home—bright little birds, ineffably blue, flying in happy companionship like blossoms that had taken life and wing and soared out to see the world that God called good.

She could hear the call of the Bob Whites, as they would go stealing through the grain fields at early morning, their voices sounding dewy as the dawn, clear as a lad's whistle to his mate. Oh, to be awakened once more from girlhood's sleep to hear the Bob Whites calling to each other in the fields back home! "*Bob White! Bob White! All right! All right!*" Cries that soothed and challenged in one breath. Oh, for a life that soothed and challenged, instead of this dead monotony of sand and drudgery and wifehood without love, of ruthless winds that were at you night and day!...

When Sourdough came back from his cattle drive, he was lean and haggard and hollow-eyed, but he had not lost his spirit. He recounted some of the hardships he and his companions had experienced in getting their herds to Devil's River.

"When we got close to the water hole at the end of the first day, the critters was so famished that they stampeded again, trying to get to drink as quick as possible. Some of 'em was trampled to death, an' some drunk so hard they wasn't able to move no more. But we finally got the most of the bunch started again next day and we kep' goin'. But it was the meanest drive I ever had anything to do with."

"Do you reckon there'll be grass enough round where you took 'em to keep 'em going till it rains here?" asked Lige, anxiously.

"Yep, I reckon. Never can tell, though. I dunno but what we'd 'a' done better to have took 'em over toward Yellowhouse Canyon, as some fellers did. But it's mostly a chanct, anyway, for who can tell where it's goin' to rain first? They say all signs fail in Texas, an' I think they're blamed right."

When he had recovered from his excessive fatigue. Sourdough began to tell Letty some of the amusing incidents of the drive, and dramatized for her his own ludicrous efforts and those of his companions to outwit the crazed cattle. He was a clown still, she told herself, facing his hard luck with a joke, laughing to hide his despair.

Letty winced daily at seeing the tragic buffoonery of these two cowboys, put on partly for her benefit, to keep her from knowing how serious the situation was, and partly because it was their nature to conceal their deeper feelings under a mask of humor. But when she looked at their faces in repose, when they were off guard, she saw more than they meant to reveal. Those stern, sad faces told a different story.

She felt an infinite pity for these two brave men, and a still greater pity for herself. All this was their life, their destiny, they were used to it, and knew how to bear it, while she had been thrust into it against her will—crying out against the sacrifice. Should she ever be able to give the faithful Sourdough the friendship he deserved? He asked so little, yet he loved her deeply in his way, she knew, as loyal to Lige as to her. Now she was too preoccupied with her own wretchedness to give much thought to him, or what she might do for him to make his lot happier.

And what of Lige? Were she and her husband moving toward each other or drifting hopelessly apart? They were like two lost figures in a mist, stretching out hands to each other, but unable to see clearly or to think of the future.

She had ideals of marriage, which she had never consciously formulated, but which had risen out of her childhood memories of her mother's loyalty to her father. Latent memories of a thousand tendernesses between them wounded her, rebuked her. She reproached herself that she was not living up to those ideals, but she shrank from the moral effort that would have involved. And anyhow, her mother had loved her father and had married him from choice, which made it different, she rebelliously told herself. She hadn't been driven to it against her will!

• • • •

One day in June, when Lige and Sourdough were out on the range, Wirt Roddy came again.

Some electricity in the air, some tingle in her blood, some prescience of spirit, had told Letty that something different was about to happen. She had begun to believe in clairvoyance, and so she had her room clean and in order, her hair smoothly dressed, her calico house dress exchanged for a little muslin, from another summer, whose blue matched her eyes and the ribbon on her hair. The dress was somewhat faded from washing, as her eyes were a trifle dimmed from her tears—still each blue was like that of periwinkles in an old-fashioned garden.

She kept looking expectantly at the road, and she was scarcely surprised when Wirt Roddy dismounted at the door. Only a leap of her heart told her that her clairvoyance had been right, that her psychic instinct was true—that she could *feel* in advance what was going to happen to her.

She greeted him simply, though she was tremulous.

"How do you do?" she said, as she gave him a chill hand, a hand that trembled in spite of her efforts to keep it still. "Will you come in? and have a seat?"

"Surest thing in the world," he said lightly.

Yet he, too, looked as if the drought, or something, had touched him a trifle. His manner was jaunty as of old, but his eyes were less glinting with alert life, he was thinner, and his face showed strain, of fatigue or anxious thought.

"Lige and Sourdough are out seeing about the cattle," she told him. "But they'll be in soon."

He seated himself in the old raw-hide chair and leaned back to take his ease.

"Are they still trying to call down rain from heaven?" he gibed. "What does it matter if all these wretched cattle do die?"

When she would have protested, he put up a hand to ward off interruption. "Not that I mind the absence of the two gentlemen in question. Their not being here doesn't distress me in the least."

She flushed resentfully at his words, his tone. Again she felt the old, fluttering fear of him that recurred from time to time. Why had he come back?

He answered her thought. "I'm on my way to see a fellow about some land—a deal I've got on. He's coming from Deaf Smith County to meet me. I thought I'd drop in and see you as I passed. There's no harm in a howdy, is there?"

106

"Why, no," she stammered. "I'm glad to see you, and Lige will be in pretty soon."

Why couldn't she be calm in his presence? There was no other that had ever upset her so, and he did it knowingly, enjoyingly, she told herself hotly, as a cat would play with a bird, watching it flutter and tremble and try to escape.

They talked disjointedly of casual things, with surface speech that meant nothing, had anyone heard. Yet underneath the commonplaceness of their words, the woman felt strange surgings of soul, riotous fears and raptures, was shaken by tumultuous emotions she did not understand, saw, as in a crystal ball at which she gazed with tranced eyes, another self, another being she had never known she was or could be. And she saw that he read her soul! He saw, too. He saw the quiet figure that sat before him, with thin hands folded in her lap, with frightened eyes fixed on his, and he saw through it this other, problematic, soul.

Why didn't Lige come home?

She stirred uneasily, and made conversation. "When do you think the drought will end, if it ever does?"

He answered gloomily. "Worst outlook I ever saw for the cattlemen. Things were getting prosperous with us, too. We'd had a boom in the cattle business for the last few years, since the early seventies."

She drew an easier breath. Cattle were such a safe topic of conversation, so impersonal. He smiled as if seeing her thought, and talked on to humor her.

"Now many a little rancher will be wiped out, and cowpunchers will have to find new jobs."

"I don't know much about the business," she said. "Only I feel sorry for the men that are losing all they have, and for the poor cattle that suffer so. I can hardly sleep at night for thinking of them all."

"Prices of beef cattle rose from about the seventies up to a year or so ago. Since then they've been going down. Too many herds have been driven to the northern markets, and too many herds are getting a start in other places, closer to the packing-houses than Texas is."

"Lige says he don't know what they are all going to do," she said, her face shadowed by foreboding.

"It's damned hard on the fellers that haven't got any backing. When a man's bunch of cattle is all he's got, and that's wiped out, where is he?"

She shivered at thought of Lige.

"Cattle business isn't the wild romance, anyhow, that it used to be. Not the same sport in it," he went on.

"Tell me about it," she said.

A reminiscent look came into his eyes, as he gazed out toward the prairie. "The Texas cowboy took up the job of the Mexican *vaquero*. He had to capture and gentle the wild cattle from the plains. Spanish longhorns descended from those that had been left behind maybe when the Spaniards quit Texas, or maybe when the Mexicans were beaten and driven back by the Texans in the Texas Revolution. These wild things had never known a lariat or a branding iron—devils they were, too."

"How could they capture wild cattle?"

He smiled. "Singing to them was one way. You don't believe it—no? The cowpunchers would scatter out so they could circle in on the bunch of wild cattle they wanted to get. Night time, pitch dark—*savez*? Then they'd begin to sing, soft and monotonous. What they sang was a sort of tune without words to it. They called it 'The Texas Lullaby'"

She remembered Lige, as he sang to the cattle that night to keep them from stampeding. "And did it work?"

"You bet! Lot o' wild things can be gentled and caught if you sing to 'em."

She visioned these fierce cattle trembling with rage and fright hearing a wordless song in the night that stilled them and led to their capture.... Long horns tossing madly in the air, bodies surging to and fro, the herd ready to stampede—bellowing and pawing the ground— and in the distance the treacherous music closing in on them!

"You make music sound cruel, and tricky and false!" she cried.

"Me? No, I wasn't doing the singing myself. I have never done much taking of wild cattle. But if it took that to save my herd, or get me what I wanted very much, then I reckon I'd try to carry a tune."

"Lige says cowboys sing to their herds all night when they are driving them up the trail, to keep them together."

"Yes, it works that way. When cattle get to milling around too much, they're liable to stampede and go over a bluff, or run themselves near to death. You got to sing to 'em to quiet 'em. Cowboys have all sorts of songs they know."

"Yes, I hear Sourdough singing them sometimes. Pretty sad, some of them are."

"Yes." He mused, tapping his spurs with the handle of his riding quirt. Presently he sang, under his breath, absent-mindedly, a song she had not heard before.

"As I walked out on the streets of Laredo,
   As I walked out in Laredo one day,
I spied a poor cowboy wrapped up in white linen,
   Wrapped up in white linen, as cold as the clay.

Oh, beat the drum slowly and play the fife lowly.
   Play the dead march as you bear me along.
Take me to the green valley and lay the sod over me.
   For I'm a young cowboy and I know I've done wrong!"

"You'd have to take him a long way from here, wouldn't you?" asked Letty, her eyes dim with tears. "Here there's no green valley, just the wilderness of sand."

"I think I mentioned to you just how cheerful it would be, didn't I?" he mocked.

Her face burned. "Much good telling me could do!"

His face clouded, sobered, and his sombre eyes gazed past her as if looking at a prospect she did not see with him. "Ah, yes, I reckon you're right about that."

Her eyes questioned his mutely as to his meaning, but he merely hummed the tune, as he tapped his spurs with his quirt.

Noon came, and still Lige and Sourdough had not come back. They must be having trouble with the cattle in some far place on the range.

So Letty prepared the meal and set the table for four, but there were only the two of them to sit down to eat.

When they had finished, he said good-bye in a manner somewhat constrained, without his lightness of tone or gesture, his teasing mystery of glance. He mounted his horse and rode away, without waving his hand back to her as he had done the other time. Why? she asked herself. Had she done or said—or thought—anything to offend him?

Scarcely had he gone when Lige and Sourdough rode up. Since they came from the direction which he had taken, she knew that they must surely have passed him, less than a mile from the house. They would know, then, that he had been there. She felt guilty of some wrong doing, though she could not have said what it was. She had not asked the man to come.

Lige and Sourdough strode into the house in a silence that struck her as foreboding. They glanced around, noting the unusual order of the room, her blue dress, the ribbon in her hair. They looked through the door into the kitchen where the table was set for four, but where dishes showing that two had eaten were still cluttered on the table that had a white cloth on it instead of the oilcloth.

Lige's face had a bleak look, like the sky before a norther comes.

"Wirt Roddy has been here," Letty said quietly. "He stopped by on his way to see a man about some land."

Her voice sounded queer and throaty to her own ears. Did it sound unnatural to theirs?

Sourdough leaned against the door-jamb and spoke with studied casualness. "Know he was comin'?"

His roach of red hair looked belligerent.

"Why, no! How could I? I haven't seen nor heard of him since the last time he was here. I never leave this place, and I never get a letter."

The smile came back to his face. "Of course, you didn't. Excuse me. But I don't like that wall-eyed perch an' I ain't achin' to see him stop round these here premises or this section."

"I couldn't help his coming, Sourdough. He just stopped, the same as other cow men do, on their way to town."

"Jes' the same, honey, but different." His eyes were affectionate as they gazed at her. "Lige an' me been fotch up with these other cowpunchers round here, an' we know none o' them's goin' to do us no dirt. I ain't so sure about this vinegarone."

"What's a vinegarone?" she inquired.

"A whip-tail scorpion, found in these parts. Way to treat it is to grind it under your heel on sight."

He turned to Lige. "If I was you, I'd put a bug in this hombre's ear, that he'd do well to make his sassiety a little scarce round here."

Lige spoke with thoughtful calm. "Twice ain't so much, if he ain't aimin' to come no more. I don't want to seem unneighborly, but—" He left his sentence hanging in the air.

Sourdough began polishing his gun, the while he sang softly another new song.

"If you come monkeyin' with my Lula gal,
   I tell you what I'll do;
I'll shoot you up with my forty-four,
   And carve you through and through!"

11

JUNE PASSED INTO JULY, July into August, and still the drought continued. "Hot as a six-shooter," Sourdough said. The sand was like hot ashes heated from the furnace that was the sky and the furnace that was the earth, while the wind was an oven blast, and the days were live coals dragged over the land.

Old Pedro had a weather prophecy for every incident, every detail he observed, and he came often to see Letty and express himself as to what was in store for them. When they heard, or imagined they did, the sound of locusts droning, he shook his gray head dolefully. "When the locusts *cantar*, that mean more drought." When the whirlwinds passed across the plain, moving spirals of sand silent and swift, he looked depressed. "That mean no rain for yet," he muttered. A foggy morning was to him a bad sign, though Letty argued with specious optimism that fog should rightly hint of rain.

"You no know this land, senorita, this *terra caliente*!" he said.

When rattlesnakes came out in numbers. Sourdough muttered, "That don't look good. They're movin' toward water an' away from a dry country."

He killed a big rattler with "Eleven rattles an' a

[*...missing text pg 256 and 257...*]

themselves?); where the oaks and the poplars and many another tree showed infinitude of restful greens, and purplish shadows, the sunlight like sifted gold making a patina in the grass.... Gray-green trunks, with lichens on them and little lizards darting up and down like idle thoughts.... Benignant spread of branches where birds sang, where squirrels frisked and chattered and little tree-toads croaked about rain.

She looked out over a desert plain!...

Her eyes ached from the hot sand that the wind blew in them, and from the glare of the sun on parched prairies where no trees shaded the earth. The wind was not so boisterous now as it had been in the winter and early spring, but it blew steadily, relentlessly, till her nerves felt she could bear no more. Never a breath of coolness, never any soothing moisture in the breeze, but a hot, dry blast that seemed to bake her brain, that drove burning sand against her burning cheeks.

She could see the heat waves eddy up from the ground and shimmer upward in the sun, visible signs of the torment the people endured. She watched the .whirlwinds race across the plain, and remembered that they were prophecies of longer drought.

She would look yearningly at the sky for hope of a cooling shower, but she saw only the heaven's awful blue, as clear, as bright as glass, with no clouds anywhere. The buzzards soared clumsily overhead.

Sometimes again there would be clouds, a pageantry of color at sunset and sunrise, a wild richness of sky that seemed like the conflagration of a world. Then she remembered that Sourdough had said those brilliant cloud effects came with drought, and she turned with a shudder away from their beauty. The only beauty that nature showed her here was a menace!

The wind blew the sand everywhere as high as she could see, so that it hung a golden gauze between her and the sun, shot through with light. She watched the coppery sun stride across the blue, day after day, and thought of Lige's saying that a coppery sky in time of drought meant more dry weather....

She saw few signs of life now. A horned toad would sometimes flash by her—its bright, beady eyes glittering, its spiked body covered with horny protuberances like a coat of mail —or an ashen lizard would slip past.

Sourdough told her one day, "Horned frogs can squirt blood out o' their eyes at you if you skeer 'em, folks says."

After that, she was more afraid of them than of rattlesnakes.

Sourdough tried to be jocose about the situation. "Well, at least we ain't havin' no cyclones," he said to Letty one day. "Folks out here say, 'Never mind the weather so the wind don't blow.'"

The plains in their terrible distinctness showed dead prairie dogs, dead jackrabbits here and there. They had perished for lack of food and water. Only the coyotes remained, and they prowled night and day, for they lived on flesh, and grew fat on the bodies of the dead. There were no song birds left, only the buzzards—carrion birds. Only the buzzards and coyotes were well-fed. The great, hideous birds were too gorged to fly high now, and flapped their wings lazily over the ground, above where the dead horses and cattle lay in stark attitudes....

The desert mocked her with its mirages, showing her across a stretch of yellow-gray sand with its clumps of bear grass and leafless mesquite bushes, the vision of green trees and still lakes with willows dipping down to them....

Sunrise and sunset on the prairies were incredibly beautiful, as if a world about to be annihilated flamed up in awful, unforgettable glory as a last spectacle for the eyes of man. But sunrise and sunset were associated with the thought of Wirt Roddy now, and so she told herself she mustn't look at them nor think of them. She must forget. She mustn't remember that she had ever thought of him!

She became nervous and jumpy, starting to hear the wind rattle the ragged dried leaves of the yucca, peering to see the uncanny shapes that dusk made to flit across the plains. She felt that if once she lost control of her nerves, they would break beyond hope of recovery, so she kept a tense restraint on herself, a restraint that was more wearing than outbursts of emotion would have been. A shrewish fit of temper, or a hysterical spell of crying would have relaxed her, would have done her good, but she did not know that. She was afraid to let go.

At times she was acutely aware of all that went on about her, as if her consciousness were purely physical, a response to sense impressions, the sting of the sand, the hot breath of the wind, the acrid smell of dust, the rasping roughness of everything she touched, the taste of the unpalatable food in her mouth, the drone of the wind, the lowing of cattle, the sight of the barren desert. At such times she felt she had no mind, no soul, but was merely a bundle of senses that rendered a message of pain for each impression they received of their world.

At other times she felt she was not there in the body at all, was unaware of anything physical, but conscious only of the psychical, of her loneliness, her longings, her despairs. She felt lifted beyond the physical into a realm of spirit that felt keener suffering, as if her body had been stripped from her to leave her soul naked to pain.

At other times she felt a two-fold suffering, of sense and soul. She began dimly to comprehend how women tried beyond endurance might sometimes go mad.

Now and then, as if deliberately torturing herself, she forced herself to face each crude, repellant detail of her environment, to let the worst of it sink into her deepest consciousness. The rough walls, on which the torn strips of newspaper were hanging, rent by the wind, the lumpy, sagging bed that no attention could make even, the chairs with rawhide seats, the table littered with pipes and tobacco pouches, the old hats and clothes hanging on the wall because there was no closet, the kerosene lamp that always seemed to smoke, despite all she could do, the sand and dust everywhere—all sickened her. She couldn't keep the rooms tidy because there was no place to put things away out of sight, no closets, no chests of drawers, no wardrobes. Her soul longed for neatness and order, but she was helpless to achieve it. In her other life, all that had been arranged for her without her thought.

Lige and Sourdough were preoccupied with the progress of their own financial tragedy. They had thrashed out in talk between them all possible plans for saving their cattle, but they could settle on no feasible means. They had no money to buy feed even if any were to be had near them. They had no wagons to haul it the long distances from the railroads, and no horses with strength enough to pull the loads.

"They say some folks have gone to East Texas to put the case before the folks there, an' see if some help can't be sent out here," said Sourdough one day after a parley that ended in no conclusion of relief.

"They can send food for the folks that need it, but it'll be a hard job to get feed-stuff for the critters, out this far, an' off the railroads an' all," said Lige dully.

"An' even if we had feed for 'em, how would we get water here?" went on Sourdough. "It'd be too much to tackle to haul water all that way for stock. All we can make out to do is to haul our drinkin' water for ourselves."

"Yeah, we've done everything we can think of to get water," said Lige.

True, they had scraped the bottoms of the old water holes in hope of finding moisture farther down. They had dug out places in creek beds, so that perhaps springs once there might furnish drink, but each effort was only a mockery. There was no water!

"You see honey, we couldn't save 'em, even if we could haul feedstuff to 'em," said Lige one day. "The water holes is all dried up."

"What is everybody else doing?" she gasped.

"Well, the big ranchers have got deeper water holes then our'n. They can dig down an' maybe get up a little water that way. Them that are closer to the railroad can haul water from there, that the roads bring in. Some of 'em shipped most of their cattle on the railroad before the drought got so bad. That has knocked the bottom out of prices, too, so you couldn't get nothin' for 'em, anyway. It's a God awful time!"

"It makes a feller plumb sick to see the dumb critters suffer like this, when there ain't nothin' we can do for 'em," said Lige one day.

"Yeah," agreed Sourdough, "it's enough to make you gag till you throw up yore toenails."

"An' this heat's enough to make your brain clabber."

Letty was sick with sympathy for the suffering that she saw all about her. Gaunt, cadaverous beasts staggered about, tortured by heel-flies that nagged them constantly, bawling in distress, searching everywhere for food and water. They had devoured every spear of the dried bunch grass, and needle grass, every leaf and bean from the mesquite bushes, every stalk of last year's weeds, and now there was nothing, nothing! They came close to the house as if making appeal to their masters not to abandon them to death.

Lige's face would twist as he turned away from the sight of them. Letty's eyes were dim with tears of pity she constantly shed for them. The lump in her throat and the weight about her heart never left her.

"Oh, Lige, isn't there *something* you could do for them?" she burst out one day.

He turned his palms upward in a gesture of helplessness.

112

"What can I do? I've got no money to pay for feed and water. No horses to haul it, no wagons to bring it, no credit to borrow on, if I could make out to get it here."

His voice was leaden, his face gray, his eyes bloodshot.

She twisted her apron in her hands and gave a shuddering sob like a hurt child. "It looks to me like I just can't *stand* to see these poor things tortured so!"

He moved restlessly. "I know. It ain't so easy for me, neither. But I'm at my rope's end."

"And they've just got to starve to death with us looking at them?" Her voice rose shrilly.

His mouth set grimly. "I reckon we'll have to turn our eyes the other way, then."

She strangled a sob in her throat, and covered her face with her hands. She had never watched anything die! Her mother had slipped away in her sleep, so there had been no fear nor horror in her going.

But to watch these helpless animals die before her eyes in slow tortures of hunger and thirst—how could she bear it?...

But she had to bear it. Unless she bandaged her eyes and stuffed her ears with cotton, she could not escape their torment.

She had to see them as they milled around restlessly, tossing their heads, their long horns glittering in the sun. They pawed the ground, as if to find food deep buried there, some greenness under the tricky sand, some water beneath the burning desert. She had to hear, day and night, their distressful bawling. Faint with hunger and thirst, they weakened themselves still further with their bellowing.... Some of them threw their heads around to the side, as if the torture of thirst twisted the muscles. Their tongues swelled, turned black, protruded from their mouths.

She had to see the cattle as they gathered round the dried-up water hole, close to the house, to die—while the buzzards waited for them to fall, one by one. The loathsome birds perched on their shoulders, and pecked out the eyes of the still living creatures.

Their mournful lowing was not so loud now, but more like long-drawn-out sobbing, human, very pitiful.

Some of them went mad from thirst and fought, goring each other to death....

One day Letty stood tense and shivering, her hands held over her ears to shut out the sounds. Lige touched her shoulders gently.

"*Pobrecita!*" he said. Poor little thing!

She caught her breath jerkily. "I saw dead cattle by the railroad track as I came out here." Her eyes showed horror at the remembrance. "Wirt Roddy said it was the trail to the west. I thought I couldn't stand it then. But they were dead, their torment was over!"

He thrust his hands deep into his pockets and turned his tragic eyes upon her. "You made a bad move when you come out to the west, didn't you? *Pobrecita!*"

She laughed hysterically. "The pastor fixed it up for me! He thought it would be the best thing I could do. He said he had prayed over it!"

12

ALL HOPE THAT LIGE and Sourdough had had of saving the cattle was gone. The last of the starved longhorns had perished of hunger and thirst, and still the gods were not appeased. The heavens were heated brass, across which clouds drifted now and then, thin wisps of cotton down, or a trailing line like that of a sea gull's wing, or a huddled mass like a flock of sheep. But they did not stay. Sometimes dark clouds banked themselves against the horizon and spread rapidly over the sky, while serpent tongues of flame flashed, and thunder muttered hope of rain, while anxious eyes scanned the heavens and suffocating hope beat at the heart.

But only a few drops would fall, and then the sun would shine as naked and as brilliant as before. The clouds would vanish as quickly as they had come, and the watchers would turn away in despair. The steady south winds blew—a bad sign in a drought the range men said, and the sand seeped in at every crevice of the house, and was patterned quaintly by the wind freaks on the level plain.

"It will rain when the good God wills," said old Pedro, over and over.

September came, and the people of the plains began to hope again, faintly and fearfully, lest a thing so presumptuous as hope might offend suspicious powers watching them. September might bring rain! But "early September blows" from the south began, and the old settlers shook their heads. "A bad sign," they said. "The drought won't break yet awhile."

And it did not.

The section was almost depopulated by now, for all the heartsick people that could leave had done so. Covered wagons had toiled across the plains, grotesque and tragic as seen in the clear atmosphere that revealed everything—the horses plowing through the deep sand, the flap of the curtains showing poverty-stricken household goods piled awkwardly inside.

"You can see a old bedstead an' a passel o' kids bangin' out of every one," said Lige one day.

Letty watched a covered wagon with longing eyes.

"Oh, Lige, can't we go, too?" she said.

He shook his head stolidly, though he moved restlessly in his chair. "We got no money to go on, an' nowheres to go to. Things are bound to take a turn for the better soon. If we can hang on and rattle with the old place till it rains, we can make it all right, yet."

"I don't know," she quavered.

"You just wait and see," he muttered, with dull defiance in the face of fate.

Lige's tall frame was thinner than it used to be, his face leaner, with haggard lines, and his eyes burned in their sockets. He was nervous, where always before he had been calm and controlled. At nights he would often mutter in his sleep, and sometimes would start up with an exclamation or a shout, then sink back to his pillow again with a shuddering heave of his big body.

Letty felt frightened as she watched him. To think of his succumbing to emotion was like seeing a mountain shaken by some internal convulsion, was like watching a granite cliff writhe in pain. His strength had been as calm, as sure, as that of the stars. Physical suffering alone would never move him, she felt certain. He would have gone to the stake, have died of torture, without uttering a groan, would have received a sheaf of arrows in his breast with no outcry.

But this mental torment and suspense were proving almost too much for him, almost more than he could bear. Was it partly, or largely because of her? Letty asked herself. Was it because he felt he had involved her in his fate, when but for him she might have managed some escape for herself from the toils in which she had been caught?

What was he thinking of, in the long hours when he sat in silence and looked at the prairie?

Her heart melted with pity for him as she watched his sufferings, his suspense, rendered all the more poignant because of his stoic silence and restraint. Then it would harden rebelliously as she turned her gaze on herself. Couldn't a man find *some* way of saving his wife from such torment?

"But I can't go 'way an' leave my outfit," he explained to her morosely, time after time. "This is all the start I got, all I ever been able to get in the world. If I pick up an' leave it, I'm busted flat, an' I won't have the heart to begin again."

"But you're busted if you stay," she importuned.

"It's bound to rain again one o' these days," he rejoined stubbornly. "An' the fellers that have stuck by the land are goin' to have the best chanct."

If only she had a family to give him a boost now! If only she had a home for them to go back to for a time! But she felt cut off from the world.

"It's like being let down by a rope into a deep well, and having the rope cut," she brooded.

She, who at home had been the sunniest of creatures, was moody, with alternations of emotion that frightened her when she stopped to think of them. At times she would be irritable, would give short answers to Lige, would feel that she must scream if anyone spoke to her or looked at her. Then again she would be plunged into despondency so profound that it seemed she could never climb up to spiritual peace and light any more, as if she were hopelessly sunk in a pit of darkness.

Such a period of gloom might be followed by one of unreasonable exhilaration. She would tell herself, after the fashion of the old king she remembered from the Old Testament, "Surely the bitterness of death is past," surely good was coming to her round the corner of the next day or hour. Her spirit would walk on rainbow clouds, her whole body would tingle with inexplicable joy. She would put a ribbon in her hair and smile at Lige, whose patient eyes would light with relief to see her cheerful.

But soon this exaltation would be followed by depression, by a lassitude of body and soul, so that she felt nothing, was a blank, swept clean of emotions as of sensations.

They hoarded their precious drinking water, which had to be hauled in barrels from the railroad. They had to share it with Lige's horse, and thus must be as niggardly as possible in their own use of it. So now it was impossible to keep clean, and Letty's daintiness revolted at the sordid grime in which she had to live.

As she washed her dishes and cooking vessels with a minimum of water, she visioned to herself the clear, cold little streams in Virginia, the full sweep of the yellow James River, the inexhaustible ocean that pounded against the sand at Virginia Beach. The thought of water became almost an insanity with her. In her troubled dreams at night, she was lost in a desert, struggling in the deep sand, her hands and face torn by mesquite thorns and cactus, her feet full of the needles of prickly pear, yet ever driven onward in her search for a water hole ... deep water, into which she might plunge, and be cool and clean once more!... Water that should wash away the sand and the tears, and help her to forgetfulness of the horrid sights her eyes had looked upon....

When she gazed in the mirror now, she was startled. Instead of the laughing girlish beauty that had once been hers, a creature almost unrecognizable stared back at her, a woman worn and faded, with tragic eyes. Her yellow hair, bleached by the sun and made brittle by the dry winds, had lost its soft waves, and instead of rippling back from the forehead girlishly, was strained back like that of an old woman. Her skin was sunburned and rough, her cheeks were sunken and sallow, and her eyes, no longer blue as periwinkles in an old-fashioned garden, were inflamed from the wind and sand, drawn in from constant shrinking from the glare, and faded from weeping.

And still the wind blew. The wind had robbed her of her beauty, her youth, her hope, she muttered to herself. Would it sometime take away her reason or her life? It shrilled round the house by night as by day—or was it the wind that she heard as she lay awake to listen to the shrill, incessant, relentless sound—the wind or the keening coyotes?...

In October in Virginia, she would be walking through the golden leaves, with the amber sunlight all about her. She thought of the evenings, tranced with moonlight that broke in silver spray over everything, or with a silky blackness lighted by myriads of little gold stars above and the nervous twinklings of the fireflies against the dark....

A mockingbird might pour his song at night, freighted with a thousand thousand loves and griefs and ecstasies.... There was a mockingbird at home that came back each spring to her garden, a bird with a broken wing that drooped, so that she could know for certain it was the same. But he was as jaunty, as careless, as if his wing were whole. His song was like iridescent bubbles that shimmered in the sunlight, that floated from his pulsing throat with joyous lightness....

Letty realized that her homesickness was more for nature than for people, since if she went back home she would be too proud to reveal her sufferings to her friends, even the most kindly. Her pride would cut her off from their sympathy. But she could fling herself upon the grass in some secret, woodland place, could give herself to abandonment of grief and feel no shame in the presence of the trees, the birds, the grasses. They would comfort, they would heal, without hurt to her proud soul....

She lived a dual life. She saw at once this sun-scorched plain, this waste of sand, whose heat rose in shimmering waves that dizzied her, those leafless mesquite bushes, the dead swords of the yucca, the bleaching bones of cattle, gaunt carcasses where coyotes skulked and buzzards perched as hideous as gargoyles.... And then she saw a far-off land, a gracious, smiling country, where pine trees were like great altar candles lifted toward the stars, where magnolias opened their waxen petals in lovely curves to show their golden hearts, where yellow jasmine climbed up into the trees to shake its laughing golden bells of perfume, where every dead stump, every post was softened and made beautiful by the grace of some wild vine....

She listened to the coyotes yelp.... With eager, straining ears she heard the shouts of hunters in Virginia, the summoning horns, the deep-toned musical baying of the fox hounds as they started off to begin the sport....

She saw the late flowers, all in a mirage that her own will called up. The tall irises, blue and white by the old flagged walk in the garden. Each particular spot of that old garden she revisited, to live over its beauty of leaf and bloom, the lilac bushes against the brick wall, that in the spring were a mass of scented purple fit for a king; her bed of Johnny-jump-ups, that lifted piquant saucy little faces, fresh with dew, the violets that edged the flower beds, the lavender, the old-fashioned flowers each in its place....

She would think that perhaps it was raining in Virginia. She could see the silver arrows falling straight and true, or else the veils shaken a little by the wind, but, oh, a gentle wind!

or else a gossamer gauze of luminous gray that misted the air while the sun still shone. She thought of flowers springing up beneath the moisture, of tall ferns in shadowy glades, of damp rocks green with lichens. She could hear the purling of brooks over rocky beds, of Little leaping waterfalls, of murmurous rivers running to the sea—rivers of living water!...

It was autumn in Virginia.... The colored boys would be raking up the fallen leaves and burning them in fragrant pyres.... Scent of leaves burning in the crisp air ... magic like nothing else. A whole litany of memories was in the thought.... Nuts would come pattering down in woodsy stillnesses, while squirrels would whisk away with their winter stores—gray squirrels, or red squirrels, saucy and chattering and timidly friendly.... Apples would be garnered, Albemarle pippins, winesaps, juicy, and with red cheeks cool to the touch. As the leaves fell, the grace of the limbs would show stark against the sky, with a beauty of line that no work of man could match, while the unchanging green of pines and cedars told of another spring....

Here there were no trees! Was hell just a place where no trees grew, no birds sang?...

Hell was a place where the winds blew all the time, winds that tormented you, but would not let you die.... Winds that drove you *almost* crazy, but didn't let you know the relief that complete insanity would bring.... Demon winds!...

Winds of the summer were bad enough, but Letty shuddered daily at thought of the winds that winter would bring.

"I don't see how this house would stand in a big wind," she said apprehensively to Lige one day in the autumn.

"It won't blow over, because it's got so many cracks the wind goes right through," he told with a gallant attempt at jocoseness.

"But it's got no foundations, Lige. Just a rock at each corner, and one in the middle of each side."

"Well, we were sorter short of rocks," he conceded. "An' that's the way we have to build our houses out here. Of course I admit that a house that's just boxed and stripped ain't so weatherproof as one that's weather-boarded."

She looked dubious. "Some of these days a hard wind is going to knock it over."

"Some of these days you shall have a sure 'nough house. You know the high-toned folks in these West Texas towns think they are aristocrats if they got a weather-boarded house, an' a cistern instead of a water barrel, and a fence round the place."

"I miss a fence," she mourned. "I feel lost without one."

"Well, we got a wind-break, ain't we?"

She looked at the wind-break he boasted of, a short stretch of fence made of rough timber and slabs, to keep the merciless winds of winter away from the horses. Sand had piled against it like snow drifts.

"You could bury a steer in that sand pile," remarked Lige. "If so be you had a steer left to bury!"

"Don't you reckon the cattle you sent away will live?" she asked, to turn her mind away from the present.

"Sure," he said, with unconquerable hope. "That'll give us a start, come spring. Seed cattle, you know...."

By now, Letty was too deadened to feel the hungers that had so hurt her in the beginning of her life on the plains, the longings for things of the mind, for books, for music, for magazines, for easy talk of trivial interests and pleasures, for social interchange of happiness. All that her senses craved now was ease for the body, surcease from the pelting sand, the wind that was at her all the time, and for cooling water in plenty.

Still the buzzards floated in the blue, their cumbersome bodies loathsomely well fed. Still at dusk the eerie shapes and shadows flitted across the plains that were so empty by day. Each day the golden gauze still hung between her and the sun....

Her mouth—once a childish, adorable mouth with its kissable cleft in the upper lip—was a thin, tense line.

Far off she saw sometimes a solitary horse and rider, or now and then still a covered wagon toiling across the sand, back toward the east, toward Virginia, perhaps!... In Virginia, soon winter would be coming, a jovial, hearty, well-protected winter, with its warmth and companionship of hearth-fires, its well-stored harvests, its still loveliness of woods, where holly trees showed their bright berries against the snow, and the everlasting green of pines and cedars showed abiding life.

In Texas, too, out on the plains, the winter would be coming on ... a winter with no healing snows, no green reminders of the spring ... a winter where lean larders would grow leaner, where a land already lonely would be more desolate, almost as empty of people as the cupboards were bare of food in the deserted ranch shacks along the way ... when coyotes would hide in abandoned dugouts that once had been homes ... when not even a covered wagon would be seen crossing the plains ... when the winds would blow harder than ever against a frail structure ... when the sky would be darkened suddenly and the northers would come!... wild stallions of the plains, swift and terrible, more than living in their might, diabolic in their cunning....

The woman shuddered as she thought of what it would be like to hear again their ghostly neighing in the night.... Wild figures would go sweeping over the prairies, their manes flying, their hoofs striking fire from the sand, their voices freezing one with fear....

And perhaps a cyclone would come, a vast whirlwind that spiraled to the sky, that would leave destruction everywhere it passed.

Oh, if one were buried deep in the grave, would one still shudder and writhe when the wind blew?...

She felt that the wind read her thoughts, knew all the emotions that she concealed even from her own soul. The wind slipped invisibly behind her all the time, could foreknow her actions because it knew her thoughts, even before they came into her mind. Maybe the wind sent them there!... Wirt Roddy had been able to read her mind, and now the wind did, too. Who gave them both that uncanny power? Did each know that the other had it?

She must be doubly careful, since the wind was so wise.... She drove back impulses, chaotic, dimly felt, primitive, out of her consciousness, as she would have frightened away a flock of marauding birds from her flower-garden at home.

The autumn was gone, and still no rain had come. Letty counted the days off on her calendar, each day a cycle of hours that brought winter nearer.

One day Lige said, "I think it'll not be long before we have a norther."

"Why?" Letty asked, cold at the very thought. Perhaps if she refused to think of winter, winter would not come.

Lige was shoveling the sand from the floor, where it had seeped in beneath the window during the night. A broom would mean too slow work. Letty stopped her dish-washing to watch him, as a hand stole to her heart.

"Oh, I dunno. It just sorter feels like a norther. Old timers can generally tell, one way or other, though they can't always know how they tell. If we had any cattle left, we could know by the way they act."

"How?" she asked quickly, and then wished she hadn't. It was pain to hear any mention of cattle now.

"They kinder bunch together with their backs to the north. Animals can tell when hard weather's coming better'n humans can. It's all the protection they got out here on the plains."

"Humans haven't that much protection, have they?" she asked bitterly, almost without realizing what she said.

His shovel clattered to the floor, and he turned sharply on his heel. He spoke no word, but his tight-lipped silence smote her.

That night as she lay awake listening to the wind as it keened around the house, she started nervously. She heard other sounds, curious, coming from a distance above them, it seemed. What could it be?

She shook Lige jerkily. "What are those noises I hear?" she cried, her voice sharp with fear.

"Jes' the wind," he muttered drowsily.

"No! above us—like birds—but there aren't any birds!"

His head lifted to listen for a moment, then dropped back to the pillow.

"Them are wild geese. They're flyin' south. Sign o' cold weather on the way."

"Will it be—soon, Lige?" she asked breathlessly.

"I reckon so. They generally move thataway, some time ahead of the cold snap or the norther," he mumbled.

He turned over and sank back into sleep.

She lay there, her mouth stifled against the pillow, to keep back her sobs, while her slight body shook with sobs. Winter coming so soon ... a norther!... From the north the wind was coming, a terrible stallion, Satanic, with flying mane and hoofs of fire!...

She lay wide-eyed until the dawn came. Then she saw through her eastern window a miracle of colors, when the great ball of fire that was the sun lighted the sky to glowing rose and amber and crimson, when the streaming clouds were like banners of battle flung across the heavens, and the prairie became, not a dead expanse of sand, but a hazy stretch of shimmering, opal colors, gray and gold and mother of pearl. The sky, filled with floating sand, was like cloth of gold, the light irradiating in every direction.

Even her pain-dulled senses quivered to a worship of beauty as she gazed. She felt again, what she had scarcely thought to experience once more, the wounding bliss of perfect beauty.... Who was it that had told her to look at the prairie some morning at sunrise and think of him?...

That day Letty's nerves were on edge because of her sleepless night, tautened by her fear, and tensed, although she did not realize it, by her electric prescience of the approach of the norther. She could not have analyzed her sensations, but she only felt that she might "fly into little bits" at any moment.

Toward noon there was a strange stillness in the air. The wind had lulled, and since there was no living creature near the house now, except Lige's horse, to make any sound, the silence of the plains was oppressive, appalling. Letty felt as if the whole world were holding its breath to hear what she should say, should think.

For she had something she must try to say to Lige. It would be hard, but she couldn't keep it back any longer. He sat in sombre silence by the window and looked out across the prairie where his cattle had once grazed, his far-off gaze fixed on infinity, filled with inscrutable things.

When she opened her mouth to speak to him, her tongue quivered impotently. She came toward him at last, with a plate in her hand, and a cloth that she was using to dry it. Perhaps if her hands were busy with something, she could find it easier to speak.

"Lige?" she began, and then stopped.

"Yeh?" He lifted heavy-lidded eyes.

"Lige—*couldn't* we go away from here?"

His face hardened. "Where to?"

"Oh, I don't know! Anywhere in the world, just away from here!" Her hands shook but her mouth set firmly.

"This is the only house we got. We can live here for less 'n we can anywheres else, till things get right again."

She took a step nearer in her eagerness. "But why couldn't we go to some town till spring, Lige? Other folks do it."

"We got no money to pay rent. No money to move our sticks o' furniture with, nor to buy any more. Towns round here are chock full o' families that have left their land, an' they got no work for more. I don't want to be a drifter. And where's a cowpuncher to get any work now?"

His tone was harsh, though he was holding himself in hand with effort. She could see that his nerves were ragged, too—perhaps because of the wind—but she could not spare him. Pain and fear made her selfish. In a way, she felt pity for this haggard, unshaven man sitting slumped there in the chair, in his dirty shirt and leather trousers, but she felt still more pity for herself. An instinct of self-preservation drove her on.

"Then, Lige, if you don't want to go, can't you let *me* go somewhere till spring?" she faltered, her heart pounding with fear at her audacity, her whole frame trembling.

He shot an astonished look at her. "Where to?" he grated.

"I don't care. Anywhere in the world, except here on these plains!" she cried with passion.

He shook his head morosely. "I ain't got no money. You know that."

"Couldn't you borrow enough for a ticket for me, Lige?"

He stared at her out of his heavy-lidded, inflamed eyes, as if he saw her for the first time, and then he laughed raucously. "There ain't nobody I know w-ell enough to be on borrowin' terms with that's got any money now to lend. This section's near 'bout ruint all round. Nothing real here now but debts and drought!"

Her voice rose shrilly, tensed with its determination. "Couldn't you sell something, then, Lige, so's you can send me?"

His chair grated on the floor as he sprang up, roused by her ruthless insistence. "What in hell have I got that anybody'd want to buy?"

His scornful gaze swept the room with its poor meagerness, and his own shabby clothes. "I haven't got no cattle left here, not a hide nor hoof, as you well know. You wouldn't 'low a cowpuncher would sell his horse or saddle or gun, would you?"

Her face whitened under his anger, but fear made her stubborn. "I've got to go, Lige, somehow! I'm just bound to go!"

"Why?" he jerked, trying to maintain his calm. His glittering eyes were fixed on her face as if to wrest her secret from her.

"I can't stand to stay here this winter, Lige, I tell you, I just can't stand it!"

"So you can't take the hard licks?" His voice was scornful.

She defended herself eagerly. "It ain't that, Lige, honest! I'm scared of the wind!"

Her hand made wide gestures as of a wind sweeping across the plains.

"Wind? That all? Huh!"

"I don't mind the being poor so much, nor having to work, nor being lonesome. It's the wind. It sort o' gets me, Lige. It near drives me crazy! I can't stand another winter of it now!"

Oh, if only he could see, could understand!

His body gave a nervous jerk, expressive of the restraint he was putting on himself.

"You got to stand it. There ain't no way out of it, as I can see."

His stiff-necked refusal to grant her plea angered her so that she gestured vehemently, and the plate dropped to the floor.

"I won't face it! I won't!" she cried stormily.

Her words dropped into an abyss of silence, as startlingly as the plate had crashed to the floor. Even the wind was hushed.

She saw Lige's tall form towering like a giant's, his face livid, his hands working.

"You think too damned much of what *you* won't stand, and not enough of what I've got to stand!" he cried hoarsely.

She reeled back, as if he had struck her in the face. "What have I done?"

"It's what you haven't done that counts! Instead of standin' by the man you married, when he's havin' such a hard time, you mope an' whine an' want to run away. Quitter!" He spat his words at her.

"What could any woman do in this fix?" she shrilled, aghast at him and at herself.

"What has Cora done, for instance? Look at her! She's boosted Bev an' chirked him up through this hard time, an' kept him alive by her spunk. You think she's got the temper of a hellcat, and so she has. You hate her. But, by God, she's a better woman than you are! She has stuck by her man!"

The veins on his forehead stood out swollen and purple, and his throat moved convulsively.

Then some insane instinct of self-defense, of anger that he should put Cora above her, tore from Letty a sentence she would have given much to recall.

"But she loved him—and I didn't love you!"

She shrank back appalled at the look on his face. If only she could take back her words!

His face grew dark and terrible, like the bleak sky before the norther comes, when the storm is gathering ready to strike.

"You married me—not lovin' me? You lived with me—not lovin' me?"

She huddled against the wall, unable to speak. She couldn't lie to him, however much she longed to take back her words. She nodded her head, mechanically. She couldn't lie to him about a thing like that, even if he killed her.

He struck his forehead once with his open palm.

"*Christ!* What sort of a woman are you?"

Then, without another word, he snatched his hat and coat from their nails against the wall. He jerked his saddle from its corner, and flung open the door.

121

She saw him catch his horse that stood shivering behind the wind-break, saddle him and mount him. Then, without even a backward look toward the house, he dug his spurs into the horse's flanks and lashed him into a run.

13

LETTY STOOD by the window, her gaze straining after the swirl of sand that marked Lige's going, until distance blurred it, then made it invisible. Where i was he going? Not to Bev's, for he was headed in the opposite direction, away from town. No house lay along that direction for ten miles, except the deserted shack where Sourdough had lived since her marriage had driven him from Lige's house. Sourdough had gone back to take his turn at caring for the cattle he and the other men had driven to Devil's River, so Lige could not hope to see him. Hube Henderson had moved. The nearest neighbor was ten miles away.

But perhaps Lige was only riding in a mad frenzy to work off his feelings, and when his horse was run down, maybe he would start back home. Then they could talk things over quietly. He had lost his head for a time, because the wind had stirred him up, too, as well as herself, had worked on his nerves till they were beyond control. That was another wrong the wind had done her!

Maybe Lige had gone to see if he couldn't borrow from somebody enough money for a ticket to Virginia for her.

She would sit by the window, watching for him, till he rode back, and maybe he would come to understand how she felt, and not be so hard on her. Lige had never been hard on her before!

She drew a chair beside the window, and sat there, still as a statue of despair, her shoulders slumped, her hands folded in her lap, her head drooping. Silence as profound as that of the grave enveloped her. Not a living thing was near her to make any noise—not a mouse gnawing in the wall, not a prairie dog that yapped above his mound, no cheerful chicken to crow, no dog to bark. Even the wind was preternaturally still, as if to add its uncanny silence as another terror.

High in the blue a buzzard floated soundlessly.

The woman felt as if she were in a vacuum, a solitude so vast that no voice, no life, no motion, could break the awful spell—in a world from which all living creatures save herself had fled—herself and one buzzard that lingered near the bleached bones of cattle long dead, the rotting carcasses of others ... Or was he waiting for another victim?...

Did an abandoned soul left to perish on some desert island feel more lonely than she? Could a mortal solitary in a world from which pestilence had swept all his companions, feel more companionless? This desolate desert was not a part of God's green earth, where people lived—it was apart from it in time and space, a land accursed, under a spell....

What would happen to her if Lige didn't come back? She hurried away from that thought, as from a rattlesnake. Should she starve to death, or lose her reason because of her loneliness and fear? But no, he would come back, of course! He was too good, too kind of heart to leave her like this....

He had gone off in a rage, because he was a man, and men couldn't understand how a woman's nerves must go to pieces because of the wind and the sand and the lonesomeness. But chiefly the wind!... But when he had time to think it over he would come back. He had felt sorry for her at first, had realized that she was just a weak, inexperienced girl that didn't know how to be a pioneer, that didn't have it in her to be a pioneer. He had called her *Pobrecita*—poor little thing!... Women of the west needed to be big and strong and full of life like Cora.... Then drought and hard work and wind couldn't break them.... If she hadn't been there, Lige would maybe have married some western girl, sturdy and plucky and gay, who could have helped him as he needed her. She had spoiled Lige's chance of happiness as well as her own—but then it was the wind's doing!

His words about Cora scorched in her memory. "She has boosted him and chirked him up through the hard times and kept him alive with her spunk. She is a better woman than you are, for she has stuck by her man!" Yes, Cora had, but *she* hadn't! And now her man was gone away in a passion.

But he'd come back, of course!...

But would he? Her body burned with shame as she heard again his last words to her.

"You married me—not lovin' me? You lived with me—not lovin me? *Christ!* what sort of a woman are you?"

Well, what sort of a woman was she, after all? She hadn't meant to be bad. Was she bad? Life had got her in a corner and had driven her to do things she hadn't wanted to, and that didn't rightly represent her. Life, in the last year, had been like a norther that battered her and scared her almost to death, so she couldn't know what to do. She had just tried to struggle on the best she could, through one hour to the next....

Maybe when Lige came back, she could find words to make him see how she felt, so that he wouldn't despise her. Men couldn't know how weak a woman's nerves were, how frail her body....

Slow hours passed, and still he did not come. Her eyes ached from staring at the yellow desert sand, the cloudless blue of the sky, the bleached bones of Lige's cattle, but still no horse and rider showed far off on the plains.

The sun was settling toward the west, bright gold against the blue. Perhaps Lige had ridden farther than he realized, and it would take him longer to make his way back. Soon, soon she would see him spurring his tired horse across the prairie, to get to her before she was too frightened. He knew how easily she was scared.

Still he did not come. The sun sank toward the level plain, and shot his lambent rays across the heavens, broad bands of rainbow light, more beautiful than words, than even human thoughts, could render.

Sunset would soon be over, and Lige hadn't come home!...

After sunset would come the short, winter dusk, and after that the dark! The thought struck a chill to her soul. The frozen finger of fear traced out her spine. "Night—the dark—alone!"

She sprang up and ran to the other window, as if, by some miracle Lige could be coming from the opposite direction. But the prairie as she looked at it there, was as empty as the other way, with not even a faroff speck that might be a man on a horse.

But in the north a little white cloud lay low on the horizon, a casual, careless little cloud like a fluff of lambswool. As she looked, it grew and darkened. It spread out and up, like a great dark wing across the sky. It was blue-black, in startling contrast to the azure it was covering.

Oh, could it be that rain was coming? Blessed rain to break the drought, and save them all from starving or from going mad? Rain that would end their troubles as by a miracle from God?

"Rain! Rain!" she babbled incoherently, stretching out her hands, cup-fashion, as if to catch the first gracious drops.

Lige could smile again, if it rained. He could be his old cheerful, kindly self, not the haggard, wretched man, with his nerves shattered by suspense and worry. Rain now would put out water in the water holes, would make the grass grow green in the spring, would make next year a time of hope instead of torment.

"Thank God for the rain!"

She flung open the door, as if to rush out to meet the rain, to let its cooling drops fall on her face, her hair, her body.

But an icy chill struck her, and she knew the truth. Not rain, but a norther, was what the cloud meant!

That was why the wind had been so crafty and so still! It was gathering its forces for a norther, to trick her and to break her spirit, when she was here alone!

Almost immediately the wind was upon her with a terrible impact. She shrieked and whirled back to flee into the house to escape it. It should not catch her yet!

She almost fell across the threshold, and slammed the door behind her, though it took all her strength to close it. She felt that a sentient brute force was exerted to oppose her, but desperate fear lent her power and she got it closed.

Then she stood in the middle of the room and struck her clenched hands together. The norther had known that Lige was gone, and it had planned to trap her!

She stood there tense, defiant for a time. When she looked out again, creeping to the window stealthily to see what her enemy was doing, she saw that the sand blew in billowing curtains between her and the sky, vast folds that twisted and writhed in mocking shapes. What monstrous, unseen terrors did those curtains hide?

Suddenly she was aware of the cold of the room. The fire had gone out, and in her absorption in her wretchedness of spirit, she had not been conscious of her physical discomfort. But now the drop in temperature roused her to realization. With shaking fingers she set about rebuilding the fire in the round-bellied stove in the room. No need of one in the kitchen, for the thought of food was enough to choke her. She made repeated efforts before she got the blaze going again, with mesquite roots and cow-chips gathered from the prairie as fuel. She held out her numb fingers toward the warmth.

Outside, the curtains of sand were stretching higher, higher, until they blotted out the last faint blue of the fading sky, and hid the round ball of the sun.

She must have light, for soon the dark would be there!

She quickly filled her lamp with kerosene, cleaned the chimney, trimmed the wick so that the light might shine as clearly as possible. She must be sure of light before the dark fell.

Night was almost on her, and Lige hadn't come home!...

New fears came to harass her. Perhaps his horse had stumbled, his foot in a prairie dog hole, and had thrown his rider. Maybe the horse had broken his leg so that Lige would have to walk all the way home. That would take him longer, of course. But he would surely come!

When darkness stole into the room, she lighted the lamp, turned it up to shine brightly, and set it on the center of the table. She felt afraid of the windows, and started to pull down a shade. How terrible if the norther should peer in and see her!

But her hand stayed in its motion, as a thought arrested her. She ought to leave the window clear, and the light burning brightly so that Lige could see how to come home! In the storm, in the driving sand, it would be hard for him to find his way, and she must leave the light to guide him.

"I've got to make it easy for him to come home!" she muttered aloud.

What if Lige should lose his way? What if he were even now driven helpless over the prairie, unable to know in what direction his home lay—with even his coyote sense of direction lost in this blinding sandstorm?

"But I reckon the horse could find his way home, even in a sandstorm," she answered her fear. She spoke aloud as if the sound of her voice would make the statement more emphatic, and hence more true. Yes, horses knew more about weather than human beings did.

What was it Lige had said? "It's their only protection out here on the plains."

The horse would surely bring his master safe home…. Still, he did not come!…

Fears worried her, as the heel-flies had nagged the helpless cattle incessantly.

If only she could know where he was!…

He had never left her alone at night before. He knew how scared she was, what a coward about the dark and the wind. He knew how the wind almost drove her crazy when it blew like this….

The wind, as if in answer to her thought of it, dashed itself against the frail house that creaked and shivered with the force of it. She could hear the timbers straining, creaking. Would they hold? How could the shack withstand such violence? Only a little house "boxed and stripped" as Lige had said, set up on rocks laid in the top of the ground, just a rock at each corner and one here and there along the side!…

The icy winds came in through the cracks in the floor, through the crevices in the wall, through the crannies under the doors and windows, so that now and then the high flame of the lamp flared a bit in a gust that seemed to come from nowhere and from everywhere at once….

Lige didn't come! Was he coming at all?…

She thought of that other night—how long ago!—when she had been terrified in the storm at night, at Bev's and Cora's house. But then, the children had been with her to companion her even in their sleep, and Lige had come to save her from her terror of the wind…. It was the wind that had driven her to promise to marry him! And now, where was Lige? Would he ever come back to her?…

Wouldn't he come back to save her, even if he despised her? He was so kind—always—until that morning!

"He was a Little crazy, too, with the wind and the drought and worrying over things," she muttered to herself. "Else he wouldn't have left me like he did."

The wind shook the house vehemently, as if to wrench it from its foundations, tear it timber from timber. Letty cried aloud in terror, "Lige! Lige!"

But she had no answer, save that which the wind gave.

Sobbing, she huddled against the wall, her fingers twisted around each other, her face distorted, her shoulders shaking.

"Lige!—if you don't come home—I'll go crazy in this wind!" she wailed.

Only the shouting norther gave reply.

Was he lost in the storm, so that he would freeze, alone on the prairie? If only she might know how to find him, and bring him home, to shelter and warmth!

But what could she do in this storm?

"Nothing! Nothing!" she moaned, as she paced the floor impotently.

She shook with horror at thought of Lige at the mercy of the norther out on the plains—the wind that was so cunning and so strong … like a devil!… the wind that went sweeping over the plain like a demon horse, with his mane flying, Ms hoofs striking fire, ready to trample her to death!

Did she imagine it? Was she going crazy?—or did she hear the thundering hoof-beats of a galloping horse?

She huddled in panic against the table, one hand on her heart. A shrill neigh sounded outside the door!...

She went almost mad with terror for a moment, and then she sprang forward, as hope leaped to life again.

She flung the door wide open. "Lige! Lige!" she cried.

A tall figure swept in out of the blackness, and slammed the door, to shut out the wind that would follow him.

"Lige!" she cried, tears of joy running down her cheeks.

But it was not Lige. As he swept off his broad-brimmed hat she saw that Wirt Roddy stood before her!

14

LETTY REELED BACK, astounded and bewildered.

The shock of seeing Wirt Roddy where she had looked for Lige made her clutch at the table for support.

"You? You?" she stammered, passing one hand before her eyes to clear their vision. If she looked closer surely she would see it was Lige after all.

"Yes, it's me," he said gravely.

Then her fear for her husband's safety sprang up redoubled. "Has anything happened to Lige? Where is he?"

"He won't be home just yet." His level gaze met hers, but noncommittally, revealing nothing of what she wished to know.

She clutched his arm. "You've seen him?"

He nodded.

"But where *is* he?" The words tumbled over each other, and her clutch tightened on his arm.

"He's back at Rube Hitchcock's place." Still his eyes, his words, cheated her of the truth.

She beat her clenched hands together. "But why—why don't he come home?"

He looked at her for a moment as if in doubt whether to tell her the truth or not. At last he spoke, grudgingly.

"He can't. He's drunk."

"But I never saw Lige take a drink! He don't drink!" she gasped, incredulous.

"Sure. That's why he's knocked out now. Went to his head, you see, because he wasn't used to it."

"But didn't he remember about me?" Her voice broke, "Didn't he think of me bein' left here alone?"

"He was laid out like a log when I saw him. He won't do no thinking about anything for a spell, I reckon. He's caved." His tone was devoid of feeling, as if he were trying to keep feeling out of it.

She gave a low sob.

"The fellers said he was tryin' to borrow money for something or other, they didn't know what. Seems he didn't say, only swore he had to have it, but they were cleaned out, too, same as him. When he found he couldn't get the money, he called for the red-eye and turned loose on it."

"Oh—oh—oh!" she moaned, the back of one hand pressed against her mouth.

"No need to worry. He'll be all right after a while. Sleep off his bat, have a hell-ter-split headache for a day, and then he'll be as gamesome as ever. I know, I've been through it."

His words brought no comfort to her.

"So I came to tell you how he was. He'll not be back for a time," he explained casually.

Her eyes of misery looked up into his. "That was—kind of you," she stammered.

"Aren't you going to ask me to have a seat?" he asked as he looked at her expectantly.

Terror fluttered wildly at her heart in an instant, fear of Lige's anger.

"Oh, no—I couldn't! Lige wouldn't like it—him being away, you know!"

"Lige left you by yourself," he countered.

"But he's drunk."

"I thought you were scared of the wind," he gibed.

The panic that leaped into her eyes answered him. "Oh, yes, yes!"

"Then you don't want me to go away and leave you here alone in the storm?"

She shuddered, but her gaze met his firmly. "I got to—on account of Lige, you know."

The wind struck the shack with concentrated fury, as if determined to wreck it, while its shrill clamor filled the air.

"And what about me?" he asked quietly. "I wouldn't think you'd send a dog out into this norther."

"But Lige wouldn't understand! He's mad with me already, and he didn't like you coming to the house the other two times."

Her eyes pleaded with him to sympathize with her situation, to understand her dilemma.

He smiled grimly. "I thought you were so tenderhearted about cattle, and animals, and all. I reckon you haven't stopped to think that the nearest ranch house is ten miles in either direction. My horse is beat out now. I couldn't make it."

She was silent for a moment, her face contorted, her body quivering with the strain of her struggle to decide what she must do. If only Lige were there!

The man's voice went on. "No ranch woman would turn anybody, even a tramp, even a criminal, away in a storm like this with no place to go. It would mean my death sure. Do you want to have any blood on your hands?"

With a shudder, she stared at her hands, expecting to see visible stains there.

The wind shrilled outside, the windows rattled violently, the lamp light flared in the gusts.

The woman gave a despairing gesture of assent.

"You needn't be afraid of me," he said gravely, as he removed his coat and laid it on the table.

His old mocking manner was gone. There was no gleam of laughter in his dark eyes, no flick of irony at his mouth, no satiric shrug of his shoulders, but in their place a seriousness that was restrained and stern. What experience, what emotion, had changed him so?

Letty sank into her chair, relieved in spite of herself, that she was not to be left again to the horror of solitude in the storm.

"The wind nearly drives me crazy," she cried. "It was you that first made me afraid of it!"

His face grew more sober. "Yes, I reckon I've got that on my conscience. And it maybe pesters me more than some other things that might seem worse."

"It was cruel!" she accused him, her blue eyes fixed on his face. "It's made me miserable, ever since I came out here. I never can get the fear of the wind out of my mind, day nor night. You put it on me like a curse! And I had never done anything to harm you!"

"I'm sure sorry," he said tensely. "I'd give a lot to take back those words. I feel like a low-down hound."

"I'm always looking for a cyclone, like you described it. I lie awake at night thinking it's coming toward me—a big whirlwind that reaches to the sky."

"But they don't come so often, even in this section," he said with attempt at cheerfulness.

"One would be enough."

"Chances are it won't ever come your way," he said soothingly, as to a child. "You were such a pretty little trick, and so bashful, I couldn't help teasing you. I ought to be hung for it."

She shook her head, and spoke with concentrated bitterness. "It wasn't only just teasing! Everything you said about the wind has come true to me, except the cyclone. It has ruined my looks, my nerves, and my disposition. It's trying to break me, and it will get me yet!"

He gazed at her for a moment in silence, and then spoke, more to himself than to her. "Your hair is not so yellow and wavy as it used to be; your skin's not so white and soft; your cheeks aren't pink any more; and your eyes aren't so blue as they used to be."

"It's the wind has ruined me!" she cried harshly, accusing destiny, the fates, as well as him. "The wind and the sand and the lonesomeness—but mostly the wind!"

"It's damned hard on the women out here," he muttered, twisting his mustache nervously. "I've thought of you a thousand times when you were up against it at first."

"But you never came to see me,—you didn't show me a way out of it!" she cried passionately.

He put his hands together between his knees and gave her a long, long, thoughtful look.

"No, I didn't come to see you, nor show you a way out. That's one thing the angel with the big book will have writ down to my credit at the last day, even if there isn't much else to keep it company. I wanted to come—and I kept away."

"Why?—why?" she flung at him.

He faced her steadily, his look of evasion gone, as well as his mockery. "I thought it all over, and wrestled it out. I was more than half in love with you—and I figured that there wasn't nothing a galoot like me had to offer a little girl like you. Even if I was to have asked you to marry me—and I wasn't a marrying man—I wasn't fit for you."

"Oh!" she cried, struggling to comprehend, to piece the facts together in her mind so that she could know the truth. He was not lying to her now, she knew, nor was he evading. The moment had come when he spoke frankly.

He went on. "And so I knew I better keep away. Girls had trusted me before, and come to regret it—to wish they hadn't. I didn't want it to be thataway with you."

She was trying to take it all in.

"But you did come, twice!" she challenged him—"when it was too late to give me any advice!"

He nodded. "Yes. When a feller's got a maggot in his brain, keeping away don't always help. I came to think that if I'd see you again I'd maybe find you weren't so pretty nor so sweet as I remembered you. And then it'd be easy for me to steer the other way. But I reckon I was just fooling myself—that was just an excuse I gave myself for coming to see you."

"But you said I *wasn't* so pretty, when you saw me!" Her words struggled forth, trying to find some flaw in his logic. "You said my hair wasn't yellow, nor my eyes so blue, nor my skin so white."

"No, that's true—the wind had hurt 'em—but that didn't make any difference." He spoke with savage constraint. "Beauty lies deeper'n complexion. The real *you* hadn't been touched."

"But you—kept away!"

"Yes—it wasn't easy, by God!—but I did. I knew I had to."

"Yes,—you had to," she whispered.

"So you see that's how it was with me," he brought out, as if speech were difficult.

She made no answer, for words would not piece themselves together in her brain—her very thoughts were inchoate, striving against each other, refusing to come clear.

His somber eyes gazed at her intently. "Life has been pretty damned hard for you, hasn't it, little woman?"

His tone of sympathy released her pent-up emotion, and she smote her palms together.

"Oh, it has been torment!"

"*Pobrecita!*"

The word recalled the other who had used the pitying endearment to her.

"Oh, it wasn't Lige's fault! He's good. It's this country, this terrible country where it never rains, and no green things grow, and no birds sing!"

"Some years there are birds," he protested with a trace of his old humor.

She gave a rasping laugh. "There are none here now, except buzzards waiting for their prey!"

He smiled grimly. "They're well-enough fed now."

"Yes, they're the only things in this God-forgotten land that isn't starved or starving! Nothing here but wind and sand, wind and sand, till it's enough to drive me crazy!"

She made a wild, rending gesture with her hands.

He watched her in silence for a moment, twisting his mustache, a frown of uncertainty on his forehead, his eyes restless.

"You need to get away for a while, for a change," he said.

"I'll go mad if I don't—but I can't!" she cried, bitter remembrance surging back into her mind. "That's what was the trouble with Lige today. I hounded him to get money from somewhere to send me back to Virginia to stay till spring."

"You ought to go."

"Yes, if I could rest and get my breath from the wind, I could be myself again. Oh, I know I'm not myself now! I feel like I'll jump out of my skin if I have to stay here through another winter and face these devil winds!"

He drew a long breath, and then spoke rapidly, as if his mind were made up and he must not let himself think again.

"Come away with me, and you shan't need to face them again, ever!"

She shrank back aghast. "Oh, no, no! How could I?"

He leaned toward her eagerly, his hands outstretched, his words coming with swift passion.

"You need to get away. You've got to think of yourself now. If you stay here—it's like you say—you'll die or go loco. And what good would that do Lige, or anybody?"

She felt the falseness of his logic, but was unable to argue convincingly, as he did, she could only protest, "Oh, no! I couldn't treat him like that. He's been—kind to me, and he's had so much to bear lately."

"He'd soon get over it. Men do." The old light of mockery was in his eyes.

"Not Lige! And anyway, it would be wrong." Her eyes widened in horror as she realized what he was asking.

"It's wrong to commit suicide, isn't it?" he demanded.

"Yes, that's a sin."

131

"Then to stay on here when you know yourself it's more than you can stand is committing suicide, isn't it?"

He leaned nearer and laid his burning hand on her wrist.

She shivered and shrank away, but she could not marshal her words to refute his argument.

The wind smote the house with redoubled fury, the timbers creaked and strained as if making a violent effort to hold together, and she could feel the structure rock and sway, with threats of leaving its foundations.

She turned to him with sudden desperate appeal. "Why can't you lend us the money for a ticket for Virginia, so I can go home?"

"Not on your life!" He shook his head vehemently. "That would mean me nor Lige either would ever see you again. I won't work it like that."

She gave a little choking sob. "Oh, I'd go down on my knees to beg anybody for a ticket home!"

"I'll give you anything but that. Anything but that, I swear it! But I won't put the country between you and me."

"You said you didn't want me to be like those others—that trusted you, and were sorry!" she half whispered, her eyes on his as in a trance.

He drew one hand across his forehead. "I don't know what I want—except that I want you!"

His passionate words seemed to echo and re-echo through the room, their sound lingering in her ears above the clamor of the storm.

"No—no!"

"Listen!" His voice was tense and stern, almost savage in its vehemence. "We can leave as soon as daylight comes and can make for the railroad. We can be a long ways off from here before Lige gets over his drunk. And then he can't stop us."

"No, no!" Her words were an incoherent cry, unreasoning, instinctive.

"But Lige can't do no more for you now, the way he's fixed. And I've got money. I'm big rich, I tell you, and I'll give you anything you want, take you anywhere you want to go."

"What sort of a woman would I be?" she cried, as memory crashed in upon her once more.

He drew back, and then he shook himself as in a dream. "Make it any way you like. You can get a divorce and we'll get married, if you say so. I want you, and I've got to have you! Don't matter how!"

Blood beat in her head, making it hard for her to think, but her thoughts struggled as through an enveloping darkness and constriction, through resisting forces.

"That would be as wicked as the other way!"

"In the name of hell, how?" Sincere amazement was in his face, his voice.

She made a gesture of contempt. "To treat Lige like that when he's trusted me? It's not his fault that he's down now. The drought and the wind have been more than he could stand, and they've nearly driven him crazy, same as me."

He caught her hand in a tense grip that hurt her. "Listen to me, Letty! You don't love him, and you never did. And I'm willing to bet anything, all I've got, that you do love me!" His tone was triumphant, his eyes exulted over her.

She wrenched her hand away and faced him in defiance. "You've got no right to say such a thing!"

"You won't deny it!" he taunted. His eyes deliberately tried now to assert their old mastery over her emotions, his very hand seemed menacing, his lips curled in a smile.

An icy terror ran along her spine, a frozen fire in her veins. She turned to flee. Better to run away out on the prairie than to stay here. Better the madness of the storm and the dark than this!

What was that roaring in her ears? Was it merely the sound of the wind outside? Wild, clamorous wailing like a troop of souls from hell!

She could vision the norther racing toward her across the prairies, a wild stallion breathing death, his hoofs of fire ready to trample her down to destruction.

Fear had her by the throat, as she paused, her hand clutching the door knob.

A shrill, prolonged neighing came from outside the door.

"Was that your horse?" she jerked.

He laughed at her panic. "*Quien sabe*?' Who knows?"

A swirl of wind swept into the room from the cracks in the floor, from the slits in the walls, from the crevices under the windows. The flame in the kerosene lamp flared up brightly for an instant, flickered, went out.

Her terror was so extreme that every muscle, every nerve, was tense as with violent action. Her fear, her wild anger against the wind, against this man, tautened her body in a strain like that of mortal physical struggle. Her breath came fast and faster, her heart beat suffocatingly, her skin was drenched with icy perspiration, her whole form shuddered as she felt the enveloping horror of darkness added to her terror of the wind and of this man.

"Who blew that lamp out?" she shrilled.

"I don't know," he answered, coming closer to her in the darkness,

"You did!—you know you did!" Fear was throttling her.

"I swear I didn't." he said, as his hand caught hers.

"Who was it then?" she chattered.

"It was the wind."

"*The wind!*"

Just at that moment a violent blast shook the house, as if to tear it in pieces and send the splinters over the wide plain. The door crashed open, and a roaring blast rushed into the room.

Half swooning with terror of the invisible, the unearthly, Letty flung herself into Wirt Roddy's arms, and clung round his neck as a drowning person would.

"The wind! The wind! Don't let the wind get me!"

"I won't!" he said hoarsely, as his arms closed round her.

15

THE FIRST FAINT GLIMMERINGS of dawn found Letty sitting huddled by the eastern window, wrapped in an old blanket, waiting for the day. She had sat there most of the night. Light-headed for want of sleep—she had not slept for two nights now—she was trying to think.

The wind that had wailed at her all night like a demon lover, had lulled now—was it by a freakish turn that a norther may take, or was it by a miracle?—and so her mind was not battered and bruised now by its noise, by its rushings at the house to overturn it. It had quieted down so that she could think. It would be at her again in a little while, but in the brief interval of stillness she must think things through.

But thought was hard!…

She tried to piece together the happenings of the past few hours. What had she done? What had she done?…

Dull, leaden misery weighed her down.…

One act of delirium that must wreck her whole life! A few mad moments out of a lifetime —that must yet ruin the whole!… There was no justice anywhere!…

She hadn't been responsible, when you looked at it right. She hadn't been herself. It was the wind, the wind that was to blame! Nobody ought to hold a crazy person responsible for what he did, and the wind had made her crazy. She could see things clearly now, because it wasn't blowing. She must think fast, before it started up again, because the wind did things to her brain that wouldn't let her think.…

The east began to glimmer with the dawn.

Only one dawn ago she had thought herself as wretched as life could possibly make her. But how fortunate she had been then, compared with now! Then Lige had been with her, good, kind, faithful Lige!…

Where was Lige now?… She pictured him lying "laid out like a log," dead drunk, because of her unreasonable complaints and pleas. Poor Lige!…

Her heart surged with rage as she thought of that other man lying there in the room, sodden with sleep. What of the moment when he would wake and she should have to face him? Oh, worse than murderer that he was!—why didn't God strike him dead?…

Perhaps He had struck him in his sleep!…

She turned toward the bed where he lay, a long mound under the heaped-up covers, and listened intently … Yes, he was breathing. He could sleep! He would rise to meet the new day with none of the anguish that was hers.…

But what of her—tomorrow and tomorrow and tomorrow?…

Soon Lige would be coming home. Home! She gave a rasping laugh as the incongruity of the word struck her.

He would come back, she knew. Sober and remorseful, he would think of her. He would almost kill his horse riding back to relieve her terrors, to tell her he was sorry for the way he had acted. He would be gentle, now that his frenzy of shock and anger was over, kind as he had always been.… So kind … dear Lige!…

A flood of warm tenderness for him rose within her. For the first time since her marriage she began to appreciate her husband. She had longed for romance, she told herself—but what lover of romance had been more tender, more considerate than Lige? She had dreamed of a cavalier with plumes and sword, a gallant figure—but what knight of legend or of history had battled more bravely against heavy odds, had been more truly chivalrous than Lige had? And always, so just, so generous!...

She looked back on what she had held as grievances against him. She had blamed him for her sufferings—but what had he done but take her from an unbearable situation, make her his wife, give her a home?... Just a poor shack, but the best he could afford....

But she hadn't made any sort of home for him! She had been selfish, wrapped in her own wrongs, cold, cold, hard to him!...

She gave a low sob as she thought how much happier she might have made his life if she had been brave and loving. And he had never once complained, until yesterday when she had driven him mad. She could see now how he must have been tortured in soul all along, where she was too selfish to care....

She saw his chiseled, haggard face, his burning eyes, his tall frame shrunken and stooped from his worry and privation, but bearing his load without outcry or complaint. Poor Lige—he'd had so much to bear, and she hadn't helped him at all. She had only loaded him with more....

Tears ran down her cheeks, and her heart softened incredibly as the realization of the truth came to her. She loved him, Lige, her husband! Now, at last, she saw him for the man he was, and loved him as he deserved!... She clasped the thought to her soul, as a mother clasps a little newborn baby, so novel, so strange, so precious beyond words!...

How glad he would be when he came home, and she put her arms about his neck and told him that she loved him. She would kiss him. She never had before—she had always merely suffered his kisses. But now she would make it up to him ... now that the wind wasn't blowing, and she had a chance to think, she could see the truth.... The wind and the sand had hidden the truth from her before....

Then, like a sword of ice and fire, remembrance pierced her!...

She was no longer worthy to be called his wife! What sort of woman was she, in very truth?...

Her body writhed....

How could she tell Lige anything now? How could she tell him the truth? Yet how could she lie to him?...

She saw his honest eyes searching hers.... She couldn't lie to him!...

Now, when for the first time she knew what it was to love him, she must slay his love for her!...

If only she could somehow make him understand that it was the wind, and not she herself, that was responsible! But, no!—he couldn't see that. And even if he did, that would not heal his hurt, his shame. The more he loved her, the more his shame would be, now ... Infinite compassion for Lige's suffering swept over her, so that for a moment she forgot her own. If only she could bear it all herself and spare Lige! He had had so much to stand for her....

What would he do when he knew the truth?...

She started up in panic? Would he kill her? Western men, she knew, had stern codes for the morality of their women. But if he killed her, that would be best—then she'd be out of it all....

But if he shot Wirt Roddy, or were shot by him? Her imagination lifted a curtain for her, and she seemed to see a fight to the death between those two—those two men, big and tall and fearless. She glanced to the wall, where the guns hung. Maybe she'd better hide them before Lige came home, or Wirt Roddy woke up. But no—she mustn't do that, for Wirt Roddy had his gun, and it would be murder to take Lige's away from him....

Her clairvoyant visioning showed her a scene where one man lay dead, with a bullet through his heart. But which one was it? She strained to see, but could not discern the features, for the wind seemed to blow a veil of sand over the face....

She saw, in fancy, another man, the murderer, led away by the sheriff, the sheriff who always got his man!... If he turned to flee, in an effort to escape, the sheriff would spit quickly and then shoot!...

The dawn glimmered more brightly in the empty sky. Soon sunrise would come.

"Will you sometimes watch a sunrise on the plains and think of me?"

Could she ever see a sunrise again, anywhere on God's earth, without her mind being soiled and tortured by the remembrance of him? Oh, if only the sun need never rise at all any more!

Day would soon be here. What would it bring?...

She must make a fire so that Lige would be warm when he came home.

She emptied the stove of its dead ashes of last night, and clumsily built a fire. She was not used to doing that, for Lige always did it for her. Would he ever do it for her again?

At last when the flame cracked and leaped, and the round-bellied stove began to glow, she turned about.

The man had risen and was sitting in the chair by the window, staring fixedly at her.

His black hair was rumpled, his face was swollen with the heaviness of his sleep. Self-loathing looked at her out of his bloodshot eyes.

Cold hatred possessed her for a moment, so that she had a mad, blinding vision of how one could commit murder—and then she felt sick, in body as well as in spirit. Her heart beat to suffocation, her limbs trembled violently. They stared at each other like two guilty souls meeting in hell ...

Silence like crossed swords clashed between them. Letty felt that she could lift the weight of the world more easily than she could speak a word to this man.

At last he spoke, with sardonic attempt at jauntiness, as if he thought by ignoring the situation he could wave it away by a word. "Good morning."

She drew a long shuddering breath, but said nothing.

The room was growing lighter now, as dawn progressed. The furniture cast grotesque shadows on the floor, and the round stove made a circle of light as well as of heat in the room, while it crackled cheerfully, disregardful of the situation as the man.

He made another attempt at conversation. "We better have a little snack and make our getaway before long."

Oh, the callous, unfeeling heart of him!

This stung her to speech. "And you can think that I am going away with you?"

Genuine surprise widened his eyes. "Sure! Why not?"

She turned on him with a look of loathing, but she spoke no word in answer.

"What else can you do—now?" he demanded.

She flung her head back. "I'd make my bed with the coyotes and the rattlesnakes before I'd go away with you!"

"So?" He nodded slightly, in meditative way, as he tried to puzzle out her feelings.

She could not endure the look in those dark, bloodshot eyes, so she turned to the window and gazed out. Outside the light was clear enough now to show the freakish effects of the storm. Sand lay in billows, wind-waved, along the plains. Some spaces were swept bare as a floor, while in others were long, irregular mounds, where there had been some slight obstruction to catch the sand and form a nucleus for a drift.

The wind-break, built to form a slight shelter for Lige's cattle—when he had any cattle!—had caught the full force of the drive, and there sand lay piled against it in a deep drift, like snow in a northern gale.

She turned round again, to hear what the man was saying to her.

"But I'd think to go away with me would be the best way out. No?"

"No!"

He chose his words cautiously, as a man picks his steps when he is walking in a bed of prickly pear.

"You mean—you hold it against me—on account of last night? You mean you can't forgive me?"

Her tortured eyes met his. "Can you ever forgive yourself?"

His shoulders heaved, and he spoke harshly, with a harshness that might have been against himself, not her. "No—but I'll make it up to you!"

"How could you—ever?"

"Well," he thrust at her in self-defense, while the look of self-loathing in his eyes belied his words. "You can't throw the whole blame on me. Weren't you—willing?"

She shuddered, and beat her clenched hands together impotently. "I wasn't! God in heaven knows I wasn't! It wasn't me—it was the wind that drove me crazy!"

"You'll not be likely to make your husband see it that way, eh?" he jeered.

Her shoulders sagged, her whole defiant pride seemed to collapse. "No, I know that," she said with dull misery.

"It ain't safe to leave you here," he argued. "No telling what he may take it in his head to do, when he finds out the facts."

"I know that," she said.

"And he'll sure find out."

"Oh, yes—I'll tell him."

Memory flashed her a picture of Sourdough polishing his gun, as he sang softly, after Wirt Roddy's last visit to the ranch,

> "If you come monkeyin' with my Lula gal,
>   I tell you what I'll do!
> I'll shoot you up with my forty-four,
>   And carve you through and through!"

Why, Sourdough himself would follow the man down and shoot him as he would a rattlesnake, would grind him under his heel as he would a vinegarone—a whip-tailed scorpion! What train of tragedies had she not started? But not she—the wind, the devil wind that could take so many forms to torment and to madden her!

Wirt Roddy tried another tack. "When we get to Fort Worth, if you want it that way, I'll buy you a ticket to Virginia and start you home."

Wild hope leaped up in her eyes for an instant, and then despair came again.

137

"I couldn't go back home to Virginia *now*!"

He smiled sardonically. "So you figure out that I've queered the whole world for you—eh?"

"Yes!" came in a broken cry.

He gnawed at his mustache in silence, a deep frown denting his forehead.

At last he rose leisurely, stretched his tall frame and stood looking down at her for a moment, as if measuring forces with her, as if asking himself could it be possible that the will of that slight creature could hold against his own.

She looked at him, speechless. How tall he was!

He had reached his decision, made up his mind, and now announced his plan casually.

"I'm not going to leave you here. Your baby face would spill the truth to your husband, and he'd take a shotgun to us both."

"He ought to!"

He smiled indulgently, as at a foolish child, "Well, I'd rather not kill him unless I'm obliged to. And I don't care to stop breathing myself, just yet. So the only way out is to pack up and vamoose before he comes. So get ready."

She only looked her contempt at him. And this was the man that had haunted her dreams for almost a year! Had he been like this all along, and she too ignorant, too blind, to see? Or had he crumbled to pieces over night?

The veins of his temple swelled and throbbed, as he stared at her. "So you think you're not coming?" he said with a derisive laugh.

"I'm not coming," she answered inflexibly.

A dark flush mottled his face, making it almost purple, and his hands clenched.

"You are coming, I tell you! If I have to throw you over my saddle like a sack of meal!"

"Then you'd have a sack of meal that way, but you wouldn't have me!" Her scorn was like the lash of a whip across his livid face.

He strode forward and seized her wrist like a vise. "You're coming, by God! I'll show you!"

Mad terror of him clutched her again, such terror as she had known last night, before despair had come. She wrenched from his grasp, and without thinking what she did, she snatched a gun from the wall.

He gave a jeering laugh. "Oh, so you think you'll shoot me, eh?"

"Yes, I will!"

Her hands trembled so that she thought the rifle would surely clatter to the floor. She had never held a gun in her hands before.

"I know you!" he scoffed. "You wouldn't hurt a horned toad, and you couldn't if you wanted to."

He advanced closer. "Stop your damned foolishness and get ready to come on with me. I'm not going to have a double killing here because you've got no brains. And I'm not going to leave you here by yourself to be shot."

He spoke between clenched teeth, his eyes savage.

Palsied by terror, she reeled backward to escape him. In an instant, his hand seized her arm to take away the rifle. Scarcely knowing what she did, she blindly pulled the trigger. A sharp crack followed, and a puff of smoke.

His hand released her to clutch at his breast. A look of astonishment came over his face.

He grasped the edge of the table for support a moment, and then lurched heavily to the floor, his fall jarring the flimsy house and making the dishes bounce and rattle on the kitchen table.

Her astonishment was as complete as his own. She stared at him, while the gun clattered to the floor—and she saw, for the first time, that it was the target rifle he had brought her for a present, and which she had never touched before.

Letty stared in a daze at the man lying there, her first impression being that he was so tall! It did not seem possible that she had shot him, but she must have. Was he badly hurt?

She bent over him to listen to his breathing. It was fainter and fainter with each gasp, and each exhalation brought a trickle of blood from his breast.

His dark eyes still stared up at her unbelievingly, till, in a few moments, they were covered by a light film.

One hand twitched, then was still.

The eyelids gradually closed, all except for a narrow slit through which the dark eyes seemed to stare at her, incredulous, accusing.

She touched his wrist, and found no pulse there.

She laid her hand over his heart—to feel no slightest flutter of motion.

But of course it would begin again! It couldn't be possible that he was dead! One couldn't be alive one minute, so full of life, and then dead right after. Life didn't work that way. He was only asleep, as he had been through the night. He would wake soon. He would wake and be very angry that she had shot him.

But he must get up soon, before Lige came. Lige wouldn't like to find him here like this ...

She crouched on the floor beside him, waiting for him to rouse.

The lids would lift slowly, the mustache would twitch, a canny smile would come over the lips, and the man would be all awake in an instant. That is the way it would come.

But he lay inert.

She put a hand on his forehead, and found it chill. But her hand was cold, too, so that didn't mean anything....

Then she began to realize, slowly, so that her reason might not topple. The man was dead! She had killed him! She—who had never hurt any living thing before—who could not have harmed a mouse caught in a trap!

She gave a low scream, and then she clapped her hand over her mouth. She mustn't lose control of herself, lest she go to pieces. She must keep her head, so she could think what to do.

Soon Lige would come riding over the prairies—and what could she say to him?

Soon the sheriff would come and put handcuffs on her, to lead her away to prison.... It wouldn't be any use to try to run, for the sheriff always got his man....

But if only she could hide the body somewhere, then the sheriff wouldn't know about it. No one would know, for who would come to look for the man here? They wouldn't know he was dead, and they'd think he had gone back to Fort Worth. If they asked her, she would *tell* them he had gone back to Fort Worth.

That was the idea—she must hide the body!...

But where?

She looked wildly round the shack, to find no hint of aid.

She thought of the old negro folk-song that Mammy used to sing;

> "I run to de rock for to hide my face,
>> The rock cried out, 'No hiding-place,
>>> No hiding-place here!'"

The lines beat in her brain.

She sprang up to flee. She would run away before the sheriff started after her. She couldn't stay here in this room, anyhow, with the murdered man lying there, accusing her with his quiet face, his still hands.

But where could she escape to?

She looked out through the window to the prairies freaked with their goblin patterns of sand, in windrows and hollows and little mounds. One couldn't hide there, where there were no trees, no clumps of bushes, no fence corners, to conceal one. Anyone could see so clearly here for such incredible distances that the sheriff would find her so easily!

Then her eyes lighted on the wind-break almost at the house, where the sand had piled in a huge drift. Lige's words flashed into her mind:

"You could bury a steer there, if so be you had a steer left to bury."

Why, that was the solution! Why hadn't she thought of it before? She would bury the dead man there in the deep sand, and then nobody need know what had happened ... not the sheriff ... not even Lige. And then Lige needn't be hurt by knowing the truth.

But she must manage it fast, for Lige might come riding over the plains any time now.

She flung open the door, and measured the distance with her eyes. Just a little way—surely she could drag the body that far—"like a sack of meal!"

She clutched the dead man by the armpits and began to drag him toward the door. He was heavy, and the task was hard. Could she make it? Terror gave her supernormal strength, and she struggled on.

Farther, a little farther at a time!... She panted and heaved and cold sweat ran down her body, but she would not give up.

Lige and the sheriff might be coming any time now!

With prodigious effort, she got him out through the doorway, and slowly, slowly, inch by inch, she dragged him to the wind-break. His body made a long path in the sand, as if a huge serpent had drawn its length across it.

She fell face forward on the sand to rest and get her breath for a moment, but fear soon goaded her up. She must finish before Lige came, so that he needn't ever know!

She ran to get the kitchen shovel to use as a spade.

She tried to dig out a grave in the sand, but the treacherous stuff mocked her efforts, sliding back almost as fast as she shoveled it away.

She had always known that the sand hated her, just like the wind did! The sand was the tool of the wind!—its weapon with which it tried to break her!

But she would outwit it—she must!

At last, with frantic efforts, she had a place made.

She dropped the shovel for terror, for a song came to her ears—from what time or space —from what other world than this?

> "Oh, bury me not on the lone prai-*rie*,
> Where the wild coyotes will howl over me,
> In a narrow grave, just six by three.
> Oh, bury me not on the lone prai-*rie*."

140

No, no, she told herself wildly,—it was not the corpse singing!

"But they buried him there on the lone prai-*rie*,
Where the buzzards wait and the winds blow free,
In a narrow grave just six by three.
They buried him there on the lone prai-*rie!*"

She must hurry, hurry and get the body buried, lest the corpse begin to sing!

She dragged the body into its place, and composed it decently, with her shaking hands. She crossed the hands over the breast—for a corpse must always have it so!

She pressed the eyelids down over the slit in the eyes. The sand mustn't get into those dead eyes ...

He was so tall!...

Then she began to cover him over with the sand, that slipped through her fingers, that slid off from the shovel, with devilish trickiness. But she outwitted it, she kept on until she had it heaped in place.

There, the sand was in a long, smooth mound now—she had made it so that it looked like the work of the wind.

Well, wasn't it the work of the wind?

At last she was satisfied, and rose to go. She gave a final glance at her achievement. The mound was high, and fairly smooth, and it covered the body so that nothing was visible. Who looking at it would suspect that a murdered man lay buried there?

Lige wouldn't guess—nor even the sheriff.

Everything was all right.

She turned to face the east. The sun had half risen above the horizon and shone like a golden wheel whose spokes shot outward and upward, glancing, glittering. Opal, rainbow lights lit the sky where clouds were softly piled, rose and amber and purple. The prairie was a vast expanse of soft gray, with golden light suffused over it, the sand giving back the glory of the heavens.

Transfixed, she watched the sun rise, across the mound, and thought of the man who lay at her feet.

Soon the intense cold recalled her to herself, and drove her into the house. She must get in and keep the fire going, because Lige would be so cold when he came in—almost frozen from his long ride. He would come as fast as he could, once he was sober and able to think again. He'd probably borrow a fresh horse from one of the boys, because his was almost foundered.

She could vision him riding across the prairie, outlined against the morning sky, spurring his horse so that he might get to her quickly, to keep her from being scared. *To keep her from being scared!*

How could she meet him when he came?

He would put his arms around her and tell her he knew how the wind had deviled her out of her senses, and he didn't hold it against her. He would call her *Pobrecita!* ...

But no!—that word was soiled now, because the other man had used it.... Was there anything in her life that could ever be clean again—or had Wirt Roddy soiled everything?...

She made up the fire again and warmed her half-frozen body before it.

She must start breakfast before Lige came, because he'd be hungry as well as cold. And anyway, when your hands were busy you didn't have to think. You could forget for a moment, maybe … Could she ever forget till the grave closed her in?

Even when she was buried deep in her grave, would she see dead eyes staring at her from half-shut lids?—hear the wind wail to her like a demon lover?…

She glanced out of the window at the long mound of sand by the wind-break. It was just as she had left it.

She would sit by the fire a little while before she began her morning's work. Strange how tired it made you not to sleep for two nights! It made your head ring queerly, too, as if the wind were blowing inside it. It made it fidgety, as if sand were seeping into your brain.

But the wind was quiet now. What was it they said out here in Texas?—"Never mind the weather so the wind don't blow!"

The wind had never been so still before. Had it blown so hard during the night that it had blown itself all off the earth for good and all—lost itself somewhere between the other worlds? Were there other women there for it to torture and drive mad? It wouldn't be happy if there weren't.

But if it had gone away for good she could be herself again.

But no!—the windows rattled, ever so slightly, as if by some faint gust. It was like the wind to fool her. It was chuckling to itself now, somewhere in hiding, to think how it had fooled her.

Well, after all, it was more natural to hear a *little* wind blowing. Nothing to be scared about in the least.

She glanced out of the window to see if she could tell whether the wind was from the north or not. Surely there wouldn't be another norther again so soon!

No, it wasn't a norther coming again—for the wind was blowing more from the east. She could tell by the little puffs of sand that were drifting toward the west.

She gave a sigh of immense relief. No norther again now!

Then she started, apprehensively. A light veil of sand was lifting from above the mound against the wind-break.

But it was only a little wind, and there was nothing to be afraid of … nothing at all.…

Besides, hadn't the wind done its worst to her already?

Could anything but the wind have made her commit murder?

There Wirt Roddy was lying under that mound of sand (a mound not quite so high and rounded as it had been a little while before!) because he had put the fear of the wind in her soul, that day long ago on the train. The wind had been listening, and had punished him for his blasphemy. Those scornful lips, those mocking eyes, would never jeer at her again—at her or at the wind!

If those eyelids lifted there in the darkness, the shroud of sand would cover them.…

The wind was growing higher now, and rattled the windows louder. She shivered as she listened. The wind made her remember—everything!

Her mind went on searching out the line by which events had happened. It was all so clear now. It was the work of the diabolic wind.

She was lost and undone because the wind had driven Wirt Roddy to the house last night. He had come because he had known Lige wasn't there.…

Lige wasn't there, because he had been in a rage with her, that made him get drunk, so he couldn't be with her when she needed him. She had tormented him with her appeals, because the wind had driven her crazy. But she wouldn't have been so easily upset all along, if it hadn't been that Wirt Roddy had put the fear of the wind on her like a curse before ever she met Lige or came to the ranch.

It was all so plain!

She looked out of the window and stared with fright at the mound. Surely she wasn't seeing right. That spot there, that white spot *couldn't* be Wirt Roddy's crossed hands showing!

Another puff of wind lifted another veil of sand, as if to convince her.

Yes, yes!

What could she do? Should she go out and cover the dead hands up again?

But no!—for then the wind would get at her again! Perhaps it hadn't done its worst to her after all. Maybe it was tempting her to come out, so that it might have her in its power. But she wouldn't go!...

If she waited, another gust of wind would blow the sand back over the hands and cover the mounded form more securely.

Those hands couldn't move anyhow. They were dead—just as she had left them. They couldn't hurt her, but the wind was different. Nobody could kill the wind!...

She stood by the window, her face pressed against the pane, her hands clenched, her eyes fixed on that mound.

Slowly, grain by grain, the sand was shifting from the treacherous mound. The wind had come from the east, so that the wind-break couldn't shelter the sand any more....

Soon the face was uncovered, the face so quiet and stern!

She gazed at it, stiff with horror. The eyelids were weighted down with sand, the sand was in the black mustache, but the face showed plainly—the dead face!...

She started. She must run out and cover up that face again from the gaze of the sun, from her own sight!

But no!—the wind's gaze was more to be feared than a dead man's face. This was but the trick of the wind to get her out from her shelter, so that it might wreak its wrath on her, might have her utterly at its mercy.

When the wind saw that it was useless to try her, that she would not come out, it would grow tired and go away, and the sand would creep back over the dead face....

The wind saw her there at the window, watching, and that reminded it of her. She would move away, and then it would forget her. That was the thing to do....

The wind was angry that she had read its thoughts so clearly, for it had risen to a gale now, and shouted round the house. It called to her to come out if she dared. It defied her, challenged her, mocked her.

But she smiled, because she was sitting in a corner with her face turned away from the window. She wouldn't let the crafty wind see her at all, and it would think she had gone away—that the house was empty. It would think that she had gone with Lige, or even that she had left for Fort Worth with Wirt Roddy.

She would be very quiet, and wouldn't talk back to it at all. She wouldn't even *think*, for the wind knew what your thoughts were. So she rinsed her mind of all thoughts, all emotions, and made it blank and empty as the desert plain.

The wind roared at her, but she didn't answer.

She sat there in her corner and smiled craftily to think how she was fooling the wind that thought itself so wise!

Still, she couldn't keep her mind entirely blank. A little thought worried her like a heel-fly. Why didn't Lige come home?

When would he be coming home?...

After a while she had to listen to the clamor of the wind, because it was so loud. She thought of Lige as he might be riding home. It would torment Lige, as it had her, since it couldn't get at her any more. It would batter him, try to turn him back, to keep him from coming to her.

But Lige would do his best to come to her. Dear Lige!

The thought of him steadied her for a moment, made her forget the ringing in her ears, the shouting in. her brain.

Perhaps he was coming now. Maybe if she looked out, she could see him riding to her across the prairies!

She rose and crept stealthily to the window to look out toward the west.

But he was not in sight.

But perhaps by some queer chance he was coming from the other way. So she turned to the window facing east.

No, he wasn't there, anywhere on the plains.

The wind had taken him! So it hadn't done its worst to her after all, awhile ago, when she thought it had!

Should she look once at the mound to see that the sand had shifted back safely over it?

Just once would she look, to satisfy herself that it was all covered again. She would peer so quickly that the wind couldn't see her.

She looked—then gave a wild scream.

There was no mound at all by the wind-break!—only bare ground, and the dead body of a man lying there, with his hands folded across his breast. A buzzard floated above it.

So the wind was determined Lige should know!

The wind was even now whispering the truth in his ears—shouting it at him!

Why struggle against a force that was a devil, and all-powerful?

She had known all along that the wind would get her!

Hadn't she even told Wirt Roddy that?

No use to fight any more! She would give up.

The wind had risen almost to cyclonic fury now. Again the curtains of sand were rolled up from the plains to the sky, wavering, shifting, their gigantic folds writhing with hideous suggestion.

What horrors did those curtains hide?

With a laugh that strangled on a scream, the woman sped to the door, flung it open and rushed out. She fled across the prairies like a leaf blown in a gale, borne along in the force of the wind that was at last to have its way with her.

THE END

Tables of contents